DANCE WITH ME

Praise for Georgia Beers

Camp Lost and Found

"I really like when Beers writes about winter and snow and hot chocolate. She makes heartache feel cosy and surmountable. *Camp Lost and Found* made me smile a lot, laugh at times, tear up more often than I care to share. If you're looking for a heartwarming story to keep the cold weather at bay, I'd recommend you give it a chance."—*Jude in the Stars*

Cherry on Top

"*Cherry on Top* is another wonderful story from one of the greatest writers in sapphic fiction…This is more than a romance with two incredibly charming and wonderful characters. It is a reminder that you shouldn't have to compromise who you are to fit into a box that society wants to put you into. Georgia Beers once again creates a couple with wonderful chemistry who will warm your heart."
—*Sapphic Book Review*

On the Rocks

"This book made me so happy! And kept me awake way too late."
—*Jude in the Stars*

The Secret Poet

"[O]ne of the author's best works and one of the best romances I've read recently…I was so invested in [Morgan and Zoe] I read the book in one sitting."—*Melina Bickard, Librarian, Waterloo Library (UK)*

Hopeless Romantic

"Thank you, Georgia Beers, for this unabashed paean to the pleasure of escaping into romantic comedies…If you want to have a big smile plastered on your face as you read a romance novel, do not hesitate to pick up this one!"—*The Rainbow Bookworm*

Flavor of the Month

"Beers whips up a sweet lesbian romance…brimming with mouth-watering descriptions of foodie indulgences…Both women are well-

intentioned and endearing, and it's easy to root for their inevitable reconciliation. But once the couple rediscover their natural ease with one another, Beers throws a challenging emotional hurdle in their path, forcing them to fight through tragedy to earn their happy ending."
—*Publishers Weekly*

One Walk in Winter

"A sweet story to pair with the holidays. There are plenty of 'moment's in this book that make the heart soar. Just what I like in a romance. Situations where sparks fly, hearts fill, and tears fall. This book shined with cute fairy trails and swoon-worthy Christmas gifts…REALLY nice and cozy if read in between Thanksgiving and Christmas. Covered in blankets. By a fire."—*Bookvark*

Fear of Falling

"Enough tension and drama for us to wonder if this can work out—and enough heat to keep the pages turning. I will definitely recommend this to others—Georgia Beers continues to go from strength to strength."
—*Evan Blood, Bookseller (Angus & Robertson, Australia)*

The Do-Over

"You can count on Beers to give you a quality well-paced book each and every time."—*The Romantic Reader Blog*

"*The Do-Over* is a shining example of the brilliance of Georgia Beers as a contemporary romance author."—*Rainbow Reflections*

The Shape of You

"I know I always say this about Georgia Beers's books, but there is no one that writes first kisses like her. They are hot, steamy and all too much!"—*Les Rêveur*

The Shape of You "catches you right in the feels and does not let go. It is a must for every person out there who has struggled with self-esteem, questioned their judgment, and settled for a less than perfect but safe lover. If you've ever been convinced you have to trade passion for emotional safety, this book is for you."—*Writing While Distracted*

Calendar Girl

"A sweet, sweet romcom of a story…*Calendar Girl* is a nice read, which you may find yourself returning to when you want a hot-chocolate-and-warm-comfort-hug in your life."—*Best Lesbian Erotica*

Blend

"You know a book is good, first, when you don't want to put it down. Second, you know it's damn good when you're reading it and thinking, I'm totally going to read this one again. Great read and absolutely a 5-star romance."—*The Romantic Reader Blog*

"This is a lovely romantic story with relatable characters that have depth and chemistry. A charming easy story that kept me reading until the end. Very enjoyable."—*Kat Adams, Bookseller, QBD (Australia)*

Right Here, Right Now

"[A] successful and entertaining queer romance novel. The main characters are appealing, and the situations they deal with are realistic and well-managed. I would recommend this book to anyone who enjoys a good queer romance novel, and particularly one grounded in real world situations."—*Books at the End of the Alphabet*

"[A]n engaging odd-couple romance. Beers creates a romance of gentle humor that allows no-nonsense Lacey to relax and easygoing Alicia to find a trusting heart."—*RT Book Reviews*

Lambda Literary Award Winner *Fresh Tracks*

"Georgia Beers pens romances with sparks."—*Just About Write*

"[T]he focus switches each chapter to a different character, allowing for a measured pace and deep, sincere exploration of each protagonist's thoughts. Beers gives a welcome expansion to the romance genre with her clear, sympathetic writing."—*Curve magazine*

By the Author

Romances

Turning the Page

Thy Neighbor's Wife

Too Close to Touch

Fresh Tracks

Mine

Finding Home

Starting from Scratch

96 Hours

Slices of Life

Snow Globe

Olive Oil & White Bread

Zero Visibility

A Little Bit of Spice

What Matters Most

Right Here, Right Now

Blend

The Shape of You

Calendar Girl

The Do-Over

Fear of Falling

One Walk in Winter

Flavor of the Month

Hopeless Romantic

16 Steps to Forever

The Secret Poet

Cherry on Top

Camp Lost and Found

Dance with Me

The Puppy Love Romances

Rescued Heart

Run to You

Dare to Stay

The Swizzle Stick Romances

Shaken or Stirred

On the Rocks

With a Twist

Visit us at www.boldstrokesbooks.com

DANCE WITH ME

by

Georgia Beers

2023

Credits
Editor: Ruth Sternglantz
Production Design: Stacia Seaman
Cover Design by Jeanine Henning

Acknowledgments

I love to dance.

That doesn't mean I'm any good at it, and when you compound that with a lack of confidence and the worry that everybody will think I look silly, I end up mostly dancing in my bathroom or living room alone. Of course, when I do that, I've got moves! You should see me! I wanted to write about somebody who doesn't think she can dance and who finds out she not only can, but she loves it. Doesn't hurt to give her a super-hot dancing partner as well, right? But we can't have it be so happy and easy…this is a romance novel, after all. So, I threw in several obstacles for poor Scottie Templeton, and for that, I apologize because I really, really like her. I hope you do, too.

Many, many thanks to Radclyffe and Sandy Lowe and Ruth Sternglantz and Cindy Cresap and Stacia Seaman and everybody at Bold Strokes Books. They keep things running like a well-oiled machine, and that makes it easy on me. My appreciation for them knows no bounds.

I'm so grateful to my friends, both writing and non-writing. I'm an introvert and being alone is my jam, but every now and then, even an introvert needs contact. Even an introvert needs to have a conversation or share a glass of wine or ask for some advice, and my people are amazing. I'm so lucky to have them all.

If you're holding my book in your hands or reading it on your e-reader or listening to the audiobook, I want to thank you. It's not dramatic to say I wouldn't be where I am today without you, so thank you from the bottom of my heart.

For all of us who love to dance but worry we're terrible.
Dance like nobody's watching.

CHAPTER ONE

Ice cream makes everything better, doesn't it?

Well. Maybe not everything. But it comes damn close. Of this I'm convinced.

"Doing okay?" my best friend since high school, Adley Purcell, asks me as she finishes cleaning one of her ice cream-making machines. Her family has always run Get the Scoop, an artisan ice cream shop that her grandfather opened when he and her grandma came over from the Philippines with Adley's mom—before *artisan* was even a thing. Last year, her grandpa retired, and Adley bought him out and took over, which means she works herself to death six days a week. She and I are tight, always have been, even before we knew that we both liked girls.

I nod as I spoon mint chip ice cream into my mouth, letting the cool freshness of it sit on my tongue for a second or two before I swallow. It's the last of today's stock and it's friggin' delicious. Adley will make more tomorrow.

"Doing okay."

"Good." Adley drapes her towel over her shoulder and blows at a hunk of her wavy dark hair—which has escaped not only from her ponytail, but also from her hat—only to have it fall right back where it had been, hanging in front of her eye. Then she whips herself up a milkshake using almond milk and chocolate almond ice cream, tosses in a little Frangelico from the not-so-secret bottle she keeps in the fridge, and *voilà!* instant frozen alcoholic shake. She takes the stool across from me at the little counter in the back of the shop, sets her forearms on the table, and looks me dead in the eye.

"Uh-oh. That's a serious stare," I say, half jokingly, 'cause when Adley gives me that look, shit is about to get *real*. "Are we about to have a serious discussion?"

"Enough already." Her dark brows meet in a V above her nose, a signal that she is not messing around. "It was one thing to mourn the death of your relationship. I get that. It took a while. I get that, too. But Penelope announcing her engagement doesn't warrant any sadness from you. You deserve better."

I sigh. Not in annoyance, but in resignation. She's right. Adley is a wise woman, and this is a no-brainer. Still, it's hard. Not to mention fucking embarrassing. I'd been with Pen for three years. I'd moved into her house. We were happy, or so I thought, and I wanted more. I wanted a commitment, something that symbolized our dedication to each other.

I should've kept my mouth shut because asking for a commitment was the beginning of the end, ironically enough. Long story short, we broke up, she kicked me out, I moved in with my grandmother, and barely a year later, Pen became engaged to another woman. *Fucking engaged.* So, clearly, she was fine with commitment. She just hadn't wanted to commit to me. That hurt. And was mortifying. And now, I feel like I can't show my face around town anymore. Which is ridiculous, but still. Emotions are tough to argue with.

"You need to get out there, get out of your grandma's house, do something. Play softball. Join a bowling league. A book club. Go out to dinner. *Something*." Adley takes a swig of her shake, and her voice gets softer. "I worry about you."

"I know." And I do. Between Adley and my grandmother and my work friends, I don't go a day without somebody gently suggesting I do something besides go home to my cats—well, Grandma's cats—and watch Netflix. And not just Netflix. Sappy, romantic Netflix. I've blown through all the sugary series with familiar tropes—big city girl comes home to small town, high school reunion leads to a second chance at love, some things are more important than my job—some multiple times. I know I'm in danger of becoming one with the couch, so maybe it *is* time to start listening to my friends. "Well," I say to Adley, "I do have something I'm rolling around in my head."

"Tell me." Adley has big, dark eyes and they focus on me. Everything about her is gorgeously brown, being half Filipino. Her hair, her eyes, her skin. She is tall and stunning to look at, and standing next to her can be rough, given how I have average light hair, average blue eyes, average pale skin, and am of average height. I grab her shake and take a sip of it before I give her my news.

"You know how Bash is getting married, right?"

"You mean Bash the Dreamy?"

I laugh at the nickname she gave him the first time they met, when Adley had marveled over how precisely he was put together. Sebastian Larue is one of my coworkers and also one of my closest friends. "Well, he wants to take dance lessons to surprise Lydia for their wedding, and he asked me to go with him, be his partner. He said it would help him and also get me *out and about*." I make the air quotes that Bash had made when suggesting the lessons to me. "It's a twelve-week course."

"That's fantastic," Adley says with a clap of her hands, and her eyes light up, and her smile gets wide, and it's clear she's thrilled by the idea of me attempting to dance and making a fool of myself, likely in front of several other people. "You're gonna do it, yes?"

"I mean, I tried to decline, but he played the I Helped You Move Out of Your Ex's card, and what could I say to that?"

"He's not wrong."

"I know. So I said yes, way against my better judgment." I eat the last spoonful of my ice cream and take my dish to the stainless steel industrial sink to rinse it, then set it on the counter to be sent through the enormous dishwasher. I turn back to my bestie. "I'm gonna be a disaster, you know that, right? I have no rhythm. Bash is going to be sorry he asked me."

"No, he's not." Adley is still smiling. "You're gonna have fun, and he's gonna learn to dance and surprise his bride, and it's gonna be great all the way around. I just know it." She slurps up the last of her shake. "Also, you *do* have rhythm. You're gonna be great. Plus, you're doing your friend a favor. That's a good thing. And you're doing *something*, and that's a better thing."

"I live to make you happy." I shoot for sarcasm, but it comes out lighter, and that's probably better. I clear my throat and exhale a resigned breath. She's right—Adley often is when it comes to giving advice to others—and I probably need to stop fighting it. I decide a change of subject is in order. "Any new flavors on the horizon? It's spring." I gesture toward the freezer. Adley is fabulous at coming up with new and creative flavors of ice cream, not to mention sundaes and desserts with unique names and even more amazing flavor combinations.

"A couple, yeah. Still in the early stages. A couple new flavors and two new dessert ideas. Gotta keep things fresh so those customers keep coming back, you know?"

I wish I had a quarter of her creative energy. "Well, you know I'm here anytime you need a taste tester." I raise my hand and give it a little wave, just to punctuate my words.

"You'll be the first one I call," she says and gives me a smile. Let me just say that having a best friend who literally makes ice cream for a living does not suck.

❖

I'm a hairstylist. I love hair. I love new styles and colors and everything about the science behind hair. It has always fascinated me, even as a little girl. All my dolls and Barbies had funky hairstyles because I was always trying out new things on them, cutting or curling or coloring.

That being said, Sylvia's, the salon where I currently work, isn't really on the cutting edge of hair fashion. Pun intended. But it's a job and I do okay there and I'm close with the stylists whose chairs are near mine. Bash is to my left. Demi works to his left. We are like the Sarcastic Three Musketeers, and one day, we're gonna leave Sylvia and her ridiculous profit split and open our own salon together.

One day.

It's Tuesday morning, and I have three grannies lined up in a row on my schedule. I don't call them that out of disrespect. That's just how we classify our senior clients who, to be honest, are much of our bread and butter because they come weekly. A wash, set, and blow-dry is basic and easy and the basis of my income. And my grandma sends me all her friends, so my schedule is pretty full most days. For that, I'm thankful.

I'm rolling Mrs. D'Angelo's hair, which is a beautiful silvery white, when Bash comes in to start his day. I can see her watching him in the mirror, like pretty much any straight woman with a pulse does…along with a surprising number of men. People always assume Bash is gay—he's a hairstylist, first of all, and that comes with a stereotype for men. Secondly, he's gorgeously put together— tall and lean, with broad shoulders, chestnut-brown hair, and a beard that is so precisely trimmed, it looks almost drawn on to his face. He's like a Disney cartoon prince. And he's mostly oblivious to the attention, which is one of the many reasons I love the guy. He's actually bi, but I never offer that up. It's not my news to share. And he's totally devoted to Lydia, who might actually be the sweetest woman to walk the earth. I wouldn't be surprised.

"Good morning, Mrs. D," he says to my client, meeting her eyes in the mirror. "You're looking fabulous today."

Mrs. D'Angelo blushes, honest-to-God blushes, and it's adorable. I half expect her to titter in delight as well, but she just smiles and says hello back. I get her all set and sit her under a dryer, and then I shampoo my next client, Mrs. Haverstein. I get her settled in my chair and comb her hair out. It's not quite as silvery as Mrs. D'Angelo's, but it's a rich salt-and-pepper. Bash has a handsome blond man in his chair and is shaving the back of his neck with an electric razor.

"You all ready for tonight?" he asks.

"Since I will never be ready to dance in front of strangers, no," I say. "I am not ready for tonight. But I'll be there."

Mrs. Haverstein meets my eyes in the mirror and raises her almost nonexistent brows in question.

"Bash is making me take dance lessons with him," I tell her with a teasing eye roll.

"Ooh," she says, drawing the word out. "That sounds like so much fun. I used to love to dance."

"It will be fun," Bash agrees and gives her a smile that makes *her* blush, too. Man, I need him to teach me that. "I'm getting married in the fall, and I want to surprise my fiancée by actually knowing how to dance when we take the floor for the first time as man and wife."

I see the blond man's face clearly fall and have to roll my lips in and bite down on them to keep from laughing. Poor dude.

"It will be fun for *you*," I say. "You actually have rhythm. And also a right and a left foot."

He shakes his head, but with a smile, because this has been my argument since he first brought it up. He's not letting me slide on it, though. "Nope. You're gonna be great. I bet you twenty bucks."

"You're my witness, Mrs. H. When he's too embarrassed to show his face anywhere because his dance partner is a catastrophe, feel free to bring up this conversation. Okay?"

She's laughing openly now, her blue eyes crinkled at the corners. She's a super nice lady that I've known since I was in high school because she used to bowl with my grandma and grandpa. Holding up her hands in surrender, she tells me she's going to reserve judgment.

The morning flies by, as Tuesday mornings usually do, and Demi finally shows up at twelve thirty for her first client, just as I return from my lunch break in the back room. While I have a clientele that skews a little older and, therefore, prefers to come in the morning, Demi's clients tend to be younger and edgier. And night owls. Her days rarely start before noon.

Today, she's wearing skintight black pants with rips in the knees. Her very shiny, very black hair is shaved close on one side and flops over on the other, and she's traded the diamond stud in her nose for a silver ring. Her eyeliner is heavy, and her Doc Martens are probably ten years old and they look it, but somehow, Demi always manages to take a bunch of worn-slash-old-slash-sloppy things and make them work. I could give her a couple plastic bags, two rubber bands, and some duct tape and she'd make it look cool. She has fashion sense to spare. I wish she'd spare some for me. I need help. A glance at my jeans and simple purple button-down shirt reminds me of this. I prefer to buy my clothes directly off the mannequin, if at all possible, because then I can be sure at least one other person in the world thinks it all goes together—the person who dressed the mannequin. When I shop online, I tend to buy the entire outfit the model is wearing, just to be safe. I can't accessorize to save my damn life.

"DeBashtie," is the first thing Demi says once she's at her station, and she keeps her voice low. Bash and I look at each other, and I tip my head to the left, while he tips his the other way. "It's a combination of all our names. *De*mi, Bash, Scot*tie*." She accents the included syllables.

"Shockingly, I don't hate it," he says.

"Me, neither," I agree.

"Add it to the list?" she asks, looking pleased with herself, and we both nod. She pulls out her phone and punches buttons.

Every few days, one of us suggests a name for the salon we plan to own together. Any of us is allowed to veto, and anything we all like goes on a list. My last suggestion was Snips. I was vetoed in about three seconds flat.

My next client is the first one of the day who's under sixty years old, and she begins my afternoon. By the time I'm pulling the smock off my last client, it's nearing five thirty and Bash is looking kind of giddy.

"It's almost time," he says, his eyes sparkling.

"I swear, you're like a little kid around this dance class. I don't know when I've seen you this excited about something." It's cute, I have to admit, even if I've had butterflies bouncing around in my stomach for the past hour. I'm not sure why I'm so nervous. I have nothing to be nervous about. It's not like I'm going to a room filled with professional dancers and I'm going to look stupid. It'll probably be a class of people who also don't know how to dance, thus the class-taking. Logically, I know this. But it doesn't matter. I'm still a ball of nerves.

"Got your clothes?" Bash asks. "I'm gonna go change."

"Okay. I'll change after you."

There's only one bathroom in the salon, so I wait until he comes back out, and then I head in with my bag. I was told to dress comfortably, so it's easy to move around, and I packed some leggings and a tank, all close-fitting. It would be just my luck to get the hem of my pants or the sleeve of my shirt stuck on something and make a spectacle of myself. Trust me, it could happen. So I made sure to pack clothes that stay tight against me. I lace up my sneakers, and I'm good to go.

We drive separately, as the dance studio is halfway home for both of us, but we live in opposite directions. It takes me three tries to get my eleven-year-old Ford started, but I manage to get there on time and slide my car into the spot next to Bash's at Ms. Tina's School of Dance. He's leaning against his Charger, feet crossed at the ankle, waiting for me. I gesture with my chin to the small building. "I hope you're ready to have your friend embarrass the crap out of you."

He ignores my shitty self-talk, and he's still grinning like a little kid on Christmas morning. "Ready?" he asks as I slam my door shut and lock my car.

No, I'm not ready. I'm not even a little ready. I'm worried about embarrassing myself. Worse, I'm worried about embarrassing him. I give him a look that must show my near panic because he throws an arm over my shoulders.

"We're just gonna have fun. That's it. Okay? Relax."

I inhale deeply, let it out slowly, and realize he's right. No need to be nervous. No reason to worry. We're just going to have fun. I nod once. "Okay. Let's do the thing."

CHAPTER TWO

Ms. Tina Alvarez must drink a ton of caffeine. It's my first thought as she buzzes around like a hummingbird on cocaine, flitting about the room, smiling, touching shoulders, laughing. She's petite, in a flowy red dress and heels, and she walks toe-heel, as if she's constantly on a stage. Her eyes are bright. Her smile is wide. Her voice is cheerful, but not annoyingly so. It's hard to guess her age, and I suspect she's likely older than she seems, but she looks like she could be anywhere from her midforties to her late sixties. Also, I like her immediately. She's got an energy about her that makes me want to smile.

The room is a good size, not too big, but not too close. The mirrors all along two of the walls help make it look bigger. The floor is shiny and gray, and there's a small cart with a laptop on it that I can only assume is where the quiet Latin music is coming through to speakers mounted near the ceiling in the four corners of the room. The studio walks a nice line between super fancy and completely affordable. I don't feel like I don't belong there, which surprises me.

"Welcome, welcome," Ms. Tina says once she finally makes her way back to the front of the room. "I will be your dance instructor for the next twelve weeks, and I'm so happy you're all here."

I look around at the other five pairs of students, and I'm surprised by the variety. There are folks older than me, folks younger than me, a same-sex couple, people of color. We're a definite melting pot, and I am so here for it.

Ms. Tina gives us her own background, how she's been dancing since she was ten, that she traveled with a dance troupe for several years, was a dancer in three different Broadway shows over the course of seven years, how she auditioned for the Rockettes but, sadly, didn't make the cut, and how she ultimately ended up back home in Northwood fifteen years ago to be closer to her children and grandkids and open her own dance studio.

"I've been teaching ever since, and even after all this time, nothing brings me more joy. I hope to instill that joy of dancing in you." She moves to the laptop and hits a button that cuts off the music. "We're going to be learning some basic dance moves, but mostly focusing on salsa. You'll be able to use what you learn here for any number of dance styles. That's the beauty of it. Now, you're all here for your own reasons, so why don't we go around the room and you introduce yourselves and tell us what you're hoping to gain from being here?"

I listen raptly as the couples introduce themselves. Neil and Jillian are a white couple that look to be in their late fifties, and they've both recently retired and are looking to stay active. "I agreed to learn to play golf," Jillian says with a gently teasing eye roll. "But only in exchange for Neil taking dance lessons with me."

"Seemed fair," Neil says with a shrug, his hand on his substantial belly.

Jamal and Kevin I'd put in their forties, maybe. Jamal is Black and very tall. Kevin is white and a good six inches shorter. They're headed on their first cruise in the fall, and they want to be able to dance the nights away.

Regina and Dale are both Black and probably in their thirties, and they're in the same boat as Bash and me. "We're getting married in September," Regina says, "and I want us to be able to dazzle on the dance floor." Dale gives her a squeeze and kisses her temple.

Davis and Linda are a white couple and look to be the oldest of the group, maybe in their late sixties. Davis makes a face that seems to be a mix of a grin and a grimace as he says, "I had a knee replacement last year and Linda here is doing what she can to keep me active. So here we are."

Pete and Katrina are a white couple in their twenties, both

perpetually smiley from what I can tell in the fifteen minutes I've been around them. They hold hands and lean in to each other as if they're afraid to not be touching in some way. It's super cute and also makes me want to roll my eyes. They've been together for only six months and decided to try something different.

Then it's our turn.

"Hi, I'm Sebastian—my friends call me Bash—and this is my good friend Scottie. I'm getting married in December, and I want to surprise my fiancée by not making a fool of myself—or her—during our first dance as husband and wife."

"And Scottie, she is not your fiancée?" Ms. Tina asks.

I shake my head. "No, I'm just a really, *really* good friend, clearly." A soft chuckle moves around the room.

Ms. Tina claps her hands together. "Well. Wonderful. I love that you all have different reasons for taking a dance class. As you know, this is a twelve-week course. We'll be touching on simple moves as well as specific ones. My focus is on salsa. By the time twelve weeks have passed, you will have all the basics you need to be confident on the dance floor. We end all classes with a recital here in class. Totally optional, of course. And there's a competition in September where all the dance studios in the area send one couple to represent their school. Always fun to watch. Does anybody have any questions before we get started?"

We do some stretches to begin with, and then Bash and I spend the next forty minutes laughing our asses off as we fumble, trip, and step on each other's feet.

"Oh my God, I'm doomed," he says at one point, through his laughter.

Ms. Tina shuts that right down. "No, no. No such thing. You are not doomed. You are laughing, and that's a good thing. We will whip you right into shape. Don't worry." She floats on to Regina and Dale, who already look like they've been dancing together for decades.

"I hate them," Bash whispers as he bumps me with a hip.

"They look fantastic, don't they?" I rub his arm absently. "We'll get there. We're not supposed to be awesome the first class."

He nods as we watch Ms. Tina move Regina's hand higher on

Dale's shoulder. They move so smoothly, like they're gliding. How they ended up in a beginner dance class, I have no idea, but I decide right then that I love watching them.

"I think I gotta call shenanigans here," Bash says good-naturedly, and a ripple of soft laughter runs through the room. Seems we're not the only ones watching.

"They're damn good," Davis says, and the rest of us have stopped to watch as Regina and Dale float along.

"We can all get there." I say it out loud, but I'm more telling myself that. Ms. Tina hears me, though, and points in my direction.

"That. Right there. That's the attitude I want." She's smiling at me, and I feel like the kid in kindergarten who just got a gold star. I feel my face get warm.

Not long after that, class is over, and I think we're all a little shocked by how quickly it went. We gather our things and file out of the studio.

"That was fun," Bash says, and I nod my agreement.

"Not gonna lie, I didn't hate it," I agree, and I'm kind of surprised. I mean, I'm still super self-conscious about dancing in front of people, but the fact that many others in the class felt the same way makes me less so. If that makes sense.

We reach our cars in the parking lot, and we wave to various other class members as we all get ready to head home.

"Will you wait until I'm sure my car starts?" I ask Bash.

He nods and stands next to his driver's side door until my car's engine sputters to life on the third try.

"Third time's the charm," Bash says as he pulls his door open. "See you tomorrow."

I'm so relieved I didn't despise class, and I'm thinking about that as I drive home. I'm not a person who dances, outside of my own bedroom by myself. Unless I've had a lot to drink, I tend to stand on the sidelines and watch the people who actually have rhythm of some kind.

I pull my car into the driveway behind my grandma's pristine and shining white Toyota Camry. Yes, this is where I live right now. With my grandmother. It's not ideal: thirty-four-year-old single lesbian residing with her grandmother, who arguably has a fuller social calendar than she does. But it works for both of us. And also, that's what I get for moving into my girlfriend's house after dating her for less than six months. Granted, the relationship lasted for almost three years, but when it ended, I was the one who had to move. Torn between renting an apartment and buying an actual house, my grandmother asked me if I wanted to come live with her. Since my grandfather passed away a couple years ago, she's been alone in a fairly sizable house that she doesn't want to leave. She also doesn't want to be—her words here—an old woman rattling around in a big, empty house. And I adore my grandmother. She's my favorite person in the whole wide world. Saying no to her is impossible.

So here I am.

"It's me," I call out as I enter through the side door. I always worry I'm going to scare her, so I announce myself every time I come home.

"We're in the living room," she calls back, and I follow her voice to find her in her favorite recliner watching *NCIS*. She hits the remote to pause the show and smiles at me.

"Are you watching your boyfriend Mark Harmon again?" I ask as I bend to kiss her cheek. She has Salt, her white cat, curled up in her lap looking happier than any cat has a right to look, and I give him a stroke. His cranky counterpart, Pepper, is around here somewhere. "Where's your bitchy sister?" I ask him as I squat down to kiss his head.

Grandma feigns a horrified gasp. "Don't you talk about her that way. She's just misunderstood."

"She's bitchy."

"And she's a little bitchy."

I laugh softly and sit down on the couch.

"How was dance class? You're here, so that means you didn't die." Grandma grins at me, and even sitting in her chair in the evening, watching TV, she looks classy and put together, dressed in a smart outfit of slacks and a colorful print top in blues and yellows. She used to have me color her hair but decided once my grandpa had passed that she wanted to go "au naturel," as she put it. And now she has a head of gorgeous silvery-white hair that, instead of making her look older, just makes her look even more sophisticated. She never leaves the house without makeup on. She has her nails done every other week, and she always smells like J'adore, the perfume she began wearing a few years ago when Charlize Theron started doing the commercials. "Why shouldn't I smell as sexy as Charlize?" was her reasoning, and who could argue with that? Now I can't smell that perfume without thinking of my grandma.

She's hipper than I will ever be.

"You're right. I did not die. In fact, I might have had a good time. *Might have.*"

"I told you."

"You did. You were right. As usual. Which is not to say I won't die at some point. Because the way Bash and I were stepping all over each other? We could be in for some serious bodily injury."

Grandma laughs, a sound I love more than just about anything. I'm the grandchild who's the comic relief. I always have been. So anytime I can make her laugh makes me feel like I'm fulfilling my given role. "I made pork chops for dinner and saved you a plate," she tells me. "In the fridge. Just heat it up."

"You're the best." I push to my feet and head for the kitchen.

"Don't you forget it." I hear the TV start back up again. And not for the first time, any shame I might feel about being a grown-ass adult who lives with her grandma flies right out the window. Because no, I won't stay forever. Of course I won't. I do want my own place. My own stuff. I want to choose furniture and paint colors and art for the walls and not always feel like I'm incidental in somebody else's space.

But for now? I kinda love living here.

❖

It's Saturday in early May, and I'm meeting my mom for lunch. Since tomorrow is Mother's Day and she's going to her husband's parents' house for the day, this is when I get to see her. I normally work on Saturdays and have Sunday and Monday as my weekend, but I took the day off to have lunch with my mom. Yeah, I know. It's a long story.

The day is lovely, a sunny spring day, not typical for upstate New York. No, typical in the spring is rain and weirdly warm or unseasonably cool temperatures because Mother Nature is clearly going through some things these past few years and is all over the place, but yeah, climate change is a hoax and don't even get me started.

I'm sitting in Jolie's, a popular diner in Jefferson Square that my mom loves, and when she walks through the front door with both my half sister and half brother, I am thrilled and disappointed at the same time. I adore my half siblings. I have four of them, total. My mom has Jordana, who's thirteen, and Kai, who's ten. My dad also has two more kids. I'm an only child, in that I'm the only offspring my parents had together, but I'm also the oldest of five kids. Oldest by a lot.

"Hi, sweetheart," my mom says as she bends to kiss my cheek.

"Hey there. Happy Mother's Day a day early." She smiles at me and takes the chair across from me as Jordana and Kai both hug me. "I didn't expect to see you weirdos," I say to them.

My mother shakes her head, blows out a breath, and motions for the waitress, then orders sodas for the kids and a white wine for herself. "Kai was supposed to have a playdate, and that fell through. Jordie's cheer practice got canceled at the last minute." She grimaced. "Sorry about that."

"No worries," I say as I reach toward Kai and rub my hand over his head. He pretends to dodge me, but doesn't really. He's such a cute kid. I love that my siblings look sort of like me, but also not. Jordana and I both have our mom's blue eyes and Kai's are hazel, but they both have Stephan's—their dad—darker hair and complexion.

"We can't stay too long, honey," my mom says as our drinks arrive. "Sam and Jojo are coming over tonight, and I need to get groceries for dinner and clean my house." She smiles, firmly expecting me to understand. And I do. She has more important things in her life than her oldest daughter. She has for a long time now. She has no idea that when she says something like how she has limited time for her visit with me, it makes me feel like I'm something on her to-do list to be checked off. Story of my life.

I take a good look at her. My mom is pretty. I've always thought so. She's about five foot six with light brown hair that she wears in a long bob and tucks behind her ears. It makes her look younger than her fifty-five years. She's a stylish dresser, and today, she's wearing dark jeans and a simple white button-down shirt to which she's added gold hoop earrings, a simple gold necklace with a *J* and a *K* dangling from it—no *S*, though—and kitten heels. I actually thought having kids in her forties would age her quicker, but it seems to have had the opposite effect. She looks younger than her age, vibrant, happy. She smiles a lot more, revealing the same high cheekbones I have, and her eyes sparkle. I try not to think about how that wasn't the case until my siblings came along, but I'm an adult now, and I do understand that she was unhappy with my father and not with me. She split up with my father, not me. But still...

I shake off the uneasiness that often creeps in when I wander down that path, and we spend the next hour chatting about Jordana's cheer squad and how Kai is going to try out for lacrosse. He also plays trumpet in the school band, and Jordana sings and hopes to try out for the junior high musical this year, which I'm told is *Godspell*. And seriously, does every school in America do *Godspell*? Mine did. Before I know it, my mom is dabbing her napkin at her mouth, and then she sets it next to her plate, a clear indication that she's done. She checks her phone for the time, then looks at me with an apologetic smile. My time is up. I realize it sadly, as I have since I was twenty-one and my mom told me she was pregnant with Jordie. Kai came along three years after that, and then my father and his new wife announced *they* were pregnant and my two other half brothers were born, and honestly, my entire twenties were spent welcoming new siblings to the family—families—and realizing that I would never have my parents' full attention ever again.

Which sucks, even well into my thirties.

I mean, it's fine. I'm thirty-four years old, what do I need my parents' attention for, right?

I stay sitting at the table in Jolie's for several moments after I've hugged my brother and sister and mom and watched them leave for the next adventure in their day. I take a sip of my water as it occurs to me that not once did my mother ask a single thing about my life. She did ask how Grandma was—Grandma's my dad's mom, but she always liked my mother—but we talked about the kids, their schoolwork, their extracurricular activities, the things they're planning to do during the upcoming summer, none of which include me, and then they were off.

The familiar stab pokes me in the chest. You'd think I'd be used to this by now, but it stings every time. Every single damn time. I have four siblings but am an only child. And wow, sometimes I really feel that.

The waitress asks if she can get me anything else, and when I say no, she slides the check onto the table with an apologetic smile.

I pay it, leave a nice tip, and decide to go bug Adley for a while.

❖

Saturday afternoons are busy at Get the Scoop, especially once it starts to get warm out. I have always been a person who can and will eat ice cream all year long. Rainy and cold out? Give me ice cream. A blizzard? I'll take a cone, thank you. Hurricane on its way? Why yes, a banana split would be lovely. But the majority of folks associate ice cream with warm weather, and I suppose I can accept that.

Because of my BFF status, I get to enter through the back door if I want to, and I do today. It's not a huge place, but it's bustling. Three employees are working out front, which I can see through the big window-sized opening that allows you to look from the back room—where the magic happens, as I like to say—into the service area. There are six or eight people in line, and a few kids are bopping around the shop, shouting for parents to *Watch me!* as kids tend to do.

Adley looks tired, but I know she often works later than she intends to, to the detriment of her sleep.

"Hey," she says, and smiles and looks happy to see me. I kiss her cheek as she asks, "It's Saturday. Why aren't you at work?" Then she blinks at me for a moment. "It *is* Saturday, right?"

I laugh softly as I shrug. "It is. I just had lunch with my mom for Mother's Day."

"*Oh*," she says, and she draws the word out, so I know she gets it. "Where'd you go? How was it?" Adley has a tall stand in a corner with her laptop on it, and she places orders, answers emails, checks inventory, and monitors sales all from that spot, rather than having an office of some kind, because Get the Scoop isn't all that big. She's looking at the screen as she talks to me.

"Jolie's. Packed. Jordie and Kai were there, too."

Adley stops typing and turns to look at me. Here's the thing about Adley: When she looks at you? She *looks* at you. Like, you can feel her probing around in your brain, flipping through your thoughts like they're folders in a filing cabinet. I've never in my life been able to hide a thing from her. Not one thing. "I'm sorry, boo." Then she sighs loudly and turns back to her screen. "Your mom never seems to get that you'd like time, just the two of you. Want me to smack her around a little bit?"

"Would you?" I grin at her and run my hand down her arm. Adley always has my back. Always. "What's new in ice cream land?" I ask, itching to change the subject. It's not like my Mommy issues are new.

Adley's face lights up, and I know I've asked the right question. If there's one thing she loves, it's creating new ice cream flavors and then trying them out on me. "I'm so glad you asked. Sit." She indicates a stool near the wall, grabs a couple small bowls, and scoops a little bit of ice cream out of a couple tubs. Then she hands one to me with a spoon and waits. This is how we do it. I take a bite and tell her what I taste, and then she knows if her flavor combinations are working.

I taste the first one. Roll it around in my mouth. It's a blast of apple, but also something warm and comforting. "Apples and cinnamon…" I take another small taste. "Sugar…brown sugar…" Adley's watching me carefully. She never gives me a hint. She's very patient. I take my time before finally looking at her. "Candy Apple?"

Her smile grows wide.

"Point for me. Next." She slides the next bowl to me, and we do this four more times. I get Island Tropics—well, not the name, but all the flavors of coconut, pineapple, and mango—Black Forest, and

Lucky Charms. Though she can't call it that without risking getting sued by General Mills, so she's still working on that. I fumble on Snickerdoodle, but Adley thinks it's because the flavors aren't quite right yet.

Spending time with her and sampling ice cream turns out to be just what I needed, and by the time I leave Get the Scoop, I feel much better about things in general.

I was hoping to have dinner with Grandma tonight, but when I get home, her car is gone and there's a note on the kitchen table for me.

Scottie—
    Having dinner out with the girls. Made a pie. In the fridge. Don't forget to feed the babies!
    Love, G

My grandma has a smartphone, and she knows how to use it. Uses it often, in fact. But she told me once that there's something about the feel of pen and paper that she enjoys more than poking at letters on a screen. Plus, she's got the most beautiful handwriting, all full of swoops and fancy. I put the note down, and out of nowhere, Pepper appears, like because I'm in the kitchen, I must be there to feed her.

"It's not dinnertime yet, Peps. But you're so pretty, so I'll give you treats."

As if the T-word was a trigger, Salt appears, and now I've got two furry things twining around my feet while I get their treat bag out. I toss a couple treats one way and then a couple the other. If I don't spread them out, Pepper will eat them all, piggy that she is, and poor Salty will get none. While they are clearly named because of their colors, I tell Grandma all the time that Pepper is the one who should be named Salt because she is, in fact, very salty. The saltiest.

I cut myself a slice of pie—strawberry rhubarb, which might be my all-time favorite—and take my plate into the living room, trying not to dwell on the fact that my seventy-seven-year-old grandmother has a more active social life than I do. As I grab the remote to see what's on, my phone pings with a text notification. I look, expecting to see Bash or Demi or Adley. Or even one of my parents. But it's none of those people.

Have you unblocked me yet?

Fuuuuuuuck.

It's Pen. Or Penelope Powell, as it says on her birth certificate. And no sooner does my brain register her name than my heart starts to pound. My armpits sweat. My stomach churns, and I'm certain I can feel the one bite of strawberry rhubarb sitting in it like a hunk of hot coal. How does she do that? How does one simple text from her have such a visceral effect on me? Initially, I changed her name to a simple emoji of a broken heart, so that's what's displayed at the top of my screen. Then I blocked her. I've had her blocked for months now. Not because she tried hard to talk to me. She didn't, I can only assume because she was busy with her fiancée. Ugh. That word feels like slime in my mouth, and I want to spit it across the room. But in a moment of what I thought at the time was maturity, strength, power, I unblocked her. Just last week. Not expecting to ever hear from her again, of course.

And now here she fucking is. Being all smarmy and acting like she knew exactly when I unblocked her.

God, *did* she know?

I give my head a shake and I scoff—which scares Salt off the couch—because of course she doesn't know. *Of course she doesn't know.* She's not psychic. None of my close friends are tight with her, and besides, I didn't tell any of them I unblocked her because they'd have given me looks. And talks. And there would've been eye rolling and head shaking, and who needs that bullshit, really? Not me.

I stare at the screen and am almost about to start typing when I see Pepper across the room. She's standing in the doorway of the living room, and she's staring at me. Just...staring. And probably judging, if we're being honest here. But then I think about what a badass cat she is, how she lives life on her own terms and doesn't let anybody boss her around, and I shock myself by setting the phone down.

"No. She can wait. And maybe I won't answer at all. Right, Peps?"

The cat blinks her big yellow eyes at me. Once. Slowly. Then she turns and walks away, and I'm not quite sure if she's impressed with me or finds me pathetic. It's confusing.

I eat my pie, which takes about eight minutes, and that's how long I make Pen wait for a response. A whole eight minutes before I pick up the phone again.

So. Yeah. Pathetic it is.

CHAPTER THREE

When I walk into the salon the following Tuesday, I'm surprised to see Demi already at her chair and buzzing the back of a man's neck with her electric razor. There's something about the way she's touching him, though. An intimacy, almost. I glance at Bash, and he rolls his lips in and bites down, gives me an almost imperceptible nod.

"Hair to Dye For," I say to them. "With dye spelled *D-Y-E*."

"Veto," Bash and Demi say at the same time and without missing a beat.

I sigh dramatically, even though I knew they'd hate it. I've decided that's all I'm offering now for names—ridiculous suggestions—since they veto anything I come up with anyway, and their suggestions are always better.

Demi finishes up with her client, and I see that he's tall with dark hair, a heavy shadow on his face even though he's clean-shaven, and a silver hoop piercing his eyebrow. Demi walks him to the front desk where he pays, then walks him to the door. Bash and I are both watching from our respective chairs as she gives the guy a kiss on the lips and watches him go. She turns back to us, and neither Bash nor I pretend we weren't just gawking.

"And who was that tall, dark, handsome man that was able to get you into the salon before noon?" I ask. Mrs. D'Angelo is in my chair again and watching our conversation in the mirror.

"That, my friends, was Micah. Isn't he dreamy?" Demi does a little spin when she reaches her chair and sighs like a Disney Princess who's just met the guy she thinks she's in love with. Of course we, the audience, know she's a hundred percent *wrong* about that. Even Mrs. D'Angelo looks down at her hands with an almost imperceptible smile and gives her head a subtle shake.

Bash and I finish our clients at roughly the same time, and when he's finished cashing his out and comes back to his chair, I try to act completely nonchalant as I say, "So, guess who texted me this weekend."

"Your mom," Bash says. "No. Your dad. No, wait. A new client. No. Jennifer Lopez."

A blink at him. "Listen, if JLo texted me over the weekend, trust me, I would not have waited until Tuesday to tell you."

"Pen." Demi doesn't look my way when she says it, just heads to the waiting area to grab her next client. But Bash turns to look at her, then back to me, and I nod.

"Yep."

"Oh God, the she-devil of Northwood? WTF?" Bash gives his head a shake, his eyebrows dip down into a V above his nose, I can see his jaw tense, and all those reactions make me love him even more than I already do. He's like the big brother I never had, and he always wants to protect me. Pen breaking up with me was actually really hard on Bash. "What did she want?" he finally asks.

"To know if I'd unblocked her yet." I say it without censoring myself and wince internally when I hear my own voice.

"You unblocked her?" Bash's eyes go wide. "Why? Why would you do that?"

"Ease up, B," Demi says as her next client, a blond woman in her thirties, sits. She unfurls the cape and drapes it over her. "She probably had a moment of strength and thought she was past the whole thing." She uses the pedal on her chair to crank it up a little higher. "After all, the opposite of love isn't hate. It's apathy."

"Damn right it is," the woman in the chair says.

"Did you text her back?" Bash asks. "Tell me you didn't text her back."

"I did," I say. "But not right away." I don't tell him that I waited less than ten minutes. That tidbit will be just mine.

"Good. Make her wait. Or better yet, don't text her back at all."

"Have you even met our friend Scottie?" Demi asks him. "She's the nicest person we know. Polite. Never rude. And not texting back would be rude."

Ugh. I hate how well they know me. I mean, I love it, but I also hate it.

"What did she want?" Bash asks, not looking at me. He and I both have empty chairs, and he grabs the nearby broom to sweep around his station.

"To see how I was doing? I guess?"

Bash snorts. "I bet. Isn't she engaged? I wonder how her fiancée would feel if she knew her betrothed was texting with her ex." He looks up at me, the broom stopping midsweep. "She'd hate it, you know."

I nod. Bash is annoyed, and I know it's at me for responding. And I don't want to admit that Demi is right about the whole rude thing. My parents may be wrapped up in their own little worlds right now, but they raised me with manners. As did my grandma. I am polite to a fault. I would rather have somebody walk all over me than stand up for myself and be loud in public where everybody can see. It's a problem. I know.

My next client arrives, and I make small talk with her even as my brain is whirring. Why *did* Pen text me? Because it wasn't actually clear at the time. She said she'd been thinking about me, so thought she'd shoot me a text just to say hi and was surprised when I responded. I always did like when I could surprise her, since one of her criticisms of me was that I'm too predictable. Not spontaneous enough. She asked about my grandma, which was one thing I will always give her credit for—she was always unfailingly kind to Grandma. I made sure to space my responses out, not to respond immediately—though, as with the first text, I didn't wait all that long—and I answered all her questions. One thing I'm proud of is that I didn't ask her any questions about her or her life or anything like that. Because a) I don't want to know, really and b) I hope her world is crashing down around her ears, but I'd never say that out loud to her. If you can't say something nice, don't say anything at all, am I right?

The day goes on in a flurry, and before I know it, it's four thirty, and Bash is closing up his station, cleaning, and putting things away.

I give him a questioning look because it's early. Dance class isn't until six.

"These shoes are killing me," he says, and we both glance down at the shiny new loafers he's got on. "I'll never make it through dance class in these. I'm done with clients, so I'm gonna run home and change and I'll meet you at the studio. Okay?"

"Sure."

I slide my car into a spot in the parking lot of the dance studio at five fifty-nine because it wouldn't start. Again. I really need to get a new car, but I just haven't been able to find the energy for a car dealer. I left my dad a message two weeks ago about going with me, but he hasn't called me back yet. Typical.

I lock my car and hurry inside and everybody is there...except Bash. For a second or two, I'm relieved that I beat him, but after fifteen minutes go by and we're all doing warm-up stretches and I still haven't heard from him, I start to get worried.

"And where is your handsome dance partner tonight?" Ms. Tina asks me.

"That is a very good question," I say.

"No matter. You will dance with me until he arrives."

To say that those words cranked my nerves up into *holy shit* territory would be a colossal understatement. We are just finishing our stretches when Bash shows up. I see him in the doorway, and his apology is written in his eyes. He sets his stuff down and crosses the room to me, limping slightly, before I have to dance with Ms. Tina.

"Where have you been?" I whisper.

"Sorry," he whispers back. "I couldn't find my other shoe. Lydia cleaned last night, and I have no idea how she managed to put one shoe away and not the other, but it took me forever to find it. Under the couch." He rolls his eyes to punctuate how ridiculous he thinks that location was. "Then I was late, and I hurried, and I missed the bottom two steps and ended up in a heap on the landing. My foot is killing me."

"Well, I almost had to dance with the teacher."

He clenches his teeth and makes a yikes face, and I laugh softly as Ms. Tina calls the class to the center of the room to go over today's class.

We learn the box step, which I'm shocked to say I pick up quicker than Bash does. I joke that maybe I should be the one leading, but when I step on his foot, he winces in pain, and I feel terrible. Ms. Tina chuckles at us and says it won't be the last time one of us steps on the other, and from the combination of laughs, winces, and irritated scolding that ripples through the room for the entire hour, I know she's right.

By the time class is over, Bash is glad, and I have had more fun than I expected to.

"Maybe you should have that looked at," I say to him as we gather our things.

He shrugs. "Nah. I'm sure I just bruised it when I fell. Probably gonna be sore for a couple days."

We head out to the parking lot. Bash is a little slower than usual, I notice, but I walk with him, and by the time he's in his car, I'm no longer worried. "Tell Lydia I said hi," I say as I give him a quick wave and head to my own car. Vehicles are filing out of the parking lot, and across the pavement, I catch a glimpse of a woman. And okay, I'm going to be completely honest here, she catches my eye because she's super hot. I'm not proud of that fact because I'm not in the habit of objectifying women, but it's the truth. I can't see a ton of detail because she's literally across the entire parking lot, but she's dressed in black leggings, a red sweatshirt with a wide neck that's sliding partway off one shoulder, and black Nikes with a white swoosh. As I watch, she reaches up to pull the elastic out of her ponytail, and waves of dark, dark hair come tumbling down over her shoulders.

My mouth actually goes dry.

I've only read about that in books, your mouth going dry, but it totally happens, and I grab my water bottle from the bag on my shoulder and take a swig as I keep staring. Suddenly, she glances over her shoulder, and I think our eyes meet, but I'm too far away to be sure. What I do know is that if I don't move in the next second and a half, it'll be crystal clear that I've been gawking at her like some creeper. I shake myself into action, force my body to move, to open my car door, to actually *get in*. Once in the driver's seat and having slammed the door behind me, I exhale loudly and hope the woman didn't notice me. I hear her ignition turn over and watch in my rearview mirror as she drives out of the lot in what I see now is a black Nissan SUV and doesn't give me a second glance.

Okay. Whew.

My phone pings a text notification before I can shift into gear, and it's Adley asking if I want to taste test for her. Since she's talking about ice cream and since I'm no fool, I tell her I'll be right over.

CHAPTER FOUR

My Saturday is a little slow.

It's my own fault. I know this. I've been dropping the ball on my marketing. I try to keep my social media updated—I have personal accounts and a separate one for my business—but I've been slacking lately, so I use the ninety minutes I find myself with between clients today to do a little research and post some interesting information to my business social media. Demi is much better at this than I am, so I make a mental note to pick her brain later. I open the small plastic bowl of grapes I brought and eat one as I scroll on my phone.

Bash pushes through the door to the break room, and he's still limping.

"Dude, you really need to get that foot looked at," I tell him for the twenty-seventh time.

"I know, I know," he replies for the twenty-seventh time. "Lydia keeps saying that, too. I really think it's just bruised."

"It's been four days since you fell. If it was just bruised, don't you think it would hurt less and not more by now?" I pop a grape into my mouth and watch him as he pours himself a cup of coffee from the machine on the counter. It's a Mr. Coffee and likely older than I am. God forbid Sylvia springs for a Keurig or something.

"Yeah, I know."

I sigh quietly, because Bash is more stubborn than my grandmother, who is a Taurus, but he's an Aries, and I know he has a weird aversion to doctors' offices and hospitals. He's going to change the subject any minute now. I slowly count down in my head from ten.

"I've got to order some of that shampoo we both like. Wanna go in on it together and get a bigger one?" I'm at four when he asks this, by the way.

"Sounds great. How much? I'll Venmo you."

So, every stylist at Sylvia's rents their space. We pay Sylvia a monthly fee to use the space in her salon, her chairs, her sinks, but we have to buy all our own tools and supplies, and even with the stylist discounts we sometimes get, this stuff ain't cheap. Going in together helps. And Sylvia raises our rent constantly. *Constantly*. After the last hike, Bash, Demi, and I went out for drinks and decided we'd eventually leave here and open our own salon together. I've always wanted my own salon, but startup costs are hefty, so the three of us doing it together makes perfect sense. Plus, we actually like each other, which I can't say for the other five stylists at Sylvia's.

"Big plans for your Saturday?" Bash asks as he sits down at the table across from me with what looks like a turkey sandwich for lunch. He stretches out his leg and props his bad foot on another chair.

"It's my grandmother's birthday, and I was planning to take her out to dinner…"

"But?" Bash asks, then takes an enormous bite of his sandwich.

"But she has requested we order in and watch movies. Which, I have to admit, I'm looking forward to."

It's no lie, either. I love spending time with my grandma, so I stop on the way home and get us a nice bottle of rosé, her favorite, and a big bouquet of flowers, which she'll scold me for, but I don't care because every woman should get flowers on her birthday. As of this morning, Grandma didn't know what she was going to want for dinner, but I predict Chinese as I drive back to the house, and when I walk into the kitchen where she's leaning against the counter and studying her phone, she looks up at me and smiles.

"How about we order from Beijing Palace?"

I grin and tell her that sounds great and don't mention to her how predictable she is.

Two hours later, we're on the couch in the living room,

sharing containers of lo mein and cashew chicken and egg rolls and dumplings and more rice than we'll ever be able to eat. Pepper is hovering, but only because there's shrimp in the lo mein, and she will do anything for shrimp, including being nice to us humans. Beijing Palace is very familiar with my grandmother, and they gave her eight fortune cookies instead of two.

"You should find a girl like that," Grandma says now, pointing her chopsticks at the TV screen where Sandra Bullock is plotting a jewelry heist.

"Well, if you happen to run into Sandra Bullock and she's looking for a girlfriend, you send her my way, okay?" I decide not to mention that Sandy's got me by more than twenty years. I also decide not to mention that the twenty years would make zero difference to me if I found her in my bed because I most certainly would not be kicking her out. I'm no fool.

Grandma waits a beat before turning to look at me, and I know she's looking at me without me looking at her because I can *feel* it. You know? And I can also feel the weight of her gaze, which tells me exactly where this conversation is going to go. I brace. Three… two…one…

"Don't you think it's time you got back out there?" she asks.

Blastoff.

I want to sigh and be put off by the question, but I don't because it's my grandma, and she only has my happiness in mind. Plus, she's probably right.

"It kinda is, yeah." She nods once and takes a bite of her egg roll. I'm surprised when she doesn't continue. "That's it? You're not going to give me a speech?"

She laughs softly, dabs her mouth, and gives her head a shake. "Nope. You agreed with me. That's all I needed."

I narrow my eyes at her because, I'm sorry, what? There will be no long diatribe about how she knows Pen hurt me, but I'm awesome and there is a woman out there just waiting for somebody like me? She glances at me, sees my face, which I can only imagine radiates suspicion, and laughs. She literally laughs at me.

"Oh, sweetheart," she says as she leans against me with her shoulder, still laughing. "You make me laugh."

I hold my suspicious face for another second or two but then break down laughing with her. 'Cause when my grandma laughs? It's the best. "You're so mean to laugh at me," I tease her.

"I'm not laughing *at* you, my love, I'm laughing with you. Because you're just the sweetest girl." Her laughter stops and her face grows more serious, though her smile stays. "You know how much I love you, right?"

"I do." And it's the truth.

"Good." She reaches across me. "And don't think you're going to hog all those fortune cookies for yourself."

"I wouldn't dream of it," I say and hand over a couple to her. I rip the cellophane off one and she does the same. We look at each other. "Ready?"

She nods.

We break our cookies open in tandem. It's our tradition. We have to read our fortunes to each other, and sometimes, they're hilarious.

She holds the little strip of paper up so she can see it and reads, "*Good luck will come to you.* Well, that's boring."

I open mine and read, "*Keep your heart open and love will find its way in.* Huh." I look at Grandma. "I think the fortune cookies were eavesdropping on our conversation."

"I think you're right."

❖

I can hardly believe it, but I'm actually looking forward to dance class tonight—words I never thought I'd say. I've been practicing the box step we learned last week alone in my bedroom, in front of the mirror. Step, side, together, step, side, together. I think I've got it down. I mean, it's not hard, it's literally three steps, so it's no huge accomplishment that I've learned it, but still. I'm pretty proud of myself.

Bash, on the other hand, has been miserable all day, limping and wincing here and there, and he has taken every opportunity he can to sit. Lydia is making him see the doctor this afternoon, fucking finally.

"I think Ms. Tina's gonna be pretty impressed with my box step," I tell him while he sits in his chair and exhales long and slow, barely disguised relief on his face.

"Yeah? Been practicing?"

"I have." I demonstrate for him, lifting my hands as if dancing with an invisible partner. "Step, side, together, step, side, together."

"Perfect. You got it." He glances at his phone, then pushes himself to his feet. "Okay, I gotta run, but I'll meet you at the studio for class, yeah?"

I nod. "Good luck," I call after him as he heads out the door. I'm a little worried. It's been a week and he doesn't seem to be in any less pain. If anything, he's in more, so I'm glad Lydia finally convinced him to have it looked at.

While I wait for my next client to arrive, I sit in my chair and scroll on my phone while I spy on Demi, who's got a very handsome guy in her chair. He's dressed in jeans and a very tight black T-shirt, which shows off two sleeves of tattoos. His hair is shoulder length and thick, the kind of hair women see and wish they had on *their* heads, all wavy and perfect. I use my toe to slowly spin in my chair so I can get a glance at them without being obvious about it. There's not a ton of talking happening, but every time my spin passes them, they're looking at each other in the mirror. Like, *really* looking at each other.

By the time she finishes with him—God, he's got great hair— I'm working on my next client. But I keep watch out of the corner of my eye even as I keep up a chat with my client, and I have a hard time hiding my shock when she kisses him good-bye. On the mouth. Lingeringly on the mouth.

"I'm confused," I say to her as I trim the ends of Missy Tate's twenty-year-old blond hair.

"By...?" Demi asks as she grabs the broom to clean up around her chair.

"What happened to the guy from last week? Micah, was it?"

"Nothing happened to him. We're going to check out the live music at Barnaby's tonight." She says it so nonchalantly that I stop moving my scissors and just stare at her for a moment. She glances up and catches me. "What?"

"You were just having eye sex in the mirror with Mr. Tattoos."

Demi's expression dissolves into what I can only label School Girl Grin. "I know. Isn't he hot? We're going to dinner tomorrow."

"You're dating them both." It's not a question because it's clear she is. And there's nothing wrong with that, I know.

"Yes, I am. I'm a big girl, you know."

I fix my face because I'm sure I'm broadcasting *disappointed* or, worse, *judgmental*, and I don't want to be either of those things. "I know, I know. Sorry. I was just surprised."

She lifts one shoulder and blows me a kiss and continues her sweeping, and I return to Missy Tate and her hair. Part of me admires Demi's ability to date more than one person at a time. I always think it sounds good on paper, but I've never been able to do it myself. Not that I think all relationships should be instantly exclusive. Or ever exclusive. I know lots of people for whom ethical nonmonogamy works great. More power to them, I say. But for me? If *I'm* dating somebody? That's the eventual goal. To be exclusive. For Demi, I guess she's just trying everything on before she settles on a final purchase. Which makes total sense.

I think I'm just envious because I'm absolutely not wired that way. Ah, well.

The rest of the afternoon slides by, and before I know it, it's time to get ready for dance class. And just like earlier, I'm looking forward to it. I change into my joggers and sneakers, having learned after two lessons that comfort is the key, at least for me. Ms. Tina is going to want me in some kind of a heel for the final recital, and I know I shouldn't wait too long before I start dancing in them so I get used to them, but I tell myself I'll do that next week. This week? Sneakers it is.

My car takes four tries before the engine turns over, and I really, really need to go look for a new one. It's just the idea of entering a dealership and having to deal with a car salesman makes me twitchy. I know I can buy a car online, that it would be so much easier, and maybe I'll do that. But also? I'm a huge procrastinator, and I know this about myself. So I shrug and shift my car into gear and push buying a new one right out of my own head. I'll deal with it later.

Bash's car isn't in the lot at the dance studio, so I figure he's running a bit late. No worries. If I have to dance with Ms. Tina, that'll be fine. She's fun, and I'm still feeling good about class and my impressive box step.

In the studio, the only ones missing besides Bash are Davis and Linda—who I remember said last week they had a previous engagement of some sort—and Ms. Tina. Those of us present are milling about, the soft buzz of conversation bouncing off the walls and echoing quietly through the studio. My phone pings in the pocket of my joggers, and I pull it out to silence it just as the studio door opens, but it's not Ms. Tina who walks in. It's that super-attractive woman I saw last week. The one who drives the Nissan SUV. The one with all that gorgeous hair.

I glance down at my phone to see a text from Bash that says simply, *Foot's broken.*

"Oh my God," I say softly as I type back, *You're kidding. Now what?*

The dots bounce, then his message comes. *Walking boot for at least 4 weeks.* What? But what about dance class? I'm about to type that question out when he sends another text. *Sorry about class, but it's paid for, so stay.* And then a smiling emoji, a ballroom dancing emoji and another smiley. *And have fun!*

I sigh and turn the phone to silent, then leave it along the wall with my stuff. I join the rest of the class, which has gathered around the woman from the parking lot. I'm in the back and can't see well, which is a shame, really.

But then she speaks.

"Hello there. You're probably wondering where Ms. Tina is. I'm afraid her mother, who lives in Florida, has become ill, so Ms. Tina flew down there to help out for a while. She's not sure when she'll be back, so I'm going to take over her classes for the time being."

And then she tells us her name.

"I'm Marisa Reyes, and Ms. Tina is my aunt, so I've been dancing with her since I was a kid…"

The rest of her words fade out because my head is now filled with fog and a screeching that I know only I can hear, but it's still so fucking loud that I worry my skull will crack from the pressure.

Marisa Reyes.

I've never seen her in person before, just a couple random photos, but I know her. I know she's thirty-six years old. I know she lives on the west side of the city, and I know that she helps out at her aunt's dance studio whenever needed. How do I know all this? Because I also know that her last girlfriend left her.

For me.

❖

Oh God, oh God, oh God.

Those are the only words that barrel through my head at the moment, and I suddenly feel like a trapped animal. What do I do? I could run. I could. Just turn, grab my stuff, and sprint out the door, never to return again, no looking back. I could stay. I mean, maybe she doesn't know me. I mean, we've never actually met or run into each other. And in my defense, I didn't know anything about her. Pen never told me she was with somebody else when we hooked up. And it's been nearly four years since Pen left her for me. Maybe she doesn't remember.

I nearly laugh out loud at that because no woman would simply forget about the person she was dumped for. Still, maybe she won't recognize me…

"Why don't we go around quick, and you give me your names so I can try to get a handle on all of you." Her smile is big and seems genuine, and her gaze slides from person to person as they tell her their names. Because I'm in the back, I'm last, and when her focus lands on me, I see a tiny flinch of an eyebrow. Her eyes flash, but I can't look away from them. They're a deep, rich brown. Like freshly ground coffee. And it feels like they're holding me prisoner.

"Um, hi. Scottie. I'm Scottie." And yeah, I'm also a fool because how many women are there in the Greater Northwood area with the name Scottie? As I expect, a shadow crosses her features, and I might have missed it if I wasn't looking for it. She's good. And oh yeah, she knows who I am. She knows *exactly* who I am.

"And where's your partner, Scottie?"

I am *this close* to answering that she left me before I realize she means Bash. I clear my throat. "Um, he just texted me that he broke his foot, so…" I shrug and leave the sentence to dangle, just like I feel like I'm dangling. But over deep, deep water. Filled with sharks.

A murmur of sympathy and *oh no*s flow through the studio. Marisa gives one small nod, then turns and walks toward the cart with the laptop. She says something about the box step we learned last week and hits a few buttons so music starts up, but I only hear bits and pieces because, *holy shit, what am I gonna do?* Not only is the dance class I'm in being taught—indefinitely—by the woman my ex dumped to be with me, but I also don't have a partner to dance with. And when you don't have a partner to dance with…

Yup.

Oh God, oh God, oh God.

Marisa Reyes is walking toward me, but she's no longer looking me in the eye. She holds out a hand and says, "Since you don't have a partner, you dance with me."

I swallow, and I'm sure she can hear it. Probably the whole room can. I stand there for a second or two or twenty-three before I put my hand in hers. It's soft, really soft, and warm, and she barely grips mine. Like, at all.

But goddamn it, I know the box step, and I'll be damned if I'm going to—

Damn.

"Sorry," I mutter after stepping on her foot. I can do this without looking. I practiced a ton. But tonight, I can't stop looking down at my feet, and I can't seem to get my counts right, and I step on Marisa one more time before I finally find my groove. Thank fucking God because I don't think I could produce any more heat of embarrassment without my body spontaneously combusting right here in the middle of the dance studio. I can feel it all without having to look. My face is red. My palms are sweating. There's a bead of sweat running down the center of my back. I swallow again and realize I just need to focus. *Find something to focus on, Templeton*, my brain screams at me. I can't seem to lift my eyes all the way up, but Marisa is taller than me by an inch or two and settling my gaze on her chin seems easy enough. Just as I can feel my body start to calm down ever so slightly, Marisa lets my hand drop and turns away.

For a moment, I forgot she's also the teacher, so she has to wander around the room and check each couple's moves. I stand there for a minute, feeling kind of silly, but then I just do the moves on my own like I did at home in my room. Step, side, together. Step, side, together. Of course, now that I'm alone, my steps are perfect.

The hour doesn't drag on quite as long as I'm worried it will. We spend it doing the box step to different kinds of music, different tempos, until we all have it down. Regina and Dale look like they've been dancing together forever, both of them not so much moving as flowing. Jamal is stressed out by the end of the night because it seems I'm not the only one stepping on toes. Kevin does as well, and by the time we're all gathering our things to go home, Jamal sits to take his shoes off and rub his toes through his socks. Kevin apologizes for about the fiftieth time, and Jamal finally smiles.

I realize I'm dillydallying, as my grandma would say, and I do *not* want to be the last one here with Marisa. I quickly grab my bag and try to rush out the door without looking like that's what I'm doing. When I get to my car, I'm a little out of breath, so yeah, I rushed out the door pretty fast. I open my car, throw my stuff in, drop into the driver's seat, and shut the door. Only then do I exhale long and loud, feeling like I've been half holding my breath for the past hour. I drop my head to the steering wheel and close my eyes, waiting for my heart to stop pounding, trying to breathe like a normal person.

The only good thing to happen in the past hour—my car starts up on the first try, and I can't get out of that parking lot fast enough.

Marisa Fucking Reyes.

I mean, seriously, what are the odds?

I feel my body relax a bit, my shoulders drop down from my ears, my back loosens. I didn't realize I'd been so tense, but how would I not be?

"Grandma is not going to believe this." I say it out loud in my empty car as I drive, shaking my head the whole ride.

"How was it?" Grandma asks as I enter the living room with the glass of wine I poured immediately upon entering the kitchen. Grandma's watching *Law & Order: SVU.* She pauses the show, Salt on her lap and Pepper on the back of the couch, and smiles up at me from her recliner.

I look at her, shake my head some more because my disbelief is heavy. I take a slug of wine—for the record, wine is really not a drink made to be tossed back like a shot, but that's what I do because I really need the alcohol to hit my system and chill me the fuck out. I feel like I've been slightly electrified for the past ninety minutes.

Grandma's looking concerned. "Scottie? What is it?"

"First of all, Bash's foot is broken. So no dancing for him."

"Oh no. That's too bad."

"Second of all, that leaves me without a partner. Bash wants me to continue on with the class because it's paid for, but I'm all by myself."

Grandma nods. "And everybody else is paired up."

I nod. "Yes. When you don't have a partner, you get paired with the teacher."

Grandma tips her head from side to side. "That could be fun. You said last week you liked the teacher. Ms. Tina, right? Did I tell you I know her?"

"Yes, Ms. Tina and no, you did not. But Ms. Tina's mom in Florida got sick and she flew down there to help out."

"New teacher then."

I tap a finger against the tip of my nose. "Now, here's the crazy part. The new teacher is Marisa Reyes. She's Ms. Tina's niece and also"—I clear my throat—"Penelope's ex. The one she left to be with me."

My grandma has developed what I call in my head her Pen face. It's a kind of grimace, like she tasted something gross, combined with a furrowing of her brow, and she makes it now. She hates how Pen treated me, and I hope the two of them never run into each other. For Pen's sake, 'cause my grandma will verbally lay. Her. Out. Which is pretty awesome to know, I admit it.

"Well," she says, after the Pen face passes. "That's awkward. Does she know who you are?"

"I'm pretty sure she did, yeah. I mean, we've never met, but if my girlfriend left me for somebody else, I'd sure as hell look her up on social media." It's a couple seconds of silence before I say, "So. I guess dance class was fun while it lasted." I add a shrug just to illustrate how much I really don't care.

Grandma, of course, isn't buying it. Her gaze stays on me as she nods, slowly, like she's thinking. "That's it then? You're just going to quit?" Her question is simple and kind. No edge. No accusation.

"I mean, I wasn't going for me. I was going for Bash."

"Mm-hmm."

"And now there's no Bash. And there's the added obstacle of Pen's ex."

"Mm-hmm."

"What's all the humming about?" 'Cause it's about something. I know her.

"I just think maybe you should consider…not quitting."

"Really?" I'm surprised, and it's clear in the way my voice goes up about three octaves.

Grandma lifts one shoulder. "You love the class. You said so yourself. You don't know how long this ex is actually going to be teaching. Maybe Tina will be back next week."

It's my turn to nod slowly. She's not wrong, and my brain starts to turn things over. There's still one bump, though. One obstacle. A big one. "But what if Marisa *is* the teacher for the remainder of the classes?"

"Well." Grandma shifts in her chair so she's facing me, and Salt adjusts as Grandma counts off her points on her fingers as she goes. "One. You didn't know about her when you got together with Penelope, right?"

I shake my head. "I had no idea."

"Two. You are no longer with Penelope. Penelope left you. Which means the two of you—you and this…what's her name again?"

"Marisa."

"Marisa. That's pretty. Anyway, you and this Marisa are now equals. You've both been betrayed and hurt by the same person. The playing field is now level."

I'm not sure Marisa would agree with that, but technically, it's correct.

"Three. You like the class. You look forward to it. I haven't seen that in you in a very long time." She drops her hands back down and strokes Salt and says simply, "I don't think you should give it up so fast." I must not look all that convinced because she tips her head to the side and asks, "What have you been saying is your biggest flaw? Ever since you and Pen broke up, what's been your biggest complaint about yourself?"

This is a test, and I know it. I also know the answer because it's stared me in the face for the better part of a year now. "I'm too nice. I bow out."

"You're too nice." Grandma says it with vehemence. "You let everybody walk on you and dictate your life, while you nod and smile instead of *fighting*." She lifts a fist and gives it a shake. "You're so afraid of conflict, and I blame your parents for that." Again, she's not wrong. My parents fought constantly before they split, and I never understood how much that affected me until Grandma pointed it out to me a few months ago. Now she pokes a finger in my direction, and the unmistakable passion in her words startles me when she says, "You deserve better than that. You're a good person, Scottie Templeton, and you deserve to be happy. Don't bow out this time. Stick with the class. Have fun. Learn to dance." And just like that, she's done. That's how my grandma is. She gets fired up, she says her piece, and then she's finished, and she relaxes, and you can do what you will with whatever opinion or advice she's given you.

"Thanks, Grandma." I kiss her on the cheek and give Salt a little scratch on his furry head.

"Think about it," she says as she picks up her remote and clicks and Mariska Hargitay moves again.

"I will. I promise." I head upstairs to my room because I realize in that exact moment that I'm freaking exhausted. Stress can wring you dry of any and all energy, and I was definitely stressed tonight.

I close my door but leave it open a crack so that cats can come in and out in the night. I undress, rip my bra off with sweet relief, and put on joggers and a T-shirt I've had since I was in cosmetology school. Then I click on my own TV and channel surf for a while until my eyes grow heavy. In that time, texts from both Adley and Bash pop up, but I'm too lost in my own thoughts to be able to focus on my friends. I'll text them in the morning.

Pepper saunters in at eleven just as I'm turning off the TV. She curls up on the pillow next to mine—I still sleep on my side of the bed. I've slept without Pen for close to a year now but haven't been able to bring myself to sleep in the center of the bed. Yet.

I sigh that last exhale before closing my eyes, feeling complete bodily exhaustion. But even as I feel myself drifting off, my mind is filled with rich brown eyes and warm olive skin and cascades of dark, wavy hair...

CHAPTER FIVE

I think May might be my favorite month. It's spring, but really spring. Not fake spring like April can be, what with its constant rain and crazily fluctuating temperatures. No, May is much less chaotic, weather-wise. The sun shows up more. Flowers like daffodils and tulips and lilacs bloom, and the world goes from brown and dull to green and lush with pops of color everywhere. It starts to warm up but isn't crazy hot. I don't love being cold and I hate being hot, so May is about the perfect happy medium for me. I wish it was four months long instead of one.

The week goes by like usual, except for my low-key stress that seems to be a part of me since my talk with Grandma last week, and before I know it, it's Tuesday again. Bash has come back to work, his foot in a walking boot. He can stand up and cut hair, but he has to sit frequently, and when he's on lunch, he props his foot up on a second chair, his relief clear.

"I still can't believe you actually broke it," I say to him as I pop into the break room to grab a Red Bull. I didn't sleep well last night—crazy dreams about dance class, which is tonight and which, as of this moment of the day, I plan on attending. That could change any second, though. I've already changed my mind seven times.

As if reading my thoughts, Bash asks, "You going to dance class tonight?"

"As of right now? Yes. Ask me again in twelve minutes."

He laughs. "I admire your honesty."

I point a finger at him. "Listen, you. I'm still pissed at you for breaking your foot. Dancing lessons by myself were not on my agenda."

"*I'm* pissed at me for breaking my foot." He frowns and shifts his giant walking boot on the chair. "I really wanted to surprise Lydia by not embarrassing her on the dance floor."

"There's plenty of time," I tell him. "You can sign up for the next class."

"Or better yet, you can teach me what *you* learn."

"I could. There's that." I haven't told either Bash or Demi about Marisa, and I'm not a hundred percent sure why yet. I think maybe I'm not ready for a bunch of other people's opinions when I'm not even sure of my own yet. I want to wait. One more class, at least. Tonight. If I go. Then I'll tell them.

My next client is a guy named Jonathan Brockman. I don't have a ton of male clients. I think a lot of them go to barbers, which makes sense. But I have a couple, and Demi has a few, and Bash has way more than both of us. Jonathan is tall and good-looking with a boyish smile and kind eyes and a body that says he spends a ton of time at the gym. He's also hinted at going out with me more than once.

"Hey, Jonathan," I say as I get him from the waiting area and lead him to the sinks. "What's new in the world of finance?" He works for a bank in the city. "Are you keeping everybody's money safe?"

"Doing my best," he says with a smile and leans back so his head is over the sink. We make small talk while I shampoo his hair, and then we move to my chair.

I'm trimming when Demi returns from her break and is sweeping around her chair. "You going to dance class tonight, Scottie?" she asks.

Jonathan seems to sit up a little straighter. "You take dance classes? What kind?"

"Oh, just some basic salsa. I was going with a friend, doing him a favor, and he broke his foot." I wish Bash was at his chair, but he's still in back with his foot up. "Trying to decide if I still want to go."

"Listen, if you need a new dance partner, I'll happily step in." Jonathan meets my eyes in the mirror, and I know he's completely serious. And for a split second, I actually consider it. But I know he's interested in me for other reasons, and I don't want to lead the poor guy on just to let him down later.

"You are so sweet," I say and lay a hand on his shoulder for a beat. "But there's another guy there without a partner, so they've paired us up. I don't want to leave him high and dry, you know?"

He nods, frowns slightly, but seems to let it go. I'm afraid to look at Demi because I'm sure she's smiling at my lie. Luckily, she doesn't say anything more, and I finish up Jonathan without having to do any more fancy footwork. I walk him to the front desk, he pays me, leaves me a generous tip, as always, and makes an appointment for three weeks out. I watch him go, and as I always do when he flirts and compliments and hints, I feel a little bad. I should just tell him I prefer girls, but I don't enjoy being forced to out myself, so I smile at him through the window, give him a little wave, and then return to my chair to clean up.

"There isn't another guy at class that needs a partner, is there?" Demi asks me, and Bash is back now, so he looks at me with curiosity.

I shake my head. "They pair you with the teacher if you don't have a partner."

"You get to dance with Ms. Tina?" Bash asks. "That actually sounds like it'd be fun."

"Well…" And then I let that word hang out there for a minute while I realize that just my saying it the way I did tells my friends there's more to the story. Son of a bitch.

"Well what?" Demi asks when I fail to elaborate. Bash is also looking at me, and I sigh loudly before telling them that Ms. Tina is in Florida with her ailing mother and there's a substitute dance teacher.

"*Okay*," Bash says, drawing the word out because he knows me well enough to know I'm not telling him everything.

"And the substitute is Pen's ex. The one she left to be with me."

Bash gapes at me while Demi says, "What?" loud enough that the other stylists turn to look.

"Yeah." I shake my head because, even a week later, it's still kind of surreal when I say it out loud. "I have spent the entire week wavering between holding my head high and continuing with the class and never showing my face there again."

"Oh my God," Demi says with barely contained glee. Bash shoots her a look, but she ignores him. "This is like a Lifetime movie or something. What's she look like? She hot?" Then they both look at me, and it's clear Bash wants to know, too.

Is Marisa Reyes hot?

That's the question, and it's certainly not hard to answer. Marisa Reyes is *smokin'* hot. Still, I try to contain myself.

"She's very attractive, yes."

Demi makes a rolling motion with her hand, telling me she wants more detail.

I sigh. "She's a little taller than me. Olive skinned. Big, dark eyes. And a ton of wavy dark hair. She's got great posture, probably seems taller than she is because of the way she carries herself." I remember something I hadn't really thought of until now. "And her voice is low. Deep."

"Sexy?" Demi adds.

"I mean, I guess?" Yes, her voice is absolutely sexy, but I'm certainly not going to admit to that right here in the middle of the salon.

"Now it makes sense why you're so hesitant to go back," Bash says. I can tell by the look on his face that he's hurt I didn't tell him, and I don't know how to explain it.

"Yeah. I've been wavering all week."

"I say go," Demi says. "Fuck Pen. And while I'm at it, fuck the ex. Actually, no. Don't fuck the ex. That would be…hmm. After hearing what she looks like, maybe you *should* fuck the ex. That'd be some fuckery right there."

Bash shoots her a look. She blinks at him, then waves a hand as if erasing the air in front of her. "Ignore me. I'm just babbling now. But I say go. Pen left her for you. Then she left you. You guys are even now."

"That's what my grandma said, too." I glance at my phone to see that time is getting short, and I'm going to need to make a decision. Like, soon.

"There's a chance Ms. Tina will be back anytime, right?" Bash's eyebrows are raised in question.

"True."

Demi chimes in with, "Or maybe she'll be gone the entire class and it'll be you and the ex for the next how many weeks?"

"Twelve," I say and try not to groan. "Well, actually, tonight is the fourth class, so eight left after that."

"Two months to go." Demi scrunches up her face like she's thinking, then nods. "You can do this."

That's the thing about Demi. She's very bold, bolder than I'll ever be, and I envy that. So something about her determined face and the tone of her voice imbues me with a little extra oomph. I nod once.

"I'll give it another shot," I say, and now the determination is mine. I feel strong. In control. Confident.

Of course, all those things slowly leach away as I drive, and by the time I pull into the parking lot and see the black Nissan SUV sitting there, they're completely gone. Marisa is here, and in response to that realization, my heart starts to pound louder. Faster. Harder. A lump forms in my throat and won't go down no matter how many times I swallow. My armpits start to sweat.

"Cheese and crackers," I mutter, forgetting I'm nowhere near Grandma and don't have to watch my language. I inhale slowly and close my eyes, willing my body to relax. To calm down. To give me a fucking break. A car door slams nearby and jerks my eyes open. I glance at them in the rearview mirror.

"Okay," I say to the car's interior, "let's do this."

❖

Marisa must be running late, despite her SUV being in the lot. I arrive in the studio, and over the next ten minutes others enter, and soon, we're all there except her. It's nearly six ten before she breezes in, her hand clutching the smaller one of a boy who looks to be about four or five. He's got a mop of dark hair, huge brown eyes with eyelashes I spend way too much money on mascara to achieve, and what looks to be a kid-sized iPad in his other hand.

"I'm so sorry," Marisa says to us. "Sitter canceled at the last minute, so…" She stops, faces us, and takes a breath. Lets it out. Smiles. God, she's pretty. "This is my nephew, Jaden. Who has promised me he'll be quiet." She gives his hand a little shake as she says it. "Right?"

Jaden nods and smiles, his eyes wide as he takes all of us in. Marisa sets him up in the corner where the laptop sits, fits earbuds into his ears, does a few things on his iPad, and then shifts her focus to the laptop. A little Latin music fills the room, the volume lower than usual, as Marisa moves in front of us.

"Okay, I think Ms. Tina told you guys that there's a recital of sorts at the end of class. You'll have a final dance, and that's what you're going to spend the next eight weeks working toward. You don't have to dance it in front of people if you don't want to. No pressure. But if you do want to, you'll be able to invite a few people. Friends. Kids. Etcetera. And the rest of the class will be here."

She looks beautiful, and I'm trying hard not to stare, not to think about what Demi said about sex. Of course, I'm not going to sleep with Marisa Reyes. First of all, that's not why I'm here. Second of all, she hates me, as evidenced by the fact that she looks at everybody but me as she talks. But God, she's pretty. She's got leggings on today. Black. They make her legs look super long. Black Nikes on her feet. The lightweight ones made of, like, mesh or something. A white T-shirt that is so worn and faded, I can make out her black sports bra underneath. There's faded black print on the shirt, but it's so light, I can't tell what it says. Or used to say. As she talks, she pulls her hair back and whips it into a messy bun, and seriously, how the hell do women do that? I've never been able to master pulling my hair up without using a mirror. Or a rubber band, apparently. And I work with hair for a living. But her hair's up now, and her neck is long and gorgeous and— "Oh my God, stop it," I mutter.

"Hmm?" Linda asks from next to me, and I shrug and make a face and shake my head because I'm clearly a super awkward weirdo who talks to herself in groups of strangers. Jesus.

"Also, for anybody who's interested, the dance studios in the area like to throw little competitions with each other. There are five schools altogether, and we like to show off our students, so if any of you decide you might like to get involved in that, let me know."

A little hum of comments goes through the room, and I can tell by looking at faces who might be interested—Regina, Jillian, Pete and Katrina—and who's definitely not—Davis, Neil, and Kevin.

"All right. I know Ms. Tina had you learning the box step because it's basic and easy, and we did that last week, but I think it's time we really get into the spice of things, don't you? You're here to learn to salsa dance, so I think it's time to get into some salsa. Yeah?"

We're all pretty excited about that. I know I am. I've always liked salsa dancing. When I agreed to do this with Bash, that was one of the reasons. Because it was salsa. And seeing Marisa's clear excitement to teach us just bolsters me.

"All right, super simple steps to begin with. The basics." She pushes through the crowd of us, and it takes me a beat to realize she's coming right at me. "Grab your partner." She holds out her hand to me, and I take it without thinking. No hesitation. And there's a split second where my brain plays a different story from where we are now. She's not the ex of my ex. She doesn't hate me. She's crossed the room to me, hand outstretched, because I'm her dance partner. I'm hers, and we do this all the time.

It's a jarring little fantasy movie, and I have to give my head a shake. And then my hand is in Marisa's, and again, it's warm and soft, and she actually holds on to mine this time. The crowd has backed away into a horseshoe shape around us, the Latin beat clear over the speakers.

Marisa stands next to me, my hand in hers. "Okay, listen to the beat, and then we're going to do this simple basic step." Holding my hand, she begins to move, her hips swaying, her other hand in front of her body as she follows the beat. "Left foot forward, one, right foot stays in the same spot, but lift it and step down, two. Feet together, three." She repeats the instructions once more as she moves, and after that, she just moves and counts. The whole time, my hand stays in hers, and the sway of her hips almost mesmerizes me. Jesus, Mary, and Joseph, she is *sexy*. "Everybody try."

The students line up, Marisa counts—"Left foot one, right foot two, together three. Left foot one, right foot two, together three"— and we all move, myself included. It's pretty easy, and honestly, Latin music is so fun and has such a great beat, it's not hard to follow it, and the next thing I know, Marisa and I are moving together like we do this all the time.

It's fucking surreal.

She suddenly drops my hand and moves away, and that's when I remember that she's actually the teacher here and needs to move around, help people. I continue with the steps and watch her while trying not to watch her, but it's hard. She doesn't walk, she floats. Glides. She's the picture of grace, and it's hard to take my eyes off her. I'm not the only one. Lots of eyes are on her. Some because they're learning the dance steps. Some because, well, because. I mean, look at her.

"Okay, let's add the next bit." She returns to me, holds out her hand once more, and we do the same thing, except we're starting with our right foot and stepping back. "Right foot back, five. Left foot stays in the same spot, but lift it and step down, six. Feet together, seven. Give it a shot." And then she and I are moving again. "Right foot five. Left foot six. Together seven. Right foot five. Left foot six. Together seven." We do it two more times with Marisa counting, and then she lets me go to wander, and my body almost cries at the loss of her. What the hell? What is wrong with me? I do my best to shake *that* off. Yikes.

I keep moving as I watch her move around the other students, helping Davis count, lifting Jillian's hand so it's in front of her and not just hanging.

"A couple details," she says, raising her voice over the music. "Keep your hands centered in front of you. It looks better than having them flapping at your sides." Jillian grins. "And don't bounce." She demonstrates bopping her head and torso to the music as she moves her feet, and we all laugh because she does look silly. "I know it's tempting to move with the beat, but focus on your feet and hips for now. Take small steps. No need for lunges. Kevin."

Kevin blushes and looks sheepish as he tries to shorten his steps.

"Okay." Marisa returns to my side and waits until she's got everybody's attention. "Now, we put it all together." She moves her feet and counts. "Left one. Right two. Together three. Four is silent. Right five. Left six. Together seven." She holds out her hand to me and we do it again, together. I keep my right hand in front of me like she told Jillian and watch Marisa's feet as I move my own. My hips sway as we step. We get to seven, stand for the beat of eight, then start again at one.

"You're really good at this, Scottie," Linda comments. Nods and murmurs of agreement ripple through the class, and then we're at eight and Marisa drops my hand and doesn't look at me.

"Okay, give it a shot." She walks around, looking at everybody's form. I am moving on my own, but watching her because I can't help it. She's...she's something.

I manage to make it through the rest of the class without getting caught staring. When I'm not gawking at Marisa, my eyes are drawn to the little boy in the corner. Jaden, Marisa's nephew. He's barely looked up once from his iPad, and I'm impressed. I love video games, but even I tire of them after a while. He's been super well-behaved, and I try and fail to imagine Drake, my five-year-old half brother from my dad, sitting quietly for the better part of an hour. No way. He'd have been running around the studio, probably shouting and waving his arms, about half an hour ago. But Jaden is sitting quietly, earbuds in, eyes following whatever's on his screen. I'm impressed.

Class wraps up with a cooldown and some stretches, Marisa telling us how important it is to keep our muscles loose. Since I'm on my feet all day anyway and today was mostly just stepping, I'm not worried. But I imagine some of my fellow dance students who have butt-in-chair jobs might be feeling this class tomorrow. I find my water bottle and realize I'm thirstier than I thought after I chug down almost half of it in one go. When I finish, I find Marisa looking at me from her corner by the laptop, but she yanks her gaze away quickly. Huh. Interesting.

We're the last group on Tuesdays, so when class empties out, the studio's pretty abandoned.

Out in the parking lot, which is emptying quickly, it's still light, the sun just making its way toward the horizon. That's my favorite thing about spring and summer, the lengthening of the days. When it's light out until almost nine at night? That's the best. I love it. I toss my bag in the back seat and take in a huge lungful of air.

Northwood isn't a huge city, and the air is always pretty fresh and clean. I exhale, drop into the driver's seat, and key the ignition. The engine coughs, I swear to God, then nothing.

I try again. Another cough, but weaker, then nothing.

"Shit."

I try again. This time? Not a thing. Not an attempt at turning over. Not a clicking. Nothing. Zero. Zilch. Nada.

"Oh no."

I try once more. Nothing.

I let my head fall to the steering wheel and mutter a curse under my breath. If Bash was here, I'd feel less at a loss. He's at least somewhat familiar with cars. Beyond filling the gas tank, I know very little. Yes, I know that makes me a bad lesbian, but what can I say? Cars don't interest me. As evidenced by the fact that I've had this one forever because I have zero interest in shopping for another.

A rapping on my window scares the living hell out of me, and I jump enough to bonk my head into the ceiling of my car. My heart is pounding as I turn to see the most unexpected sight.

Marisa Reyes is standing outside my car. "Trouble?" she asks, and it's clear she's less than thrilled. But I glance around and see the parking lot is empty except for my car and hers.

I roll down my window. "Yeah. It's dead."

"I'll give you a ride." She says it not as an offer, but as a foregone conclusion.

"I mean, I can call an Uber," I say.

"I'll give you a ride," she says again. Then she turns on her heel and heads back to her car as if she knows I'm going to follow her.

I stare after her, weighing my options. It's after seven and I haven't been home since I left this morning, and I'm tired and hungry and, "Fuck," I mutter, grabbing my things and pushing out of my dead car.

I follow her.

CHAPTER SIX

Marisa's SUV smells lovely as I climb into the passenger seat. Like fresh air and sunshine and coconuts.

I try to be discreet about looking for the source, and when I can find no air freshener anywhere, I finally realize it must be her. I quietly inhale, because it's a wonderful scent, warm and inviting.

"Hi. I'm Jaden." The boy is in a car seat behind me, and I turn to smile at him.

"I know. I was in the dance class. Hi. I'm Scottie."

Jaden snort-laughs. "That's a boy's name."

"It is. It was my grandpa's name."

Jaden studies me for a moment as he seems to think this through. Finally, he says, "Cool," and apparently, that's the end of the conversation.

Marisa gets behind the wheel and starts the engine.

"Thank you for this," I say. "I'll call and get my car moved tomorrow."

She gives a nod. "No worries." She plugs her phone into the dash and chooses some quiet kid music for Jaden. We back out of the spot, and she turns to me, actually looks at my face for what seems to be the first time. God, her eyes are dark. Stormy. Gorgeous. Her eyeliner is slightly smudged under one eye, but that just makes her seem more human. "Where to?"

I give her my grandmother's address, and I can see the slightest surprise register on her face. I assume she knows Pen and I split, given that Pen's engagement announcement has been all over social media. Of course, maybe she's blocked Pen everywhere. Who could blame her?

"I'm really liking class so far," I say by way of small talk, because the lack of conversation in the car is deafening.

"Good. Sorry about your friend's foot."

"Yeah, me, too. He wanted to surprise his fiancée."

She nods but says nothing more.

Ugh. Yeah. Not awkward at all, this ride.

I swallow and then turn back to Jaden, who's looking out his window. "Jaden, how old are you?"

"I'm seven," he says.

"You're four," Marisa corrects him. He holds up three fingers.

"My mommy and daddy are in heaven," he says, and it's so matter-of-fact that I'm speechless for a minute and just blink at him. I turn to Marisa just as she's looking at him in the rearview mirror.

"That's right," she says. "And who takes care of you now?"

"You do!" he says and points excitedly at Marisa.

"You got it." I see Marisa's throat move as she swallows. She must feel my eyes on her because she turns the kid music up a bit before she speaks. "My brother and sister-in-law were killed in a car accident last year." They're shocking, her words, both because they're just awful, and also, God knows she doesn't owe me any explanations.

"Oh my God. I'm so sorry." I say it very quietly, so only she can hear me above the sound of what I think is supposed to be a fish singing. "That's terrible."

A nod. She keeps her voice low, too. "It's been hard. I'm his legal guardian now."

What the hell do I say to that? Instant toddler? Plus, you get to explain to him the loss of his parents as he grows? Wow. "I can't imagine," I say, and it's the truth. I try to think about having to take in any of my siblings. Say, Drake and Noah, who are five and eight. "Your life must have changed so much."

"It did. Completely." She glances in the mirror again. "But what else could I do? He's my family and I love him." The simple statement looks good on her. Her face lights up, and her smile is tender, and her love for her nephew is crystal clear.

"I admire you." It's the truth. And honestly, what else is there to say? Not that there's time even if I thought of something because we're turning onto my grandma's street. I direct her to the right house, and again, she looks a little confused, like she wants to ask, but she evidently chooses not to.

When she pulls to a stop in the driveway, I turn to the back seat. "Bye, Jaden. Thanks for the ride." I hold out my hand for a high-five and he slaps it with exuberance as he says bye. He's adorable, and I like him already. I turn to Marisa. "Thank you. I really appreciate it."

She nods. "You're welcome," she says simply.

"Maybe I'll see you next week, J. That's what I'm calling you now. You're the J man."

Jaden giggles with delight as I slide out of the SUV. Marisa waits until I'm in the side door before she shifts into reverse, a chivalrous thing I've always liked.

"Who was that?" Grandma asks from the front door, where she's clearly looking out the window.

"Excuse me, ma'am, are you spying on me?" I tease her, setting my crap down and then crossing to her to give her a kiss on the cheek. Her J'adore is spicy, and she's still dressed in nice clothes, and I remember she had dinner with friends tonight. "How was dinner?" I ask.

"First, where's your car? Did it finally give up the ghost?"

I groan. "Ugh, yes. It wouldn't start, and I had to leave it at the dance studio."

"Who drove you home?"

"Yeah, that was Marisa."

Grandma blinks at me, and I can almost see her reaching into her memory banks. Her eyes go wide. "The ex?"

"The very one."

And my sweet, loving grandmother? Laughs at me! A full-on, deep from the belly, amused-by-my-pain laugh. "Oh, I bet that wasn't awkward at all. At. All."

I let myself be indignant for a moment before I join her because, as I've said, my grandmother has the best laugh. "It was… interesting."

"What did you talk about? How much she probably hates you? Ways she's planned your murder?"

I shake my head as we both head for the kitchen by mutual agreement, and she grabs wineglasses from the cabinet while I choose a nice Syrah and go to work with the corkscrew. "Surprisingly, no. I told her I could call an Uber, but she insisted on driving me." I pop the cork. "She had her four-year-old nephew with her, and I found out that her brother and sister-in-law were killed in a car accident last year and now she's raising him. Isn't that sad?"

"Oh my. That is sad. I vaguely remember hearing something about that in my circle. Oh, that poor boy."

"He's a cute kid. Funny. I think he likes me." I pour wine into the glasses and we each pick one up and touch them together. Grandma and I always do cheers. It's bad luck not to. She taught me that.

We spend the rest of the evening watching a true crime documentary on Netflix, because when I tell you my grandma is obsessed with true crime, I mean she is *obsessed with true crime*. We watch in entertained horror as the story plays out, trying to outguess the other, and by the time it reaches its conclusion, we're both kind of speechless.

"Man, people suck," I say.

"So much," she agrees.

And we both head to bed.

Alone in my room, I'm able to shift my thoughts back to earlier in the evening. The dancing. The closeness of Marisa. Her hand in mine. I give myself a shake because these thoughts are ridiculous. So she's hot. So what?

"I can look, though," I mutter on a pout as I change into my pajamas. "Nothing wrong with looking."

And then my brain throws me an image of Marisa's face in the SUV as she talked about Jaden, about loving him. That gentleness. The softness in her eyes as she said it.

They stay with me as I slip under the covers and as Pepper sneaks in and curls up on the pillow next to my head and as I drift off. I dream of warmth and coconuts and Latin music.

❖

"Pen has been texting," I tell Adley on Friday. We're in the back of Get the Scoop. She's making ice cream and I'm sitting on a stool and watching. Friday evenings, I tend to spend in the shop with her, and then we'll often go out for drinks after she closes.

Adley glances over her shoulder at me. "Like, more than just the once?"

I sigh. "Yeah. A couple times. Very innocuous. *Have a great day. Weather's great today.* Stupid stuff like that."

"Why?"

That's the question, isn't it? I've asked myself the same thing a hundred times since her fourth text of the week came this morning. *Happy Friday, hope yours is great.* That's what she said. See what I mean about innocuous? "I have no idea."

Adley shakes her head. "Isn't she engaged?"

"Evidently."

More headshaking. "She's sketchy."

"You thought that about her when we were together."

Adley pins me with her eyes. "And I was right, wasn't I?"

Yeah. She was. I really should listen to her more often.

"You're not texting back, are you?"

"No," I tell her. "I did when she first texted, but I've kept my responses very sporadic."

"You shouldn't respond at all." Adley finishes with a tub of that tropical ice cream, which is mango pineapple with coconut flakes throughout. The scent alone has the whole back room smelling like an umbrella drink on the beach. "Here, take this out front for me, would you?"

"Sure." I never question it when Adley asks me to do a task that she could easily have an employee do, for two reasons. One, she's my best friend, and I am always happy to help her. And two, she gives me free ice cream. All the damn time. I mean, the least I can do is carry a tub of it from the back of the shop to the front, right?

Friday nights are super busy at Get the Scoop, especially once spring hits. Adley's open all year round but runs a skeleton crew in the winter. Not a ton of action in the ice cream game when it's twenty degrees out, but she does more than just sell cones and sundaes. She caters dessert for events and gatherings, works closely with local schools and sports organizations, and is always networking. But once the weather warms up and Northwoodians venture out of their houses once more, she gets very busy.

There's an impressive line of people waiting for ice cream tonight, but everybody seems happy. I hand off the Tropical Dream to one of the kids working behind the counter and turn to head back where I came from when a mop of dark hair on a small human catches my eye, and before I can make sense of it, I hear my name.

"Scottie! Hi! Over here! It's me!" Jaden Reyes is waving like a nut at me, a huge smile on his face as he bounces on the balls of his feet. His other hand is tucked snugly in the hand of his aunt Marisa, whose dark eyes meet mine, and whose expression I can't quite read. It's not hate or disdain, though, I'm pretty sure, and that's a huge relief.

I scoot around the counter. "Hi, Jaden. What are you doing here?"

"I'm getting ice cream," he tells me, and while he doesn't actually say *duh*, it's definitely implied. I hear Marisa chuckle softly and I meet her gaze.

"Hi," I say.

"Hey," she says back, and her smile seems genuine.

"Do you work here?" Jaden asks.

"I don't, but the owner is my best friend."

"Really? I bet you get all the ice cream you want. I wish my best friend had an ice cream shop."

"You know…" I meet Marisa's dark eyes again. God, she looks good, dressed simply in jeans with a hole in one knee and a red top. "If it's okay with your aunt, I can take you back there, and you can see the ice cream being made."

"Yeah!" Jaden jumps up and down. "Can I, Aunt Mar? Please?"

I worry a bit that I may have stepped on toes, but Marisa is surprisingly easygoing about it.

"Sure." She moves his hand to mine and lets it go. "I'll wait outside."

I mean, I could probably bring them both to the back, but I don't think of that until Marisa is walking away and my eyes are glued to her ass. I give myself a mental shake, tightening my grip on the small hand in mine. "Come on."

Adley loves having kids in the back. She loves to show them the machinery and the ingredients. She's a person who was really born to be a parent. I hope she finds somebody soon who has the same dreams.

"Jaden, this is my best friend in the whole world. Her name is Adley. Adley, this is my very new friend, Jaden."

I watch as Adley's face lights up, and she comes around the table to squat in front of Jaden. She always wears a white coat, similar to a chef's coat, and it makes her seem larger than life somehow. Her dark hair is in a ponytail, and she's got a white hat on. "Do you like ice cream, Jaden?" she asks in a conspiratorial voice, as if she and Jaden are about to share a secret.

He nods with the vehemence only a four-year-old can display.

I stand aside and watch as Adley and Jaden become the best of friends. She tells him all about the steps that go into making different flavors of ice cream, and he is riveted, his dark eyes big, nodding at everything she says. It's adorable. By the time she finishes with him, he has a huge sundae that he made all by himself.

"Should we get something for Aunt Marisa?" I ask him. "What's her favorite?"

"Mint chocolate chip with chocolate sprinkles," he replies without missing a beat.

I meet Adley's eyes. "You heard the man." And a couple minutes later, Jaden and I are walking out the back door and around the building to the parking lot where Marisa is leaning against her SUV and looking at her phone. When she glances up at us, her eyes go wide for a split second before settling back to normal.

"Well, look at you," she says, her eyes on Jaden's sundae. She brings her gaze up to meet mine, and I give her a sheepish grin, wrinkling my nose in the hopes of looking cute enough to forgive for the enormous amount of sugar I just gave her nephew.

"And this is for you," I say, handing over the mint chocolate chip cone. "Complete with sprinkles."

She smiles in what looks to be pleasant surprise, then takes it from me without meeting my eyes, and I feel the warmth as her fingers brush mine. "Thank you. My favorite. How'd you know?"

"Seems your nephew pays attention to important things like favorite ice cream."

Marisa directs Jaden to a nearby picnic table before he can drop his entire sundae. I stand kind of awkwardly because I don't want to invite myself, but she didn't ask me to sit with them.

I jerk my thumb over my shoulder. "Okay, well, I'm gonna get back."

"Sit with us," Jaden says, but his words don't register because I'm too busy watching Marisa run her tongue around her cone while trying not to watch. Holy shit. If I've ever seen anything sexier, I can't think of it in this moment.

"Oh, um…"

Marisa meets my gaze for a split second before looking away. "Sit," she says simply, and my ass drops to the bench faster than I do most any other thing in life. "Thank you for this," she says politely, and I nod. "You know the owner, huh?"

"Adley Purcell. We've been friends for years. Her grandparents owned this shop. Her parents didn't want it, so when her grandparents retired, she bought them out. She loves the science of it, the mixing of flavors. She's fantastic at coming up with new combinations."

Marisa nods. "I've noticed they've got some really unique flavors. Things you wouldn't normally find at your everyday ice cream shop."

"She prides herself on that." I turn to Jaden. "How's the sundae?"

Jaden holds up his thumb while shoveling a huge spoonful of chocolate chip cookie dough ice cream into his mouth. It makes me laugh and ruffle his hair.

I feel like I could sit here forever, but at the same time, conversation is understandably a bit awkward. If Marisa feels anything like I do, this whole thing is just…weird. That fact hits me strongly all of a sudden, and I push to my feet. "Okay, well, I'd better get back." I give Jaden's hair another tousle, thankful that he's there to be a buffer. "Thanks for visiting. I'll see you next time." I shift my focus to Marisa, who's watching me now, and she gives me one nod, then looks away.

"Thanks for the ice cream."

"Anytime."

"Jaden, what do you say to Scottie?" she asks him.

"Thank you," he says and then surprises me by getting off his bench, wrapping his arms around my waist, and hugging me tightly.

I'm momentarily speechless, and Marisa looks almost as surprised as I am. Without a word, Jaden lets go and goes back to his sundae.

"Okay. Well." I give a dorky little wave because smooth is about the last thing on the list of cool stuff I can pull off. "I guess I'll see you next week."

Marisa smiles, and I turn and walk away, and I swear to God I can feel her eyes on me.

Back inside the shop, I thank Adley for the great tour.

"Are you kidding? You know how much I love kids. And he was adorable. How do you know him?"

Oh. Right. I didn't give her that info, did I? "Um, he's Marisa's nephew." I wait for her to put the pieces together, because she's busy working on another new flavor, and she's not great at split focus.

"Marisa." She bobs her head once as if she knows who that is, but I can almost hear the wheels turning in her head. Five, four, three, two... Her head snaps up. "Marisa, Pen's ex, Marisa? Dance instructor Marisa?"

"Yeah. That very one."

"Oh my God."

"I know."

"How...? What...?"

"Yeah." I drop back onto my stool.

"That's *so* weird," she says, drawing out the word *so* to last a good three seconds. "Like, how?"

"How what?"

"Like...*how*?" She looks so baffled that it actually makes me laugh softly. The truth is, I don't quite get *how* either.

"I saw them standing in line when I brought the ice cream out and...I don't know. Jaden called my name and was waving and jumping up and down." I shrug. Give my head a shake. "I just...went over and said hi. And Jaden's so cute and excited, and I don't know why, but I thought he'd like a tour and..." I shrug again because I'm not really telling Adley anything both of us don't already know. And I'm not coming close to answering the question of *how*. "It's really weird."

"It's *really* weird." She gets a spoon from a drawer, scoops out some of the ice cream she's been working on, and holds it out to me. "What do you taste?"

I take the ice cream into my mouth and let it sit on my tongue for a few seconds. I've learned this is the best way to taste Adley's concoctions. Let it sit, then roll it around with my tongue and feel the flavors as they either burst forth in a taste explosion or slowly seep over my tastebuds in a soft, subtle way. This taste is the second version, and I close my eyes and concentrate.

"Vanilla first, but subtly. Creamier, though. Cinnamon? No. Wait. Clove? Nutmeg. There's definitely nutmeg." My eyes pop open. "Eggnog!"

Adley points at me with a nod. "Yes!"

I take another spoonful. Now that I know what it is, I can't untaste it, and it's delicious.

"I haven't decided if I want to make a batch of it now or save the recipe for the holidays." It's how Adley keeps customers coming during what's not necessarily considered ice cream season—she makes holiday flavors. Last year, she came up with a pumpkin pie ice cream that was unbelievably good, despite not being a traditional ice cream flavor.

"I say save it." I lick the spoon clean and take it over to the industrial stainless-steel sink.

She bobs her head a couple times. "I'll do that."

"Summer's on its way." I jerk a thumb over my shoulder. "And there was a pretty good line out there earlier. I love seeing that."

"Me, too."

"Hey, you should come over this weekend. Have dinner with Grandma and me."

Adley smiles. Her expression seems a little far away, and I imagine her brain is off on some new flavor, as it so often is. "Yeah, maybe I'll do that," she says, her focus on the middle distance.

She won't, but at least I got her to smile.

Chapter Seven

"S ylvia is raising the fucking rent again."
These are the first words I hear when I walk into work on Tuesday. Bash is still in his boot and still limping, but he's livid as he yanks a sheet of paper out of my old-timey mail cubby on the wall—Sylvia has no clue how to email or text us like a person living in this century—and hands it to me. It's clear he wants me to join him in his indignation, and I likely will, but I literally just walked through the back door and haven't even had a chance to let my eyes adjust from the sunlight to the much dimmer atmosphere of the back room of the salon.

I stow my purse and take a large gulp of my mocha latte and burn the roof of my mouth, and my eyes water as I try to pretend I didn't. Then I look down to scan the paper. I meet his eyes and let his words absorb into my brain. "Wait. She just raised the rent, what, five months ago?"

"Yes. What the fuck?" Bash was stage-whispering, which always makes me laugh because the walls in here are pretty thin. Also, pretty much everybody here hates Sylvia. We're just more vocal than most. Bash shakes his head. "I've got to pay for a wedding at the end of the year."

I frown and nod my commiseration. I certainly understand what it's like to be thrown for a financial loop. I mean, hello? I live with my grandma.

He bitches a bit more, and I nod and agree, and then we head out onto the floor to work.

I very much dislike Sylvia, but I love the specific hustle and bustle of a busy salon. I always have. The soft hum of various conversations, the splash of water spray from the sink, the buzz of an electric razor and the snip of scissors and the whoosh of a blow-dryer. And the smells. Perm solutions, keratin, shampoos and conditioners, and hair products galore. People constantly moving. Coming and going and sitting and standing and spinning in chairs. It's the soundtrack of my working life, and it's the soundtrack I always wanted for my working life from the time I was a young teenager.

"Untangled," I mutter to Bash as we walk to our respective chairs.

He opens his mouth, I'm sure to veto me, but then he snaps it shut and makes a thinking face. "Hmm."

"Yay! Put it on the list," I say as I check all my supplies and get ready for my first client.

"Good morning, folks," Sylvia says loudly as she enters the main floor through the front door. She does that. Makes an entrance. She's in her sixties, her hair dyed a deep auburn. I'm surprised to see her, as she prefers to sit back and rake in money rather than actually do hair. Granted, she's the owner, and therefore, she can do that if she wants to, but it's always bugged me. We've started to feel like she's a little bit out of the game now, not really keeping up with trends or changes. Most of us are constantly reading, surfing the internet, watching other salons to see what they're doing. The beauty industry is continually in flux, and you have to change with it if you want to stay relevant. And keep getting new clients. But Sylvia doesn't seem interested in that anymore. "I trust you've all received my letter."

We're not officially open yet, so the only people listening to her are stylists. Nods and muttered words ripple through us all, and nobody looks happy.

"You just raised the rent less than six months ago," Bash says, and I shoot him a look.

"It's true, and I'm sorry to do it again, but I don't control inflation." Sylvia's blue eyes flash even as she pastes a smile on her heavily made up face. "Prices have gone up on everything. Electricity. Heat. Things that I have no say in."

I can see the muscles in Bash's jaw flexing, and I know he

wants to say more. How the prices of the things we have to pay for out of our own pockets are also going up—products and tools and subscriptions—and that Sylvia raising the rent on us for the second time in less than a year is grossly unfair. I implore him with my eyes to keep quiet. His nostrils flare as he looks at me, but thank God, he doesn't say anything more.

Sylvia doesn't stay long—she never does—and within a half hour, she's gone, and the atmosphere in the salon has relaxed a bit, and we're working a usual Tuesday.

Demi arrives around eleven and the three of us chat about everything and nothing as the morning morphs into the afternoon. Demi gives a trim to a very handsome guy in a business suit. He's got sandy hair, a neatly trimmed beard, and I hear her call him Ben. When he kisses her good-bye on the mouth, Bash and I exchange looks.

"Demi, seriously, *another* one?" Bash asks.

She raises her dark eyebrows in question, like she has no idea what he means.

"That's three guys you've kissed in here in, like, three weeks," I point out.

"And?" she asks. Then she gives us her best shit-eating grin. "I'm playing the field."

"Do they know that?" Bash asks, and I'm not surprised. He is very much a one-woman or one-man kind of guy. He doesn't look away from the woman in his chair as he asks.

Demi lifts one shoulder in a half shrug as she sweeps up around her chair. "Guys do this all the time."

I'm not sure I agree with that generalization, but I let it go. Bash looks like he's going to say more, but then doesn't, and I'm glad. I don't like when he and Demi get into it. Which they do fairly often. They love each other, but they fight like brother and sister. *Teenage* brother and sister.

"Hey, it's Tuesday," Demi says after she sweeps hair into the central vac hole in the floor behind her.

"All day long," I say as I comb out Mrs. Sheen's salt-and-pepper hair.

"Dancing with the hot instructor again?" Demi asks but doesn't look at me. Neither does Bash.

I squint at them both. "How do you know she's hot?" I mean, she totally is, no argument there. But I'm not sure how they'd know that unless…

"You told us," Bash says.

"Oh. Right." And I realize I may have shown my hand by being all accusatory. Mrs. Sheen is following all of this in the mirror, looking very engrossed. "Well, *A*, I don't know if I'm dancing with her tonight. I assume so. And *B*…" I give them both my best stern look before I give up and sigh dramatically. "Yes, she is very hot. Also, I had ice cream with her on Friday."

"What?" they both say at once, loudly enough to garner looks from other stylists and other clients, and I have a moment of great satisfaction at saying something neither of them expected. Like I said, I'm not exactly known as the Queen of Spontaneity.

I had worked on Saturday and saw both Bash and Demi, but I'd been so…discombobulated is the word to describe it…around Friday's ice cream thing that I didn't know what to do with it. So I didn't tell anybody. But that's changed now because I clearly can't keep my big mouth shut.

"Spill," Bash orders, one hand on his hip, the other pointing at me. "Right now."

"Don't you point your comb at me, mister," I tease. Then I meet Mrs. Sheen's eyes in the mirror and frown at her. "I'm so sorry we're subjecting you to this, Mrs. S."

She waves a hand under her smock and gives me a smile. "Are you kidding? This is better than my stories. Go on. Spill."

I shake my head with a grin because I think I'm ready to talk this out with my friends. I tell them all of it, how I was visiting Adley and saw Marisa and Jaden in line. How I pulled them out and offered Jaden a tour. How much Adley liked that, and how we brought ice cream out to Marisa, and she invited me to sit with them.

"It's so weird," I say, recalling how Marisa's face would change so quickly. "I think she'd get comfortable and then remember who I am. It was like she went back and forth the whole time. Like a switch kept flipping. Which makes sense because I kinda felt the same way."

"I think if you look up *awkward* on dictionary-dot-com, there's a picture of you two having ice cream together," Demi says, then laughs at her own joke.

"You're probably right." I'm rolling Mrs. Sheen's hair, and she's riveted to the conversation. For giggles, I say, "What do you think, Mrs. S?"

She tips her head to one side and really seems to think about it. "This girl is who, now?"

"She's the ex of my ex. So my ex dumped her to be with me."

"And now neither of you are with the ex."

"Correct. The ex is now engaged to somebody new."

Mrs. Sheen's blue eyes widen. "Sounds like you're both better off."

I snort at the same time Bash scoffs and Demi nods and mumbles, "You got that right."

"And what's the dancing bit?" Mrs. Sheen asks, so I explain the dance situation and how I ended up there. "Oh, that's something," she says to more nodding from the three of us. "Awkward, but also sexy, yes?"

I blink at her, this woman my grandmother's age, getting to the heart of the whole thing after five minutes of explanation. "Both. Yes. Very much so."

"Sounds like the Universe is messing with you."

I laugh through my nose. "Sure does."

"So. What do I think?" She meets my eyes in the mirror. "I think we're all living vicariously through you, so you need to be brave and stick it out and keep dancing with this girl and then fill us in. We want to see how it ends."

At this point, not only are Bash and Demi nodding along, but so is Bash's client. I shake my head and grin because yeah. I'm going to keep dancing with Marisa.

I want to see how it ends, too.

❖

I'm much less nervous for dance class number five than I have been for the previous four, and I'm not sure what I should do with that, but it's on my mind as I shoulder my bag and head into the studio. Yes, I notice Marisa's SUV in the parking lot, so I'm assuming she's teaching again. I head inside with a little spring in my step.

It's when I lay eyes on her that the nerves come screaming back because, my God, she looks incredible. She's wearing a dress today. A red one with sequins. And heels. Silver ones. Her hair is all fancy, with corkscrew curls and ringlets, and she looks absolutely stunning. I'm clearly not the only one who thinks so as I look around the room. Everybody has noticed her, especially the men. Even Jamal and Kevin are doing a little bit of gaping.

Regina is the one who finally says what everybody's thinking. "Wow, Marisa, you look fantastic."

Marisa smiles—and is that a blush I see on her cheeks? "I just came from a recital at an elementary school where I teach an extracurricular dance class. I was going to change, but I thought this would be a good time to talk about traditional salsa. Actually, most paired dancing, really." She points to her feet. "Heels. I'm sure you've all heard the old adage about Ginger Rogers doing everything Fred Astaire did, but backward and in heels, yes?" Nods and murmurs ripple through the class. "Obviously, heels aren't really a factor for the women in a recreational class like ours...or women who are not leading, I should say." She glances at Jamal and Kevin. "Or for the men." They chuckle.

"What does that mean?" Davis asks, his brow furrowing. "Women who are not leading."

"Well," Marisa says. "It may seem a little sexist, but the man traditionally leads in a dance." She starts to move in my direction, and to say she's *walking* is just...wrong. Marisa doesn't walk in the dance studio, I've noticed several times now. She glides. Floats. Seems to skim the surface of the floor. But however she's doing it, she ends up in front of me with her hand out. "But if both dancers are women"—she waits until I put my hand in hers, and the warmth and softness register in my brain instantly—"one of them has to lead, right?"

And before I realize it's happening, she's pulled me toward her until our bodies are pressed close, her hand at the small of my back. My hand that she's not holding goes up all by itself and settles on her shoulder, and suddenly we're moving to nonexistent music, and I swear to my goddess Adele, for just a few seconds, the room fades away and there's nobody but us. Just me in my leggings and sneakers and Marisa looking like she should be on Broadway, and our hips are moving, and her dark eyes have captured mine, and I can't look away, even if I want to, which I absolutely don't because as I've said many times now, I'm not a fool and—

"Oh, right," Davis says, and is he extra loud? It seems like it. Then he clears his throat and Marisa stops moving and lets go of me, and I want to cry. I blink a lot—like, a lot—and try to get my bearings because what the fuck was that? I feel like everybody was looking at us, and suddenly, nobody is, and what the hell just happened? I glance at Marisa, who looks away quickly, and it's clear that whatever that was affected her, too, and I'm so confused right now.

Class goes by in a blur. I don't even know what we learned. I moved a lot. There was hip swaying and the steps we learned last week and something new that I must've succeeded at understanding because I have several moments of being close to Marisa. Of my hand in hers. Of swaying with her. Of watching her mouth while she calls out instruction to the others. By the time class ends, I'm feeling embarrassed, lost, and more than a little bit weirded out. I think she is, too, because she avoids any and all eye contact with me the second the clock hits seven and class is officially over.

I pack up my stuff, feeling a little bit dazed by the evening, almost a little drunk, and I wander slowly out to my car. I wave to each person who says good-bye to me, but I'm feeling a bit like I'm walking in a fog, and suddenly, I feel like I need to talk to Marisa. Everything in my brain screams for me not to, to just get into my car, pray it will start, and go home.

But I don't.

I move slowly on purpose, taking my time opening the car door, putting my bag in, and before long, the lot is empty except for my rattletrap and Marisa's black SUV. For all I know, she could be staying for another hour or two, but I keep dragging my ass, pretending to do things like adjust my seat height, dust my dashboard and just as I mutter aloud, "What the fuck am I doing?" she appears, no longer in the dress and heels. She's traded them for gray joggers and a blue hoodie. Her hair is up now. I watch as she locks the door of the studio, and before I can even think about it, I'm out of my car and walking across the lot to hers, and when she turns away from her driver's side door, probably to see whose footsteps she hears, I blurt. I don't talk. I don't casually mention. I stop when I'm about a foot away from her, and I just blurt.

"I didn't know."

She blinks at me, obviously surprised. Probably puzzled. "I'm sorry?"

"I didn't know. Back then. When I started seeing Pen. I didn't know about you."

More blinking. Maybe a slight hardening in her eyes? Her throat moves in a swallow as I try to figure out what she's thinking. It's hard for me to tell, though, through the shrieking of my brain telling me to shut up, for fuck's sake, and just go back to my car. "I'm really sorry," I go on because why would I listen to my own brain? Why? "If I had known…but I didn't. I didn't know. She didn't tell me."

Marisa looks down at her feet, and God, I wish I knew what she was thinking. Or maybe I don't. When she raises her gaze, she looks past me. Over my shoulder. Sighs softly. "Yeah, that's not something she's ever been good at. The truth."

A little scoff finds its way out of me. "That's for sure." We stand there for a moment, awkwardly but also not. Which I can't even begin to understand. "Anyway," I finally say, "I just wanted you to know that." I lift one shoulder and turn to head back toward my car.

"Hey, do you…"

My entire body halts in place like I've been hit with a freeze ray when I hear her voice. I slowly turn to look her way.

She hasn't moved, and she shifts her weight from one foot to the other as she tips her head to her left. "Do you feel like ice cream? I don't know. I kinda feel like ice cream."

"Ice cream?"

"Ice cream."

Slowly, I start to nod. "I could go for some ice cream."

"Good." Her gaze moves behind me again. "I should probably drive. I don't think your car can be trusted." Her grin takes away any perceived insult. Because let's be honest, she's not wrong.

"You're a smart woman." I grab my purse from inside, lock my car, and try to avoid actually skipping with joy across the parking lot to her SUV. Last time I was in it, I smelled coconuts, and this time is no different. There's still no air freshener to be seen, and I remember when I was dancing close to her, the warm, sweet smell of coconuts drifting into my awareness.

"You did great today," she says, and I blink in confusion for a moment before I realize she's talking about dance class.

"Oh. Thanks. I'm really enjoying it."

"You've got natural rhythm." We pull out into traffic. "That's not something you can learn. Some people just…don't have it."

I'm amazed at her words because here I am, living my life assuming I got skipped the day they handed out rhythm. Apparently, she disagrees. "How did you get into dancing?"

She gives a small shrug as she drives. I want to look at her—because she's talking and that's the polite thing to do—but I'm afraid of staring. Gawking. "Aunt Tina has always been a dancer." She glances at me. "She told your class her background?"

I nod. "Oh yeah. Very cool."

"She's always been kind of a superstar to me. When I was a kid, I wanted to be just like her."

I grin because tiny Marisa must've been adorable.

"But I'm also practical, and the chances of me making it as a dancer in New York or something were super slim. Plus, I didn't want to leave my family. So I dance where I can, and then, you know the saying. Those who can't do, teach." She grins, but I think I catch a minuscule sliver of sadness in her expression.

The sky has clouded over as we pull into the parking lot of Get the Scoop, which is about half full.

"What would you like?" Marisa asks. "My treat."

"Are you trying to keep me from getting us free ice cream?" I tease.

"I am doing exactly that. Your friend is in business to make money, I'm betting."

"You are not wrong." I grin at her, and my brain gives her points for taking Adley's livelihood into account. "I would like a small ube cone, please."

"You got it. Stay here."

"Yes, ma'am." And there's something alarmingly sexy about Marisa giving me orders. I chuckle to myself as I watch her walk to the serving window on the side of Get the Scoop. "Careful, Templeton, your bottom is showing," I mutter. I people-watch while Marisa is gone, and when I see her coming back, two purple cones in hand, I jump out of the car to help. "You got ube, too!"

"I was curious," she says and slams her door just as a light rain starts.

"Adley introduced me to it. Her mom's Filipino, so she cooks with it quite a bit." I take a lick of my cone, the nuttiness of the ube similar to pistachios.

"This is good," Marisa says. "Subtle. Kind of vanilla-like, but a little nutty."

"Exactly." We sit and eat our ice cream quietly for a few moments, and it's weird because it's not weird. It's not at all uncomfortable to be sitting in silence in Marisa's car, eating ice cream with her and watching the rain, and I don't understand how that's possible.

"So, what do you do, Scottie?" she asks over the sound of the raindrops on the roof of her car. It's picked up a bit now, sending customers who are waiting in line up against the building so they're under the eaves and the small awning on the front. Some give up on the window and head inside the shop instead.

"I'm a hairstylist," I tell her.

"Really?" Marisa's eyes light up. "Do you cut kids' hair?"

"I do. Not super often. It's not, like, my specialty. But yeah, I cut kids' hair."

"Would you be willing to cut Jaden's?" She kind of grimaces, as if she's asking me some huge favor. "He's kind of funny about letting people touch his hair, but he seemed to really like you last week…" Her voice drifts off, and the only thing on my mind is how much I want to help her.

"I'd be happy to." I ask where he is, and she tells me he's got a playdate, and then we make a plan for her to bring him by after school on Thursday, her night off from dance class. "Do you do something other than teach dance?" I ask, because I've been curious about that.

"Sadly, teaching dance classes a couple nights a week doesn't pay the bills. Especially with a kid now. I'm a financial planner, which gives me material security and control over my calendar, usually. Important both for my dancing and now for Jaden."

"Wow," I say because that's about the last thing I would've guessed.

"Wow? Why wow?" She tips her head in clear curiosity.

"I guess the creativity of dance and the logic and math of financial planning seem to me like they're on opposite ends of the spectrum. I would not have been surprised if you'd said you were... an art teacher. Or a photographer. Financial planning? Nope. Never would've guessed. You are clearly a multifaceted woman."

"I've always been good with numbers. And I like mapping things out. Plans for the day. Hiking paths. Futures." She gives a little laugh and it's super cute. She uses the flat of her tongue and pushes what's left of her ice cream down into her cone, and I have to consciously not stare. Why we keep doing something that shows off Marisa's tongue talents, I don't know, but I'm suddenly very warm.

"I don't mind numbers, but I've never loved them."

"What do you do when you're not cutting hair?"

I think about the question, and when a couple minutes have gone by without my answering, I laugh softly. "Apparently, that's a very good question. I mean..." I stop talking because I was about to say something that might take this whole lovely evening and toss it in the toilet.

Marisa seems to read my mind. "It hasn't been all that long since you and Pen broke up and you're still figuring life out?" Her dark eyes find mine, and I'm surprised to see nothing but kindness in them.

"That." I point at her. "But I'm getting there. I like movies. My grandma's teaching me to cook—something I should've learned years ago, if I'm being honest. I love trying new restaurants."

"That's a good list," Marisa says with an approving nod.

We finish our cones within two bites of each other. It's still raining, but there's something comforting about being in this small space with her, warm and dry. "Can I say something?"

"Only if you're going to tell me how weird it is that this doesn't feel weird," she says, and I'm pretty sure I gape at her.

"Yes. That. Exactly that. Why? Why isn't it weird? I don't understand it."

Marisa shakes her head, and a couple of escapees from her messy bun slide free. "I don't either." She lifts a shoulder again, and I realize the half shrug is a regular mannerism of hers. "That's the weird part."

We sit with that for a moment.

"I love the sound of the rain," she says softly after a few minutes. "There's an element of peace to it."

I completely agree and nod, and we stay in her car, just listening to the rain in companionable silence long after our cones are gone. I have no idea how much time has gone by when she finally turns to me with a soft smile and says, "We should get you back to your car."

And I smile back and agree and watch as she starts the car up. The frightening part is that if she—and let's remember she's my ex's ex—asked me to go home with her tonight? I absolutely would.

No question.

No hesitation.

A ridiculous realization, that.

Chapter Eight

I'm nervous.

It's Thursday and almost three thirty, and Marisa is bringing Jaden in so I can cut his hair, and I'm nervous.

Also, I didn't tell Bash. Or Demi. So when I drop my scissors for the third time, Bash gives me a look like he's wondering if I might be drunk. I shake it off and manage to style the hair of my clients without doing something klutzy like chopping off a chunk or dyeing somebody's head green. Believe me, though, it's a close one.

And then the electronic ding sounds, telling the stylists somebody's come through the door and is in the waiting room, and I glance out the window near my station and see Marisa's SUV in the parking lot, and my heart starts to pound. Like, *pound*. Like I've got a jackhammer in my chest.

I give myself a moment. A few seconds. A full minute. Two. I give my arms a shake and pretend I don't see Bash giving me a look. Then I head to the waiting area.

"Hi," I say, forcing what's probably too much cheer. But both Marisa and Jaden smile at me, and that somehow eases the freak show that is me just a bit.

"Hey," Marisa says. "Thanks so much for doing this."

"Of course. No problem. Jaden? Ready?"

He jumps off his chair, then turns to look at Marisa and asks, very quietly, "Can you come, too?"

"Oh, sweetie, I don't know that there's room," she begins before I interrupt to let her know that of course there's room.

They both follow me to my station.

I help Jaden up into my chair, and he's immediately giddy. "This is like a *space chair*!" he says, so of course, that means I have to spin him around several times until he's giggling his little head off. Marisa's sitting in an extra plastic chair behind me, and I meet her gaze in my mirror.

"That'll be lots of fun until he throws up all over your stuff," she says, but her voice holds amusement, and her eyes are smiling. Bash and Demi are both paying very close attention to everything going on, but thank all that is holy, neither of them makes a comment.

"Good point." I stop the chair. Jaden makes a sound of disappointment but gets over it quick. "Okay, what are we doing to this mop?" I ask, ruffling his hair with my hand. Between him and Marisa, I get the idea of what he wants, and I get to work, wetting him down, combing his hair, trimming. It's funny because, nervous as I am with Marisa watching, I am very much in my element. I know how to do this, and I'm very good at it. Kind of like me watching Marisa dancing, I guess. Jaden and I talk about school and his favorite video games, and because I have my little brothers in my life, I can almost keep up with him, which earns me points, I can tell.

"You've got great hair," I tell him. Not that a four-year-old boy cares about such things, but he does have great hair. Thick and dark and soft, and I absently wonder if his aunt's hair feels the same.

I blow him dry, which makes him laugh, and all too soon, we're finished. I walk him and Marisa out to the front desk where she pays me and tips me generously, even as I protest. Then, she says something that takes me completely by surprise.

"Can I set an appointment for myself?"

I blink at her for a beat before shaking myself into action. "Sure. Of course. No problem." I have an opening on Saturday and put her name in my schedule, and now I know I'll be a catastrophe on wheels until then.

I see them off and stand at the door while they cross the parking lot. As Marisa reaches her driver's side door, she looks back and smiles at me, and I swear, it reaches right in and stirs up everything inside me. Confusion, delight, arousal. I sigh and let the door close, then head back to my station to sweep up Jaden's hair.

"Well, she was stunning," Bash comments as he rolls rollers into his client's hair. "Wow."

"Definitely a MILF," Demi adds. "And her kid. What a cutie."

"Not her kid," I say. "Her nephew."

"Haven't seen them before," Bash says. "Referrals?"

I clear my throat and consider several lies before giving up. He's going to find out anyway at some point. "Well, you'd know her if you hadn't broken your foot. She's teaching our dance class."

"Wait," Bash says, midroll. "That's her? *That's* her?"

"That's who?" Demi asks as she replenishes some of her products. Her chair is empty at the moment. She stops what she's doing, and her eyes go wide, and I know she's figured it out. "Wait. That's the ex?"

I nod. "That's her."

"Holy crap," Demi says, still seemingly frozen in place. "I mean…wow." Though I don't think *wow* is what she was going to say.

"Yeah."

"Well, I can tell you this," Demi says then, continuing on with her chore. "She's into you."

My eyes snap to hers in her mirror.

Bash is nodding in agreement. "Totally."

"No," I say. "No, she's not. She knows who I am, and I'm sure I'm the last person on earth she's interested in. Besides, how would you know?"

"Well," Bash says, "here's the thing. It's very complicated, so do your best to follow along, okay? You see, Demi and me? We have *eyes*." He widens his comically and points to them, and Demi cracks up. I can't help but laugh, even though I try not to.

"She was watching you the entire time you were cutting that kid's hair," Demi says. "And I mean *watching you*, if you get my drift."

Bash is nodding with enthusiasm, as is his client, a regular of his, a woman in her fifties whose name I can't remember.

I shake my head with another soft laugh. "You're all ridiculous." I do my best to brush it off because, really, this isn't something I want to think about. It's not something I should be thinking about. Is it?

Could they be right?

"She made an appointment with me for Saturday," I blurt, then want to slap myself when the three of them gasp in surprise.

"And I rest my case," Demi says.

Bash nods in satisfaction.

Thank God my next client arrives then because I have no idea what to do with any of this.

❖

Today's the day.

If I thought I was nervous to do Jaden's hair, then I have no idea what nervous actually is, because right now? I feel like I want to crawl out of my skin and run away.

My phone pings a text notification, and I glance at Adley's name.

Just breathe…

God, she knows me well. I text back, *Can't seem to remember how. What is air?*

She sends a laughing emoji. Then two more. *You got this. Come see me after.*

She means at the ice cream shop, of course, since that's where she is the majority of her life. I often head there on Saturdays when I finish up anyway, so it's already in my plans.

Thank God Saturdays are busy at Sylvia's because the last thing I think I can handle is having my hands in Marisa's hair when there's nobody else around. At least we'll be surrounded by others.

Bash took the day off—I have mixed emotions about that—but Demi is here. I think she knows this is weird and confusing and new territory for me because she doesn't tease. Instead, she leans toward me and whispers, "A Cut Above."

I realize she's offering a name for our future salon, so I roll it around, make a show of considering it. "I don't hate it," I say as the doorbell sounds. I turn to look.

She's here.

In all her jean-clad, red top glory, she's here.

I swallow. Hard. Glance at Demi, who gives me a smile and one nod. It's so strange to me how I haven't really delved into the emotional stew my brain has become around this whole thing, but my friends seem to understand. I feel like Demi gets it, and that's something, right?

"Hi," I say to Marisa as I meet her before she can sit. "Nice day out there." *Good, Scottie, talk about the weather.* I have to consciously not roll my eyes at myself.

"June has made a very sunny entrance," she says, and her eyes dart away from mine, and for the first time, I wonder if maybe this is all freaking her out a bit, too.

I can't bring myself to ask, though. Because seriously, how would I? *Hey, do you find it odd that your ex's ex—the one your ex dumped you to be with—is super ridiculously attracted to you? Is it messing with your head?*

"Follow me," I say and lead her to the sinks. She sits and leans, then I'm standing over her, and there is eye contact. I'm looking down at her and she's looking up at me, and for the first time in my entire career of hair, it occurs to me just how vulnerable a position somebody is in when they're at my sink. Lying back, neck braced by the sink, throat exposed. There is an element of trust I never really grasped before now.

I run the spray and let it warm up, and when it's the right temperature, I wet down Marisa's hair—which is thick and soft, just as I suspected it would be—and she closes her eyes. Okay, so vulnerable and intimate. Wow. Her eyes are closed, my hands are in her hair, and...

I swallow again—swallowing for no reason is apparently a thing for me now—and I work in the shampoo, its watermelony scent filling the space between us. I scrub her scalp, the lather thick and bubbly, then rinse it out. Next up is conditioner. As my fingers press and massage, I glance up and see Demi watching me. She raises her eyebrows in question, and I lift one shoulder, and just like that, we had a silent conversation that consisted of her asking me if I'm doing okay and me telling her I have no fucking clue.

I silently thank the Universe when I wrap a towel around Marisa's head and instruct her to sit up and walk back to my chair. Okay. I survived what turned out to be an unexpectedly sensual experience, and I wonder what's going through her head in that moment.

She sits and blows out a breath. I towel her hair a bit more, drying the ends gently, taking my time. Wet, her hair falls about to her shoulder blades, and I see that her curl is natural.

"So." I meet her eyes in my mirror. "What are we doing? Trim?"

She nods. "Please. Take off the split ends and maybe…an inch or so? It's been a while since I had it cut."

"You got it." I get to work. "How's Jaden? He like his haircut?"

"Loves it." She smiles at me in the mirror. "You did a great job. His hair is crazy thick, and sometimes people have a hard time cutting it evenly."

"Must run in the family, that thick hair," I say with a grin, giving hers a gentle tug.

Her smile widens to show teeth. "True. My brother and I had the same hair. Jaden inherited it."

"Well, it's gorgeous," I say and mean it. "Take it from somebody who has average hair in every way. Color. Thickness. Etcetera."

"Are you kidding? You have great hair."

The compliment sends color to my cheeks as I thank her. I know because I can see it in my reflection, and I hope she doesn't notice. Demi does, though, because when I glance her way, she's grinning down at her broom as she sweeps up after her just-departed client.

"Where's Jaden now?" Her nephew seems to be a safe topic, so I steer us back to him as I comb out her hair.

"With my mother," Marisa says. "I think they were headed to Target, which means he'll come home with several things he doesn't need." The affection in her voice tells me this is a common occurrence and that her annoyance with it is probably fake. "My house is full of so much stuff that's not mine."

"I'm sure my grandma feels the same way about me," I say with a chuckle as I use my scissors on the ends of her hair.

"Was that your grandma's house I dropped you at? I didn't know you lived with her."

"Yep. For almost a year now." I can see her doing the math in her head and likely figuring out that I went from Pen's place to Grandma's, so I clear it up for her. "I wasn't sure what to do after I was…asked to move out. My grandma has lots of room and lives alone and asked me to stay with her for a bit." I shrug. "A bit has turned into a lot of bits."

She smiles a little sadly. "Yeah, I remember how that felt."

Ugh. This is a topic I didn't really want to touch on, but I also know that just because we don't touch on it doesn't mean it's not a thing. Because it's totally a thing.

"Sorry," she says before I can comment. "That's a weird topic for us both, I think."

I drop my arms to my sides, scissors in one hand, comb in the other, and look at her in the mirror. "This is odd, right? Like, I'm not the only one who thinks so, am I? This is..." Another shrug because I'm lost for words.

"Freaky? Weird? Confusing." She takes a beat, holding my gaze. "Unexpected?"

I point my comb at her reflection. "That's a good one. Yeah." Our gazes hold for a moment, and it's charged. Oh, it's definitely charged. It's in that moment right there, that exact second, that it becomes clear to me that everything I've been feeling about Marisa, she's feeling, too. I pull my gaze away and return my focus to her hair. I'm keenly aware that Demi is only one chair over and doesn't have a client yet and probably heard that whole conversation, but instead of being annoyed by that, I'm glad. I have a witness.

I finish cutting Marisa's hair and then blow it dry. She closes her eyes here and there, and those are the times I study her face. Her olive skin that looks so smooth and soft I can barely keep myself from touching it with a fingertip. Her full lips—especially the bottom one—that still sparkle with a light coat of gloss, despite the fact that she's been here and talking with me for almost forty-five minutes. Her dark eyebrows that, rather than arching, are almost completely straight and angle up from the top of her nose, thick and dark and sexy, so it looks like she's always slightly serious.

"Your hair has a little bit of red in it," I comment when I've finished drying and neaten it up. "Not a ton, but a few strands here and there. It's really pretty."

Her smile is soft as I spritz her with a little hair spray to hold the style. "My dad. His hair's quite a bit lighter, more of a reddish brown."

"Well, it suits you. You've got fantastic hair." I meet the reflection of her eyes. "And I would know. I mean, I'm kind of an expert." I smile, letting her know I'm being a smart-ass.

"You totally are," she says as I remove the smock, and she stands. "This looks great. I love it."

I'm always thrilled when a client is happy, but this is beyond, well, because it's Marisa. "I'm so glad." She follows me to the front desk, and I always feel awkward charging somebody I know, but Marisa's ready with her phone and Apple-Pays me on the spot, complete with a very generous tip. She puts her phone away and glances up to meet my gaze, and there's a moment of…I don't know what. Uncertainty? I'm not sure. My next client is sitting in a chair and stands up.

"Thank you so much," Marisa says, and then she sort of hovers for a moment before giving one nod and turning to go.

I must stare at her for a long time because my next client clears her throat behind me, jerking me back into action.

I apologize and smile and lead her to the sinks. As I wash her hair, the only thought in my head is how her hair isn't nearly as soft as Marisa's.

CHAPTER NINE

I'm surprised by the return of Ms. Tina the following Tuesday at dance class. Surprised and, I admit it, slightly disappointed. That is, until Marisa walks in a few minutes before we start. Her gaze meets mine across the room, and I swear to the little tiny baby Jesus, I can feel it in my blood.

And I am honestly so confused by what's going on. I've thought about nothing else since Saturday. When, I don't want to forget to add, I got another text from Pen. Just one of her generic *Hey, hi, how you doing?* texts that confuse the hell out of me because why? Why are you texting me? You didn't want to get married. You don't like the conformity, the feeling of being put into a box society creates for women. No, it didn't matter that I really wanted a traditional wedding. You didn't. End of story. Then you leave me, kick me out of the apartment that, let's be honest here, *I* made into a home. And then? Not only do I find out you were sleeping with somebody else before you broke up with me, but you end up engaged to her within six months. Six months! Engaged! Clearly, it wasn't that you didn't want to get married. You just didn't want to get married to *me*. So tell me, why are you texting me random hellos?

Yeah, I didn't say any of that to her, though. Of course I didn't. I just set my phone aside and watched *Downton Abbey* for the dozenth time.

And now, here I am, trying not to stare across the studio at the ridiculously hot woman Pen left to be with me, and what the actual fuck, Universe? I am so confused by all of it that my head hurts.

"All right, my friends," Ms. Tina says, clapping her hands and moving to the center of the room as she gets our attention. "I'm so sorry to have left you so early on, but I trust my niece has taken good care of you. She is going to continue to do so, as I am only here for this week, and then I must fly back down to the alligator-infested sauna that is Florida to get my mother set up in her new home." She looks tired and a little drawn. She's forcing the cheer, I think, if the dark circles under her eyes are any clue, and I wonder if her mom's new home is some sort of assisted living. I think about how hard it would be if I had to move Grandma into something like that. She'd leave her house kicking and screaming. "Go ahead and warm up, and we'll get started." Ms. Tina moves to the laptop on the corner cart where Marisa is standing, punching keys. As the Latin beat fills the room, and I stretch out my hamstrings, Ms. Tina and Marisa lean close and have a conversation I can't hear, which includes both of them looking my way.

My heart rate kicks up several speeds. Because of course it does.

And then they're both walking toward me, and Ms. Tina says, "Scottie, I know you're without a partner, so Marisa's going to be yours for today. Okay?"

I nod because my voice has apparently gone shopping or something. I hope it buys me something pretty. And then Ms. Tina calls out some instruction, and Marisa holds her hand out to me. I grasp it without hesitation, and it's warm and soft as it always is, and class begins.

I'm sure it comes as no surprise to say that dancing with Marisa is nothing at all like dancing with Bash. Even though he and I only took one class together, there's a definite shift, and it feels like it's in the very atmosphere. I've danced with Marisa in short spurts with her as an instructor—she danced with me for a few moves, and then she had to move through the class to help others while I danced with an invisible partner. But having her as my dance partner for the entire class is…God, it's so many things.

It's nerve-racking. I don't want to screw up, so I'm concentrating extra hard. And let me add, doing pretty well if I say so myself.

It's warm and smooth, odd ways to describe dancing with somebody, but they fit. Marisa is always warm—I'm learning that about her—but also, we move very smoothly together. She's taken on the traditional male role in our pairing, and she gently directs me with her body, though I'm not quite sure how. I can tell when I'm supposed to step back or forward or to the side. There's a gentle pressure. She's not pushing or pulling me, just gently leading me in the right direction, and I have zero problems following.

It's crazy sensual and sexy. I'm trying my hardest not to think of her that way, especially after getting another text from Pen. Being attracted to Pen's ex is just too fucking weird for words. I have vowed more than once to myself since the haircut on Saturday that I really need to chill. Just take a breath and chill. But now that I'm dancing with Marisa, now that I am literally in her arms, gliding across the floor with her, all I can think about is what she feels like. What she smells like. How well we fit together. God, how well we *move* together.

Ms. Tina must agree because she calls us out more than once, making the rest of the class watch as we dance the newest steps.

Class is over way too soon, as far as I'm concerned. I'd like to dance with Marisa forever, and the second I realize that, I give my head a shake. I'm gathering my things together when Ms. Tina approaches me, her tired face smiling.

"Scottie, do you have a moment?" she asks.

"Sure." I stand up straight—that seems to happen automatically when I'm next to Ms. Tina and her perfect posture—and give her my full attention.

"Do you remember when we mentioned how the local dance studios put on a little friendly competition once a year?" I nod and she continues, "It's basically to showcase not only the studios and the instructors, but also an occasional student." She rubs at her chin with a red-tipped finger. "Among the studios that participate, I've been dancing the longest. I have a reputation for not only stellar teaching, but I also try to add a little…pizzazz, if you will. Each year."

I have no idea where she's going with this, but I nod some more like I totally get it. Also, I'm super curious.

"I'd like you to dance with Marisa in this year's competition."

Well. I don't…what? What did she just say?

"You two move so well together," she continues, and now her face has lit up, and she doesn't look as tired as before. In fact, there's an element of excitement, a sparkle in her eyes as she speaks. "You make a very natural pairing, something we don't see in every class. Plus, the fact that you'd be a same-sex pairing adds a level of modernism I think we can use in our contest, which can stick so tightly to tradition that it becomes a little…stodgy."

I glance across the room to where Marisa is shouldering a duffel bag. She meets my eyes, gives me an uneasy smile paired with a small wave, and leaves. Well, okay then, I guess. Ms. Tina follows my gaze and waves a hand dismissively.

"I haven't mentioned it to Marisa yet, but I know she'll be fine with it. She dances in the competition almost every year."

To say I'm relieved that Marisa isn't fleeing the scene because of all this is a colossal understatement, and I hate myself for it. I do wish she'd stayed so I could at least see what she thinks. Of course, this is a job, so maybe she doesn't have a choice and she *has* to dance with me. I don't like that possibility.

"What do you say?" Ms. Tina asks, her eyes still bright. "It's a lot of fun. I promise."

For some reason, when I look at her face, at the gentle smile, I think of my grandma, and I know I can't let her down. "Okay. Sure. As long as Marisa's okay with it." I add that last line because I feel like I have to.

Ms. Tina claps her hands, clearly delighted. "Fantastic! It's not until September, so you'll have plenty of time to practice. I'll choreograph. I already have some great ideas." Any trace of her being tired or sad has simply melted away. She's thrilled now—it's evident on her face, in her voice—and for a beat, I'm really happy to have been the person to have done that for her.

It's not until I'm alone in my car that the question blasts through my head on a mental bullhorn.

What the hell did I just agree to?

❖

"Wow."

That's all Adley can seem to manage half an hour later as we sit together at Vineyard, a cute little wine bar not far from Get the Scoop. Much as I love sitting in the back of the ice cream shop and chatting with my bestie, I also know she needs to get *out* of the ice cream shop every now and then—sometimes, I have to drag her out—so I begged until she agreed to meet me, luring her with the promise of some ridiculous news I wasn't sure what to do with.

"Wow." She says it again, takes a sip of her Tempranillo, and blinks at me. "This is, like…" She gives her dark head a shake. "You can't make this shit up."

I drop my head and blow out a loud breath. "You *cannot* make this shit up."

"So you're gonna do it?"

"I mean, I said I would. Before I gave it much thought, but…I said I would. I can't back out now. Ms. Tina was so happy." I groan and take a sip of my semidry Riesling, which hits my tongue with a tang and leaves an essence of pear and honeysuckle. It's friggin' delicious.

"You are a people pleaser," Adley says, pointing at me. "You know that, right? Especially when it comes to mother figures. Or grandmother figures. You have this thing where you can't let them down."

I sigh because she's right. "I know. It comes from my parents' divorce, I think."

Adley nods her agreement. "You were so worried about adding to their stress when they were fighting that you did whatever you could to be the good girl, the girl who does everything right. Even to the detriment of your own happiness." She sips again, then pins me with those dark, dark eyes of hers. "You've never stopped doing that."

"Facts." Isn't it crazy how deeply you can be affected by your childhood? How one simple behavior can inform the rest of your life? Carry into adulthood? "It's too bad you like ice cream so much. You should've been a therapist." It's not the first time I've said this to Adley because it's true, and she laughs.

"I've told you a hundred times, I'd be a terrible therapist. I'd want to just come right out and tell people what their problem is and how to fix it. To hell with taking months or years to get them to figure it out on their own. I'd give them solutions in two appointments. And then I'd starve."

We laugh together, and it's easy. It always is with Adley. Don't get me wrong, I love my half brothers and half sister, but Adley's the sister I never had growing up. Both my parents were only children, so I don't have cousins. Before the divorce and the remarriages, my family was pretty small. Now it's pretty sizable on both sides, and I've never felt less a part of it than I do now.

"What if Marisa says no?" I ask, steering us back to the original topic. "Like, she's been super nice to me—I have to give her credit. She knows who I am. She knows exactly who I am, and I wouldn't blame her if she hated me."

"But you told her you didn't know about her, right?"

"I did. And she didn't seem terribly surprised."

"How long was she with Pen before you?"

I squint, trying to recall what Pen had told me. "Three years? Four? Though, who knows if Pen was telling the truth."

Adley snorts, and it's the perfect response. "I bet she won't say no."

"You don't think so?"

She shakes her head. "You said she's the teacher's niece, right? And dances in the competition every year?"

"Yeah."

"Sounds like this is a job for her, a yearly thing. Maybe she's even expecting it."

"I'm sure she is. I just don't know if she's expecting to dance with *me*."

Adley leans in to me with her shoulder. "All she has to do is get to know you, Scooter. To know you is to love you."

"Are you tipsy?" I ask with a laugh, because alcohol makes Adley super affectionate. When she's affectionate is when her nickname for me makes an appearance.

She holds her forefinger and thumb a tiny bit apart. "Maybe a titch."

"That's what happens when you only eat ice cream all day," I tease.

We're quiet for a moment, sipping our wine and eating from our shared charcuterie board, dinner for both of us.

"I hope she doesn't say no." I say it softly, almost to myself, but loudly enough so Adley hears.

"Yeah?"

I nod, and I can feel her studying me. Nobody knows me as well as Adley does. I turn to meet her gaze, and she holds mine for what seems like a long time. I feel like she's got things to say, lots more than the, "Just be careful, all right?" that she finally speaks. "I worry."

I nod my promise that I will, and we're quiet for a moment or two. Then I hold up my glass for cheersing. "To summer and ice cream sales that are through the roof."

"To dancing in a competition and not falling on your ass."

I shoot her a look of horror as she touches her glass to mine. "Thanks so much for putting a worry I hadn't even considered straight into my head. You suck."

And Adley laughs and laughs, and it's a sound I love, deep and throaty. Adley laughs with her whole body, and I can't help but join her.

That night, as I feared, my dreams are filled not only with me dancing, but of me dancing and falling. Dancing and falling to a laughing audience. Dancing and falling to a laughing Marisa. Dancing and falling to a laughing audience and a laughing Marisa. Dancing and falling to a laughing audience and a laughing Marisa while I'm stark naked...

CHAPTER TEN

Why are there so many people in the grocery store at four thirty on a Thursday?

I don't understand it, and I have to consciously not growl at a woman who has stopped her cart dead center in the damn aisle so she can browse the crackers.

Somebody's grandma, somebody's grandma, somebody's grandma, I repeat in my head as I maneuver around her and do my best not to make any noise that indicates my irritation.

I don't mind grocery shopping, but I prefer to go early in the morning or later in the evening when there are fewer people, and I can browse and take my time. But this morning, I used up the last of my toothpaste, which somehow did not make it onto my grocery list. And when I say used up, I mean squeezed every last little blob I could possibly get out of that tube. There is no waiting if I want to brush my teeth anymore today. And I do. My mistake was asking Grandma if she needed anything. Because I'm a good granddaughter, and that's what a good granddaughter would do. As luck would have it—or not have it—she needs several things, and instead of a quick trip to Walgreens, I'm in the middle of Wegmans on a Thursday afternoon with every parent in the greater Northwood area who picked up their kid from school and needed to swing by the store quick.

I love early June, and the sunshine beaming through the front windows of the store does help to lighten my mood a little bit. So there's that. I'm making my way to the cosmetics and bathroom stuff when I hear my name called out loudly in a little kid voice, and before I can even comprehend the sound, my lower body is hit by what feels like a rocket. And then Jaden's arms are around my waist and he's hugging me, and I can't remember the last time somebody was that excited to see me. Makes me happy.

"What are you doing here?" I ask, ruffling his hair. Which looks damn good if I say so myself.

"We're gonna make cupcakes," he said, and his eyes have the sparkle that only little kids get when they're giddy about something.

"Cupcakes? What kind? Will there be frosting? Sprinkles? I need details, man!"

He dissolves into little boy giggles. "You're hilarious, Scottie." And his use of such a big word at his age makes me laugh in surprise along with him.

"I get that a lot," I say.

"Get what a lot?" The voice comes from behind me, and it sounds—feels—coated with honey, warm, sweet, and inviting.

"I told Scottie she's funny," Jaden says, filling her in.

"Actually, you said I was *hilarious*." I can feel myself brace as I turn and meet Marisa's eyes because I know it'll have an effect. And it does. Right down to my... "Hi."

"Hey. Fancy meeting you here." She furrows her brow. "What does that mean exactly, anyway? My mom always said it. Fancy meeting you here. Is it fancy that I'm meeting you here?"

"I mean, I guess it could be fancy." I glance down at my very unfancy jeans and T-shirt. "Though I'm not really dressed appropriately for fancy."

"You look great," she says, as she stands there looking like she just stepped off the home page of a trendy clothing website, in her cool, pale yellow jumpsuit and olive skin. And then we just kind of grin at each other, and it occurs to me that we keep running into each other in random places and how weird that is. Finally, I find my voice.

"So. Cupcakes, huh?"

She glances down at Jaden, whose attention is running short, I can tell by the way he's looking around the store at other things and kind of bouncing on the balls of his feet. "Somebody was having a craving for chocolate cake."

I lower my voice. "You mean you, right?"

She puts a finger to her lips. "I like to let him think it was his idea."

"Understood."

She looks into my handbasket and takes in the grapefruit, bran flakes, Metamucil, and Alka-Seltzer and raises her eyebrows in question. "Well. That's quite an assortment you've got there."

"And I haven't even added the whitening toothpaste yet."

"Grandma asked you to pick up a few things, did she?"

I nod. "Yes, and why is everybody in Northwood here right now?"

"I know, right?"

We laugh together, and then the laughter dies down and we're left standing, not quite awkwardly, but not exactly not awkwardly. Jaden tugs on Marisa's shirt.

"Come on," he says in that way only little kids can, like he'll absolutely *die* if they don't go right now.

Marisa lifts and lowers her eyebrows, smiles at me, and takes a few backward steps. "Catch you later, Scottie."

"Make awesome cupcakes," I say back, then spend the next half hour wondering if that was a totally ridiculous thing to say. I decide yes. Yes, it was. I have no game. Zero game. Zero. I should just accept that.

Grandma isn't home when I get there. She's having girls' night, and I'm a little embarrassed by the intensity of my jealousy. I put away her groceries and read the note she left me telling me there's some pasta in the fridge for me for dinner. Okay, that makes me feel better. I feed the cats and eat my dinner in front of the TV watching *Law & Order: SVU*. Jesus Christ, I'm becoming my grandmother, but forty years early.

It's not until I'm in bed later that it occurs to me Marisa never mentioned the dance contest. That makes me wonder if Ms. Tina hasn't said anything about it to her yet. And that, of course, sends me off on a whole new course of worry.

❖

I completely forget until I arrive at work on Saturday morning that I have an appointment in the afternoon to do my half sister

Jordana's hair. When she and my mom arrive around three thirty, the salon is buzzing with business. Bash is on his sixth client in a row. Demi's got that tall guy with the eyebrow piercing again—Michael? Micah?—in her chair. And Jordie is all excited. Bouncy. I haven't seen her with this much enthusiasm since she turned thirteen. She hugs me, hugs Bash, gives Demi a wave, then plops into my chair.

"What are we doing?" I ask, meeting her eyes in the mirror. My mom is sitting in a chair behind us along the wall, scrolling on her phone. "Just a trim?"

"No." Jordana pulls out her phone and shows me a photo of the back of a woman's head, her hair in a complicated braid-slash-bun type thing with pieces hanging down in pretty corkscrew curls. "For my dance, remember?"

No, I don't remember because I was never told. My mother glances up at me in the mirror. "Didn't I mention that?" she asks.

I shake my head but shrug it off because I can do what Jordana wants, no problem. "What dance is this?"

"The junior high Spring Fling," my sister says, and her excitement is so clear that I can't help but smile at her. "Mom and I got this gorgeous dress. Wanna see?"

"Duh," I say, then look at her phone again as she shows me photos of her in a beautiful royal-blue dress that makes her look so grown-up it almost brings tears to my eyes. "Do you have a date?" I ask, wondering to myself if thirteen is too young for one and deciding yes, it absolutely is.

"No, a bunch of us girls are going together. We got a limo and we're going to dinner and it's gonna be awesome."

"Sounds like it. Where's dinner?"

She names a pretty upscale restaurant, which surprises me and also doesn't. As I spend the next forty-five minutes styling my little sister's hair and listening to her exuberance about the upcoming evening, thoughts roll around in the back of my mind. Memories. I recall my very first school dance. I was sixteen, and my mom had little to nothing to do with any of it. I went shopping with Adley and her mom with money that my mom gave me. Adley and her mother helped me pick out a simple but elegant blue number that sparkled. I remember Jason Carter had asked Adley to go with him, but she said no because she knew I didn't have a date—this was before either of us realized we liked girls better—and so we went together. My mom had been on a date with Stephan that same night. There aren't even any prom photos of me except ones that Adley's mom took.

But none of that is Jordie's fault, so I put my best effort into her hair, which comes out looking pretty incredible, if I do say so.

I glance up at my mom several times as I work, and she's either scrolling on her phone or gazing at Jordie with so much love on her face it makes my heart ache a little bit. But there is one moment when I meet her gaze, and there's something on her face… Sadness? Regret? I don't know. It's hard to tell. But I finish up and have to argue with them about payment. My mom insists she should pay me, and I insist that I'm not charging my own sister, and we go back and forth for a good five minutes before I finally win.

Jordie hugs me hard, and that makes it all worth it. "Send me pictures, okay?"

"Thanks, Scottie. Love you." And she's out the door. My mom kisses my cheek and follows her, and I stand at the window and watch them pull out and drive away.

"You okay?" Bash asks me softly. He knows my story and is surprisingly intuitive for a guy.

I inhale a deep breath and let it out. "Yeah. I'm good."

"Her hair looks fabulous," he says.

"It does, doesn't it?"

"You do good work."

"Thanks. It helps that she's gorgeous." It's true. My little sister's going to be a knockout in five years.

Demi has taken her sweet time with the tall, dark, and handsome guy, which isn't surprising, as they've spent much of his appointment having eye sex in Demi's mirror. Bash and I have made eye contact and have shaken our heads several times as we've worked on our own clients, and when Demi finally takes the cape off him, he stands and bends down to kiss her on the mouth.

When the doorbell tells us the door has opened, I'm facing Demi, and I swear to God, every drop of color drains from her face as I stand there. I quickly look over my shoulder to see the other guy she kissed recently, the one with sleeves of tattoos, standing there looking stricken.

Uh-oh.

I meet Bash's eyes, and he grits his teeth and makes an *oh shit* face, and we watch as the tattooed guy turns to leave and Demi runs after him, leaving Eyebrow Piercing to gaze after her, probably wondering what the hell is happening. Then he heads outside as well, and Bash and I try not to be obvious about watching out the window as Demi stands between the two men, her head turning from one to the other, her hands flailing about as she, I assume, tries to explain herself.

I do not envy the woman. At all.

"That's exactly why I could never *date casually*," Bash says quietly, making air quotes around the last two words. "I always wished I could, but I was always afraid of that happening." He points out the window with his scissors, as his client, a woman in her twenties, nods her agreement.

The two of us give up any pretense of not watching and we gawk. Stare. Ogle. The guys are pointing at each other and shrugging and lifting their arms in tandem *What the hell?* gestures, and Demi looks like she's about to cry. Something I've never seen before. And then the guys walk away in opposite directions, leaving Demi standing there facing the building. She glances up at us, and we quickly turn away and busy ourselves, like there's any way in the world she'd not know we were watching. She comes in through the front door, walks right past us, and heads for the back room.

Bash and I look at each other. He indicates his client sitting in his chair, and since I don't currently have one, I'm elected. With a sigh, I follow Demi into the back.

There's an employee bathroom back there, off the makeshift kitchen area, and she must be in there, the door closed and her nowhere else to be found. Thank God it's Saturday, which means no chance of Sylvia popping in, because she'd have words to say— probably words like *lollygagging* or *dillydallying*—even though we don't work for her.

"Demi?" I knock softly at the door. "You okay?"

She doesn't answer right away, but I can hear her sniffing, then a blow of her nose. I wait a couple more minutes, and the door finally opens. I've known Demi for a while now, and emotional is not a word I'd use to describe her. Stoic. Tough. Even-keeled. Very chill. All those apply. So this teary, mascara-smeared waterworks before me is a surprise, to say the least.

"I suck, Scottie."

"No, you don't." I don't ask if she wants some tea, just move to the electric kettle on the counter and click it on. My grandma always makes tea when somebody is upset, so I guess it's ingrained.

Demi moves to the table and drops into a chair like her legs have given out. "I do, though. I was selfish and self-absorbed and ended up hurting two really great guys because of it." She sighs loudly.

"You still have the third guy, right?" I ask and make a face because that is in such poor taste, but also, I kinda hope it'll make her laugh.

She blinks at me for a second, and then a laugh bursts out of her, much to my relief. "I guess I do, yeah."

"Well, there ya go. Not the end of the world after all." God, I'm bad at this. I busy myself making us both a cup of tea, and I sit across from her.

"They were both really good guys. They didn't deserve that. I mean, I never claimed to be exclusive with either of them, but…"

"They assumed."

"They did. And I knew that, and I let them." She sighs and sips and then meets my eyes. "Why is dating so hard? Why is *love* so hard?"

"That is something I definitely do not have the answer to. Wish I did."

"I mean, all I'm trying to do is not be alone in life. You know? I just want somebody to keep me company. To have my back." She's gazing out the window now, and I think she's just thinking out loud, so I stay quiet and let her talk. "It's not a lot to ask, right? Just… somebody who looks out for me while I look out for him? Somebody who will rub my feet after a long day or hug me when I feel sad or pick up my favorite candy bar or bag of chips when they're at the store just because they were thinking about me."

It's not too much to ask, is it? I want those same things. Don't we all?

"I mean, look at you. You had it, and then Pen goes and just… leaves. Just decides she doesn't want any of that with you anymore."

Um, okay, ouch. Facts, yes, but still. Ouch.

Demi waves a hand at me. "I'm sorry. I don't mean to be so blunt. I just don't understand it is all. Why is it all so freaking hard?"

I shake my head. "I wish I knew." I sit with her for a while longer, and we sip our tea together in silence until it starts to get close to five. I have one more client and then I'm outta here. I finish my tea and stand. "Are you going to be okay?"

She waves a hand at me and makes a *pfft* sound. "I'll be fine," she says and gives me a sad smile. "My own fault, you know? Thanks for sitting with me, though. I appreciate it."

I nod and round the table and give her a hug. Demi's not really a hugger, but she holds on to me, and we stay like that for a moment before I head back out to my chair.

For the rest of my shift, I can't help thinking about her words. All of them. Not just how Pen up and left, decided I wasn't her person after all. But all of it. All those things that we as human beings want. That we need. We're not meant to be alone. *I'm* not meant to be alone. If I learned only one thing during the wretched breakup I went through not so long ago, it's that. I want all those things Demi mentioned. All of them. And more. I want somebody who wants to be near me all the time. Just in the same place. I want somebody I'm so into that I know where they are in the room at all times, even if I'm not looking for them. I want somebody who's the first on my list when something good happens and I want to make calls. I want somebody whose perfume I recognize from yards away. I want somebody who makes me laugh. I want somebody who takes time in their day to text me just to see how my day is going. I want somebody who wonders about me when they're not with me. Somebody who'll cook for me. And not just cook for me, but cook my favorite things. Somebody who knows how I like my eggs and my hamburgers, and that I drink almond milk but prefer half-and-half in my coffee.

All these thoughts swirl in my head as I work on my last client, a woman in her early sixties whose daughter-in-law recently gave birth to her first grandchild. I smile and nod and look at photos on her phone, but the whole time, those thoughts about what I want in life roll around in my head like bingo balls in a ball mixer. Is it too much? Am I asking too much? Expecting too much? I thought

I had that stuff with Pen…well, most of it. Okay, some of it. Pen doesn't cook, so forget about the eggs thing. She rocks ordering food, though, and did know pad thai is a favorite of mine. I can't remember what her perfume smells like, though I do know it's in a square bottle. I used to text her daily from here, telling her little anecdotes about clients or fellow stylists, but it always took her hours to get back to me. If she got back to me at all. She told me more than once that she just forgot to text back. Which is a pretty clear sign that you're not at the top of somebody's list, right?

I finish up and check my client out, then spend the next hour cleaning up and putting things away, since I won't be back until Tuesday. Bash asks if I want to grab a drink, but I realize I'm not really in the mood for that.

What I am in the mood for is pad thai.

At home.

With a glass of wine and something on Netflix.

And probably my grandma.

CHAPTER ELEVEN

Tuesday at work is insane. Between overbooking myself—because I clearly don't know how to keep an accurate schedule—and the woman who brought in her twelve-year-old daughter who had green hair because she was trying to color her hair at home and hadn't followed the directions, my stress levels are pretty high all day. By the time I get to dance class—with about thirty seconds to spare, thank you very much—I'm pretty sure I'm just going to short out like a robot that's been running too hot all day. A couple zips, a flash, and I'll just power down and stand against the wall.

"Hi." Marisa comes right up to me as I put my things in a corner. "You look frazzled. Everything okay?"

I find myself torn between being mortified that she can tell I'm frazzled by looking at me and kinda thrilled that she already knows me well enough to tell I'm frazzled just by looking at me. I give her a small groan. "Crazy day."

"I hear that," she says, and her smile is soft and her eyes are sweet and, holy crap, I'm going to be in trouble with this woman. The thought hits me, fresh and hard and out of the blue. So. Much. Trouble. "Dancing always helps me. Softens the edges." She reaches for my upper arm, gives it a rub. "Hey, do you have a few minutes after class? I'd like to talk to you."

I nod and watch as she heads to the front of the room to get everybody's attention, and class begins.

Here's what I'm finding: The more time I spend with Marisa—be it cutting her hair or running into her at the grocery store—the more of an effect she has on me. The more I dance with her, the more aware of her I am. Does that make sense? Like, she's not doing anything any different in dance class. We are dancing together like always, her leading, me following, my hand in hers, her other hand on my back. Lots of touching, our bodies are very close, but there's nothing sexual about it.

Wow, okay, that's a huge lie, because starting with this class—class number seven—all I can think about are sexual things. I don't know what happened, where that line was that I not only clearly crossed over but blew the fuck past, but I am suddenly completely turned on anytime she comes near me tonight. It's like a switch flipped and now everything she does floats my boat. Pops my kernels. Cranks my knobs. The way her hips move. How she smells like coconuts again. That there's barely an inch between her breasts and mine. The way just the tip of her tongue darts out to wet her bottom lip as she concentrates on the steps we demonstrate for the rest of the class.

Oh. Right. There's the rest of the class here.

I'm pretty sure my face is flushed for the entire hour. I *know* my underwear is damp. I also wonder if Marisa is feeling any of this because she doesn't make eye contact. At all. Once we start dancing, once we're actually touching and moving together, she finds a spot somewhere around my forehead, and that's where she looks anytime we're face-to-face.

The hour flies by. I do a double take at the clock when Marisa calls time and tells us all what to work on for next week. I'm torn again, this time between grabbing my crap and sprinting for the door, and hanging around after everybody leaves. I know I have to do the latter because Marisa asked me to, but it suddenly feels… *dangerous* to be alone with her.

I take my time gathering my things and wait for her to shut down the laptop. I check my phone for messages, and when I finally glance up at her, she's looking at me, but then looks away really quick. The way you do when you've been staring and then get caught, but try to pretend you weren't staring, even though you *know* the other person knows you were staring.

"So," Marisa says from her spot behind the laptop cart, "my aunt wants us to dance together for the contest in September."

I nod. "She mentioned it to me, yeah."

"You up for it?"

Another nod and a half shrug, 'cause yeah, I'm breezy. Nonchalant. Unaffected. "Sure. You?"

"I mean, it's my job, so..." She lets the sentence dangle unfinished in the air between us, and I don't like it. I don't like that answer, though I'm not sure what I would have preferred instead. She must feel my slight bristling because she quickly adds, "I think it'll be fun. We"—she clears her throat—"we dance well together."

A beat passes while the two of us look at each other from several yards apart, and then the words push themselves from my mouth before I even realize I'm about to speak. "It's weird, right?"

"*So* weird," she says, clearly relieved that I brought it up first. And then we stand there and sort of chuckle and shift our weight from foot to foot, and it's only a little awkward and only for a minute or two. Marisa takes a breath—I can hear her inhale—and steps out from behind the laptop cart to walk toward me. "We'll need to practice. I can help my aunt with choreography. I've got some stuff in mind. Is that okay?"

"Sure." My body reacts as she gets closer, and it's so strange. So odd. I can't recall that ever happening, not even with Penelope, who I was totally in love with—or at least I thought I was. But I never felt my body literally preparing for her the way it seems to be doing for Marisa. More wetness to the south. A softening of my stance. An itch in my hands, like they're just waiting until she's close enough to touch.

Jesus Christ on a cheesecake, what is happening?

She stops about four feet from me, and that makes me wonder if she's feeling it, too. If she's feeling something. She clears her throat again, and is that her tell? Is that what she does when she's nervous? Because that's the second time in about five minutes. "I don't know what your schedule is like," she says, and while I'm sure she's trying to be all business, her voice is soft, and again, the eye contact is fleeting. "I mean, we could practice pretty much any night. I'll just need to make sure Jaden has a sitter, which my mom can help with, most likely."

"Okay," I say. Helpful, Scottie. So helpful.

"And Aunt Tina will be here to help out when she's in town

because it'll be hard for me to be objective when I'm also dancing. Like, watching our overall moves and stuff."

"Sure." Clearly, words have left me. I'm only allowed one at a time, I guess.

"We'll want to start rehearsing soon. Next week? The week after?"

I nod. "Yeah. Okay. I'm pretty open."

"Great. How about I take a few days to come up with some ideas, listen to some music options, and then I'll let you know, and we'll pick a day?" Her shoes are suddenly very interesting, apparently. It's cute, though.

"That sounds perfect." And it does. And also, nerve-racking and worry-inducing and arousing and so many other things that my brain can't begin to list them. But I smile, and Marisa gives one quick nod, and that's that. I pack up my stuff and head out to my car where only it and Marisa's SUV are left. Again.

I don't wait, though, this time. I can't. My heart can't take it. I've had enough awkward weirdness for one night. I start my car—which takes three tries, goddamn it—and head home.

"Hi, sweetie," Grandma says where she's in the kitchen pouring herself a glass of pinot grigio from the fridge. She grabs a second glass without asking me and pours me some, too. "How was class?"

"Class was fine, but I'm dancing in a competition between local dance studios in September with Marisa and we start rehearsals soon and it just feels awesome and weird and wonderful and horrifying." I blurt it out without even saying hello.

Grandma blinks at me and takes a sip of her wine before she speaks. "Well. I'd ask how you're feeling about it, but the fact that you're speaking at a hundred and twenty miles an hour with no pauses for air is all the answer I need."

I grab the wine, take a slug, and blow out a breath. "Yeah." Then I fall into a kitchen chair and take another slug.

Grandma pulls out the chair opposite me at the small table and sits, and I feel her studying me for a moment. "Sweetie, what exactly is the problem here?"

I gape at her. Is that a real question? How does she not see the problem?

"I mean, I know why you feel weird about it, but is there any reason to? You and this Marisa seem to be doing okay. Right? You told her you didn't know about her during the Pen years, so she's aware of that. You've been dancing with her for—what?—five classes now?" I nod. "And you seem to be enjoying yourself, for the most part. Do you think maybe you're freaking out for no reason?"

A snort. "But that would be so unlike me," I say, my voice heavy with sarcasm, because yeah, it would be exactly like me to freak for no reason.

Grandma laughs, and just like that, the mood lightens considerably. Maybe she's right. Maybe I just need to chill the fuck out. After all, I'm about to be in a dance competition with one of the most gorgeous women I've ever had the privilege of meeting.

Perhaps I need to focus on that and let the rest fall away.

❖

School ended this week, and at the same time, summer programs and sports and such started up. My half brother Noah has started playing Little League baseball. He's only eight, so going to watch isn't so much catching a game as watching kids learn the game. That is to say, it's boring as hell. But when Noah calls me himself and asks if I'm coming to his game, how can I say no?

As with my mom's new family, I love my dad's sons. While there are a myriad of issues I have with my parents, none of them are the fault of my half siblings. So I do my best to be a good big sister, and I attend games and plays and concerts, especially if one of them personally asks me to.

The hardest part when it comes to those things is remembering how very few of them my parents actually attended for *me*. I played softball and basketball in school, was in several plays, and played the flute in the marching band. I can count on one hand the number of games or performances or parades my parents came to, and if I dwell on the unfairness of it, it will wreck me. It has before. So I do my best not to dwell, just to show up and cheer on my little brothers and sister. Like I said, none of my Mommy or Daddy issues are their fault.

I find my dad and his wife, Connie, in the bleachers, and I climb up to sit with them. My dad hugs me back and I give Connie a wave, and she smiles. She's nice to me. Always has been. But we're not what I'd call close, and that's on me as much as it's on her. I could make more of an effort and I know it. I just don't.

My dad is alarmingly into the game. He's alarmingly into everything his boys do now, and it takes everything in me not to focus on the possibility that maybe if I'd been a boy, I'd have gotten more attention from him. But I squash that down into a tiny dark corner and leave it there for later analysis and focus on the game instead. It seems to last forever. I absently wonder if we are now in tomorrow, but no. It's still Friday. Thank God they only play five innings or we might be sitting on these bleachers all weekend. But when the game finally ends and we all climb down and Noah throws himself into my arms and asks if I saw his base hit, it's all worthwhile. He's an adorable kid, sweet and kind and gentle. Unlike his little brother Drake, who's got dark hair and eyes like Connie, Noah looks more like me. His light brown hair is similar in shade to mine, and we both have blue eyes like our dad. I rustle his hair when he takes off his cap and tell him he needs a haircut.

"Gotta get you to the barber," my dad says to him happily, seemingly ignoring the fact that his daughter—standing directly in front of him—is a goddamn hairstylist. I poke the inside of my cheek with my tongue but don't say anything. As usual.

An hour later, I'm sitting in a bar in Jefferson Square called Martini's, nursing a beer and waiting for Adley to arrive. It's Friday night, and it was hard to convince her to leave the ice cream shop for a short time to grab a drink with her bestie, but I did it. She's coming through the door as I sip, moving at extra quick speed the way Adley does everything.

"Do you ever slow down?" I ask her as she sits on the stool next to me. "Move at a normal pace?"

"Listen, I don't have time for normal paces. I am busy." She snaps her fingers a few times to punctuate her statement, and it makes me laugh.

"Oh right, I forgot."

The woman behind the bar has a mass of dark curls that I'd kill for, and I immediately start wondering things about it. Occupational hazard. What shampoo does she use? Is that natural curl? I think it is. Does she love it or hate it?

Adley orders a gin and tonic and teases me, telling me to stop analyzing the poor woman's hair. She knows me well. "How was the game?" she asks, and we're off on another topic.

"Long and boring, but Noah was adorable and had a base hit."

Adley thanks the bartender when her drink is delivered and takes a healthy sip. "Those boys are the cutest."

"Yeah, I told him he needs a haircut, and my dad promised to take him to the barbershop." I roll my eyes.

"Right there in front of you?" Adley asks. I nod and she shakes her head. "Jesus."

"Yeah." I swig my beer and sigh because this isn't new. Adley's heard it all before, but she's a sweetheart who lets me repeat all the stories all the time. I change the subject. "What's new in the wonderful world of ice cream?" We're talking about how business is down from this time last year, but Adley's got a couple ideas for new sundaes when my eye is caught by the front door opening. A group of about five women come into Martini's, and it's like somebody's reached a hand into my lungs and just pulled all the air out. I blink. I stare.

"Hey," Adley is saying, but I can't seem to shift my gaze. "Scooter. What's up?" She turns to look at the group, then swivels back to me and, in typical, hugely observant, and intuitive Adley fashion, whispers to me, "Is that her?"

Marisa is wearing cropped jeans and a black tank with a pink denim jacket she's sliding off her arms as she and her group of friends take two of the high-top tables and push them together. Her dark hair is partially pulled back, leaving waves skimming her shoulders. She's laughing and relaxed, and it's a version of her I haven't seen before. It's nice. No, it's beautiful.

"Yeah," I say with a nod, and Adley, never one for subtlety, openly gapes until I elbow her. "Well, don't stare. God."

"Which one is it?"

I pinch Adley until she turns back to face the bar with a whine. "Ow!"

"She's the one in the black tank." I say it without looking. I don't know if Marisa has seen me, but I don't want her to catch me ogling her. "This is, like, the third time we've been at the same place at the same time, and it's seriously weirding me out."

"Somebody up there is trying to tell you something," Adley says, subtly pointing up.

"Hey, Scottie," comes the voice from behind us, and I feel my own eyes go wide with surprise. Clearly, she *did* see me.

I turn around and those dark, dark eyes capture mine. "Hey, Marisa." I glance over her shoulder. "Girls' night out?"

She smiles and nods. "Coworkers, yeah." Her gaze lands on Adley, and I mentally shake myself until my manners show up.

"Oh, this is my friend Adley Purcell. Adley, this is my dance instructor—and dance partner, turns out—Marisa Reyes."

As they shake hands, Marisa squints at Adley, then repeats her name twice before saying, "Do you own Get the Scoop?"

"I do," Adley says, and I notice she sits up a little straighter. Pride'll do that to you.

"Well, my nephew loves, loves, loves your ice cream, and he loved that you had him in the back. He talks about it a lot. We'll definitely be back again soon."

"Jaden, right?" Adley asks, and both Marisa and I nod. "He was a sweetheart. He's welcome anytime. I'll take him in the back again, and he can help me make a new flavor."

"Oh my God, don't say that if you don't mean it." Marisa laughs and then the bartender is there, and she orders a rum and Diet Coke, a pitcher of light beer, and two glasses of white wine. First round is clearly on her.

"I definitely mean it. Bring him by anytime." She lifts her G&T and touches it to Marisa's glass.

The bartender helps her carry her drinks back to the table, and Marisa gives me a smile and says she'll talk to me later and then I can breathe again.

"Man," Adley says. "You've got it bad. Just ask her out already."

I hope my face shows the *What the hell are you talking about?* that I feel because what the hell is she talking about?

"What?" Adley says. "She's obviously into you. You are *absolutely* into her. Might as well, right?"

"That will not be happening."

"Why not?" Adley asks, and as if Pen is sitting right there with us, participating in the conversation, my phone pings an incoming text and there she is.

I hold the phone up so Adley can see. "That's why not."

Just thinking about you, says the text, followed by a smiling emoji surrounded by hearts.

"What the hell is she doing?" Adley asks, and that is the question, isn't it?

I shake my head and sigh. "I don't know." I finish my beer and signal to the awesome-haired bartender for another. "I really don't."

"Have you responded?"

"No," I say, probably too vehemently, because Adley squints at me.

"But you want to."

"No." I sigh. "I mean, maybe?"

"*Why?*" Adley asks, and draws the word out so it's about seven syllables. "Why would you want to? She ripped your heart out. She kicked you out of your own home. She told you she wasn't the kind to get married, and now she's engaged to somebody else. Why would you even give her the time of day?"

Adley Purcell, voice of reason, everybody.

"I don't know." But that's not exactly true, is it? I lift the fresh beer the bartender slides me and take a big swig of it before I admit the real reason to Adley. "I feel like I have all the power right now. I've never had the power when it comes to Penelope. Not once in the entire time we were together. So I think I'm just...reveling in that for a bit."

Adley tips her head from one side to the other and seems to take that in. "All right. Fine. I'll let it slide for now." She sips her drink and adds, "But I do wonder what's going on with her."

"Me, too," I say.

Adley stays long enough to finish her drink, but then tells me she's gotta get back to Get the Scoop and help with closing. I wave away her attempt to pay, hug her, and tell her I'll see her again soon, and then she's gone, and I'm sitting alone at the bar with an almost full beer. I'm glad my back is to Marisa and friends because if they were in my line of sight, I'm afraid I'd stare like a creeper. Instead, I pick up my phone and scroll back through all the messages Pen has sent in the last week or two. There aren't a ton, but there are more than she ever sent in that span of time when we were together. And Adley's words come back to me because I, too, wonder what's going on with her. She's engaged. She should be planning her wedding and canoodling with her fiancée, shouldn't she? Not sending vague, random texts to her ex.

I'm seriously considering what kind of a response I could send when Marisa appears next to me, and I drop my phone, then quickly snap it up and make the screen go black.

"Looks like we're the holdouts," she says, and when I glance over my shoulder, her table has cleared out, and her friends are headed toward the door. "Jaden's spending the night at my mom's, and I'm just not ready to go home yet."

"That was the fastest girls' night out I've ever seen."

She laughs and it's pretty. Soft and musical. "It was. Everybody's got people to get home to."

"Not you?" I think we both realize that I'm asking if she has somebody besides Jaden at home, because it occurs to me that I have no idea. Maybe she does. I mean, look at her. Why wouldn't she?

"Nope." She takes the stool next to mine. "Do you mind?"

"Not at all," I say. And I don't. Spend time sitting next to this gorgeous woman who, according to my bestie, the powers that be are putting in my path for a reason? Yes, please.

"How was your day?" she asks, and I love the simplicity of the question.

"It wasn't bad, as Fridays go. I worked, was pretty busy, then went to watch my little brother play baseball. Then I spent way too long convincing Adley to leave the ice cream shop for half an hour to meet me here for a drink. And here I am."

"That sounds like a pretty good day," Marisa says, signaling the bartender. Turns out the rum and Diet Coke was hers, and she orders herself another. "Does your brother play in college?"

I laugh because I tend to forget that when somebody doesn't know my backstory, of course they would assume my younger siblings are merely a few years younger. "No, he plays in elementary school."

Marisa's eyes go wide. "What?"

"Yeah, my parents split when I was thirteen. Then they both got remarried a few years later and then both had kids a few years after that. So I have a sister who's thirteen and three brothers who are ten, eight, and five."

"Wow," Marisa says.

"Right? I was in my twenties when everybody was born."

"Was it hard for you?" And believe it or not, Marisa is the first person to ever ask me that right off the bat. I blink at her a couple times before answering.

"It was. Yeah. Still is sometimes." I sip my beer. "I often have to remind myself that my parents are much different people—and much different *parents*—now than they were when I was a kid."

"That's really observant. I bet not a lot of people would get that. Are your siblings being raised differently than you were?"

I snort what's supposed to be a laugh but ends up being more sarcastic than anything else. "In every way. Yes."

"I bet that can suck."

"In many, many ways." I grin at her. "You're really intuitive, you know that?"

She lifts one shoulder. "I come from a big family. Lots of ins and outs and family dynamics. Family can be complicated."

"So complicated." We're quiet for a moment, and while I debate internally for that time, I decide maybe it's okay to ask her about her situation, since she just learned a whole bunch about mine. "So, you took in Jaden after his parents died. That's…incredible. Selfless, loving, and I bet hard."

She inhales a deep breath and lets it out very slowly before she speaks. When she turns to me, her dark eyes are filled with so many things, emotions in quick succession. Grief, happiness, worry, joy. "It's been…so much. So many different things. Jaden is a good kid. A really good kid. And my heart breaks for what he's been through. He sees a therapist, and he's pretty good about talking to me about things. But he also has nightmares. And sometimes, he just wants his mom, you know?"

"Ugh." I can feel my heart aching in my chest for the poor kid. "I can't even imagine."

"I guess…this is going to sound awful, but I think part of me is glad that, if this was going to happen, if he was meant to lose his parents, he lost them at the age he did. He's got memories, but not so many that the entire scope of his life is changed." She grits her teeth and makes a face like she's worried what she just said might be tactless. "I mean, that's stupid, of course the scope of his life has changed. I just…" She seems to struggle for the right words, but I put my hand on her forearm, stopping her.

"I get it. I totally understand what you mean." She tosses me a look of gratitude. "So, you said you have a big family. What made you decide to take him in?"

"Well, my mom wanted him. Was all set to move him in. But my dad uses a cane, and my mom is pretty sprightly for being almost seventy, but they babysat Jaden when he was two, before he went to preschool. And I watched them do it. It was only three days a week, and they loved it. But they were *exhausted* by the time Friday rolled around. They'd spend their weekends recovering only to do it again on Monday. And I just knew having him full-time would take a toll on them, healthwise. They're only recently retired. They should be able to take vacations and travel and just relax, not raise another kid from three years old."

I love listening to her talk. I realize that in the middle of her story as I just sit there with my chin in my hand and listen. The timbre of her voice. The way her glossy lips move. How she turns her glass in a slow circle with her fingers as she speaks. I am entranced. Thoroughly entranced by this woman. "So, he's been with you for a year?"

"About that, yeah. I have a little house and had the extra space, and he's my godchild. We were always close."

"Sounds to me like he's a very lucky little boy to have you." I almost wince when I hear my own words because Jaden is obviously *not* lucky. He lost both his parents, for fuck's sake. But Marisa smiles and thanks me, and I'm relieved.

"No kids for you, right?" she asks.

I shake my head. "No. Not yet."

"You want them, though?"

"I do." I give a nod to go with my words. "I wasn't sure when I was first out. My childhood was such a mess, and I really struggled with the possibility of messing up another kid the way my parents messed me up. But…" I look into my near-empty glass, my past struggles and indecision around the subject flashing through my brain. "But yeah. I'd love to have kids." I glance up and meet her eyes, and there's something there that I can't identify, that gives me a little flutter low in my body. I clear my throat and change the subject, if only to stop her looking at me like that because it's just too…I don't know. It's too *something*, and it's doing things to me. "Why financial planning?"

If Marisa is surprised by the shift in topic, she doesn't show it. Again, she lifts one shoulder, and I'm kind of starting to like that little half shrug. "I have always wanted to be fully in control of my future, so when I was younger, I'd do lots of research on things like stocks and investments and Wall Street. I almost moved to New York City to work there."

"Really? Wow. That's impressive. What stopped you?"

"I didn't really want to leave Northwood. I always thought I did. Couldn't wait to get out of town and live somewhere big where nobody knew me. But when it came right down to it, I realized that I actually love this little town." She sips her drink. "Plus, it would've killed my mother." And then she laughs that musical laugh again, and it worms right into my stomach. And lower.

"It's still so interesting to me that your two jobs are so opposite. One is logic and numbers. The other is creativity and emotion."

"What can I say? I guess that makes me well-rounded."

"I guess it does. Not a lot of people are."

Our gazes hold, and something zips between us. I think we both feel it because we each look away quickly.

We finish our drinks, and while I'm tempted to have one more, Fridays aren't actually Fridays for me, since I work Saturdays. "I should probably get home," I say. "I've got a client at nine tomorrow morning."

"I forget you work on Saturdays. You're off on Mondays?"

I nod. "Hairstylists and some restaurant folks. We have our own weekends." We both slide off our stools and prepare to settle up tabs. For a split second, I want to pay for Marisa's, but then I realize that could be seen as kind of presumptuous, and I don't want to be that. We sign our own slips and slide them back across the bar, gather our things, and head out together.

We get to Marisa's SUV first, and we stop and sort of stand there. "Well. I'm glad I ran into you tonight."

"Yeah?" Her words surprise me, but I'm not sure why because I feel the same. "Me, too."

She swallows. I see it and hear it. When she looks back up, she seems to hesitate before saying, "Listen, I know you're working tomorrow, but want to grab a drink later? Or some ice cream?"

When I tell you I am *this close* to squealing in delight and jumping up and down like a tween girl, I am not even kidding. I try really hard not to grin like a weirdo, but I'm pretty sure I do. "I'd love that."

Her smile seems to be a combination of joy and relief. "Okay. Good. Perfect. I'll text you. Or you can text me when you're done. Or whatever. One of us should text."

I laugh because she's so stupidly cute right now. "Okay. Sounds good."

She gives a quick little nod and opens her car door and gets in. I back away slowly, watching her face in her side mirror for a minute before I turn and walk to my own rattletrap. And the weirdo grin breaks through. I see it in the rearview mirror, and I shake my head at myself, but I also keep right on grinning. I make eye contact with myself and point at my reflection.

"You, my friend, have a date tomorrow night. I think."

CHAPTER TWELVE

Saturday's weather is gorgeous. Stunning. Sunny all day long. About seventy-five degrees. Just absolutely perfect early summer weather.

People might complain about being inside on a weekend day when it's so nice out, but honestly, I've worked in a salon for many years now, and I don't even consider Saturday part of the weekend anymore. My weekend is Sunday and Monday, so I'm not upset to be cooped up on a gorgeous day.

That being said, it's also my date day, and *that* makes me not want to be here. While I'm very aware that chatting along with my clients often makes the day go by faster—the one exception being if I have somebody in my chair who insists on talking politics and their politics are the opposite of mine—I'm being kind of quiet today, doing more nodding than participating.

"What's going on with you?" Bash asks me after my fourth client heads out the door.

"What?"

He waves a finger up and down in front of me. "You're being weird. What's going on?"

I haven't told him about Marisa, and I'm still not sure I should, but I also know he'll bug me all day until I can't take it anymore and I crack, so it's probably better to just come clean.

"Okay. Fine. It's possible I...have a date tonight."

"What?" he says. Loudly.

I look around quickly, then make a face at him. "Shh. Seriously. I don't need the whole place to know."

"I can't believe you're just telling me this now. I'm hurt." He pouts. I laugh.

"Stop that. You are not."

"Tell me," he orders, and since we both have empty chairs for the next few moments, I figure I might as well.

I spill the details. All about the dance lesson last week and the competition and running into Marisa at the bar last night and how we ended up talking, just the two of us for a bit, and how she asked me to drinks or ice cream tonight.

He stares at me as I talk, clearly rapt with attention, and the more I say, the farther open his mouth falls until he's completely slack-jawed by the time I finish. "Holy shit," he says quietly. Then he repeats himself. "Holy shit."

"I know, right?"

"Going for ice cream is just the cutest date thing. It's like… rom-commy. What are you going to wear?" The question takes me by surprise, and I glance down at my jeans and simple top. When I bring my gaze back up, Bash is shaking his head. "No. Just no."

"I agree with Bash," Demi says from her chair, and now I know that she's been listening as well. "Plus, you're gonna have little hairs all over you. Come on."

Well. So much for not getting all nervous about tonight.

"Jeans are fine," Demi says, and Bash nods his agreement. "But maybe cropped ones. And wear that cute light blue plaid sleeveless button-down you have."

"Yes," Bash says, agreement clear in his voice. "That's perfect. But put a white tank on under it and then leave it unbuttoned."

"Oh, good call," Demi says. "Ice cream is casual, so you don't want to overdo it. What about those cute white sneakers you have? Wear those with no-show socks."

"And pull your hair partially back." Bash reaches for my hair, gathers some of it, and holds it behind my head while he plays with what's left still hanging, arranging hanks of it here and there. He turns to look at Demi, who nods enthusiastically.

"Perfect."

So, yeah, that's how I decide what I'm going to wear tonight.

❖

While I don't love waiting in line forever, I'm always thrilled when Get the Scoop is busy. I pull in, and the lot is almost full, so it takes me some time to find a spot. Kids are running everywhere, some with cones, some with no cones but ice cream on their faces. I get out of my car and glance around. No Marisa yet, which is a bit of a relief because now I have extra time to *really* let my nerves build. I roll my eyes at myself and lean against my back bumper, just watching the kids. I'm sure Adley is inside, in the back, brewing up some new flavor combination, and I know I could go in the back, grab some ice cream that way, but I don't like to take advantage. No, I will wait in line like every other customer. Maybe I'll scoot back there and say hi later, though. Depending on how things go.

She's here.

It's like some kind of weird sonar in my head, but I turn toward the parking lot opening at the exact moment Marisa turns her SUV into it. There's really only one place she can park, so she does, and then a couple minutes go by before the car door pushes open and she slides out. That's what she has to do—slide out. Her SUV is much taller than my small car, and I've noticed she turns in her seat so both legs are out and then she slides to the ground. It's cute. Fun to watch. Especially today, since she's wearing shorts and those legs are on full display. Dancer's legs. Wow.

We meet halfway between her car and mine.

"Hey there." And her smile says she's happy to see me. At least, that's what I choose to believe it says. I know mine says that about her.

"Hey yourself. How was your day?"

"Busy. Saturdays usually are. But it's done and I'm here with you now, so my day is excellent." Oh, the gushing. Yikes. *Dial it back a bit, Templeton.*

Marisa's smile gets a little wider, which is a relief. She looks devastatingly pretty today in her simple shorts and T-shirt, white sneakers with no-show socks on her feet giving me as much leg as possible, and it's honestly hard for me not to gape at them. I'm saying it now: Marisa has the sexiest legs I've ever seen. Long. Shapely. Muscular and pretty. I give myself a mental shake.

"How about you?" I ask. "What did you do today?" By

unspoken agreement, we stroll toward Get the Scoop and decide to wait in line at the outdoor serving window rather than go inside.

"Well, when Jaden's not home, I take advantage. I cleaned like a woman on a mission. His room. The bathroom." She turns to look at me and asks, "Do you have any idea how much toothpaste a four-year-old gets not in, but *around* the bathroom sink?"

"Can't say that I do."

"It's a lot, Scottie. Trust me. It's a lot."

We laugh together over that as we take our places in line.

"Then I vacuumed my house, mopped my kitchen floor, and took a glass of wine out onto my deck where I actually sat and read a book, uninterrupted, for an entire hour."

"An entire hour? Wow. That sounds lovely. I honestly can't remember the last time I did that."

"Blissful, I'm telling you. Blissful."

And then there's a beat or two of quiet where we just stand there. Just stand next to each other. Looking around at the other people. Smiling softly. Being in each other's presence. It's weird and wonderful and exhilarating.

"I'm really glad you asked me to do this," I say.

"Me, too," Marisa says, her eyes on the menu board posted above the window. "I mean, you turned me on to this place, and now I'm hooked. You're like my dealer."

"Adley pays me well to bring her sacrifi—er—new customers."

That gets another smile, and I decide right in that moment that I would like that to be my job forever, making Marisa smile or laugh. It feels really, really good somehow.

"What do you recommend?"

"No mint chocolate chip for you today?" I remember that's what Jaden had me get for her last time. He said it's her favorite.

"That's always my solid fallback. And it's definitely a favorite. But there are so many fun flavors on this list. I think I'd like to try something new."

"Okay, well, let's see. We've done the ube." I scan the board with her, trying not to notice that we've stepped very close to each other. I can smell that hint of coconut that always comes from her, which makes me say, "I highly recommend Tropical Dream. That's mango pineapple ice cream with flakes of coconut." She nods. "And Baby Bear is honey ice cream with pieces of doughnuts in it. The honey is really subtle, though, so it's not cloyingly sweet. Took Adley a long time to get that one right." As I go through various flavors, giving my opinion of each, I can feel Marisa's eyes on me as if they were fingertips, skimming softly over my skin and leaving goose bumps in their wake. She's looking me over, taking me in. My underwear is instantly damp, and somewhere in a corner of my brain, that power of arousal she has registers and glows. "Stop that," I say, just above a whisper, and I can feel how my face has heated up.

"Sorry," she says back softly, but when I turn to face her, she's looking at the board and smiling and clearly not sorry at all, and I absolutely love that she knew exactly what I was talking about.

What is happening here?

It's a silly question because *duh*. I know what's happening here. But it's so incredibly unexpected that it's kind of thrown me for a loop, as Grandma would say.

"What are you having?" she asks as we get closer to the window.

"I feel like my old standby tonight. Chocolate almond. It's my favorite. It's almost equal parts almonds and chocolate. Delish. And I will get sprinkles. Of course."

"Of course."

And we stand there some more. And it's so incredibly…I don't even know how to describe it. Buzzy? Is that a word? Because I feel like my entire body is abuzz when I stand near her. Like everything is thrumming somehow. Electrically charged. It's a crazy, weird, awesome feeling, and I don't want it to end. Ever.

Which is a super intense realization, and it makes me swallow hard. I'm busy hoping Marisa doesn't notice as it becomes our turn. We place our orders—Marisa surprises us both by choosing a Peach Cobbler sundae instead of a cone—and she insists on paying for both of us. I do my best to protest, but she wins with the old standard—"My invitation, my treat"—and I let her. But not without my own caveat.

"I get the next thing, then," I say, sounding way more confident than I feel.

"Deal," she says, surprising me. And now I know there will be a next thing, and I'm kinda giddy. I have to roll my lips in and bite down on them to keep from smiling like some kind of weirdo.

The kid who hands me my ice cream cone gives me a look. I think he recognizes me and realize I'm right when he says, "Do you want me to get Adley for you?"

"Oh no, don't bother her. I'll catch up with her later." I wave a hand as another kid hands over Marisa's sundae. There's something sexy about the fact that she ordered it, rather than, like, a kiddie cone or something. She *eats*, and I love that. Because I eat, too. Why wouldn't we? Ice cream is friggin' delicious.

"Ooh," Marisa says, and I follow her gaze to a little table that has just opened up in the seating area outside. It's a small space. Adley would rather have customers sitting at tables inside where they can see all the flavors in front of their eyes instead of on a board mounted to the front of the building. But I told her last summer that having space out front where people are sitting and noshing on their cones and sundaes would be a draw for people driving by. She agreed with me and created a little roped-off space with a handful of tables and chairs.

It's a warm evening and my ice cream gets soft pretty quickly, so I go to town on it, and that's when I realize that maybe Marisa made the smarter choice. I am using my tongue and spinning my cone in a circle. Marisa is using a spoon and watching me.

She's watching me.

My heart rate kicks up several notches. I keep eating, trying to be neat about it, but I hold her gaze for a moment.

"I'm so glad you ordered a cone." Her voice is low and there's a quality to it I haven't heard before. A sexy quality. A flirty quality. And then she winks. Actually winks! I didn't think people did that anymore, but she totally winks at me and it's totally sexy and oh my God, what is happening here?

Again, a stupid question because again, I know exactly what's happening here. And it's hot. And sexy. And turning me on in the biggest of ways. She grins at me as she puts a spoonful of her sundae in her mouth, and it makes me think she knows exactly the effect she's having. Okay. I can play this game. Can't I?

"Well, I'm a little sad you didn't get one."

"I had one last time we were here. And the time before that. You got to watch then." She raises and lowers her eyebrows just once, and the grin stays. Oh my God, she's telling me she knows I was watching her last time. The last *two* times.

I laugh. I can't help it. I laugh and shake my head and eat my ice cream and… "I'm really glad we're here." It's a simple statement, but nothing I could say right now would be a truer one. I'm thrilled to be sitting across from her at my best friend's ice cream shop, eating ice cream and flirting with each other, and this is so not what I expected even two weeks ago.

"Me, too," she says, and then we eat in silence for a moment or two. "The weirdness factor is easing up a bit, don't you think?"

I nod. "I've noticed that, too." And we eat and we look at each other, and while I'm still a little nervous and a lot turned on, she's right. It feels less and less weird by the second. "The only thing I'm sure of is that I really like spending time with you." I'm a little shocked I actually say the words, but it's too late to take them back now.

"Same. Hey, how do you feel about taking a walk by the lake?"

Seriously, how many more romantic things can we do in one night? Because twenty minutes later, bellies full of ice cream, we drive together in Marisa's car to the public parking lot at Black Cherry Lake. It's a busy place on a Saturday night in June, but we find a spot and then casually stroll to the shores of the lake. There's a walking path, and we find it, joining many other couples and families out for a stroll.

"What's your go-to movie genre?" Marisa asks out of the blue.

"Oh, is this the getting-to-know-you part of this date?" I bump her with a shoulder as I take a moment to think about my answer. "Thrillers followed by romantic comedies."

"Me, too," she says, a tinge of surprised excitement in her voice. "Same with TV?"

"With TV, I'm partial to crime procedurals and true crime shows, but I do like an occasional sitcom. You?"

"Same. Though you have to throw in some *SpongeBob* and some *Bluey* 'cause I have a kid, you know."

"Ah, I see. Nothing wrong with a good cartoon here and there." We pass a couple holding hands, and I don't know if that gives

Marisa ideas or what, but the next thing I know, her hand is brushing mine, and then she takes it and our fingers lace and it's so fucking perfect, I almost want to cry.

"How did we get here?" she asks with a quiet laugh and a shake of her head. She holds up our linked hands to punctuate her point, then leads me to a bench off to the side of the path. It's still light out, but the sun has gone down now, and the bench is in amongst some trees, a bit of cover. Dusk will hit soon. We sit but continue to hold hands.

"I have no idea," I say, and it's true. "Do you believe in things like, I don't know, fate? Or the Universe talking? Signs? I mean, if Sebastian hadn't broken his foot, and your aunt hadn't had to leave, we wouldn't have had to dance together. I wouldn't have had a chance to tell you that I didn't know you and Pen were still together when we started dating. I wouldn't have met Jaden. Or cut either of your hair. Yours is looking fabulous, by the way." She grins. "We wouldn't be dancing in the competition together."

"We wouldn't be doing this," she says, then leans in, and almost before I can even register it, her mouth is on mine, and she kisses me. Softly. Tentatively, like she's testing the waters. She kisses me slowly. I kiss her back, and there's no hurry here. I can taste the peaches and the vanilla ice cream from her sundae, which mix really well with the raspberry lip gloss she put on in the car. She pulls back just enough to look in my eyes. Hers have gone darker. A little hooded. Sexy. I realize that she's checking in, making sure this is okay with me. I let her know it is by sliding my hand around to the back of her neck and pulling her to me again.

I'm not sure how long we kiss. Time kind of falls away. So does sound. Awareness. Worry. It's all gone, nothing existing except Marisa's mouth. Marisa's lips. Marisa's tongue. Marisa's hands, one on my thigh, the other in my hair. I close my fist in hers and give her head a gentle tug, revealing the long column of throat. I want to lick it, to run my tongue up and down the entire thing, but my consciousness comes suddenly screeching back, and I remember that, though we're sitting off the path, we can still be seen. I opt for just kissing her neck softly, then let go of her hair and meet her gaze again when she opens her eyes.

Her breathing is rapid, her breasts rising and falling and drawing my eyes to them. She laughs softly. "Probably a good thing we stop, huh?"

I nod, feeling joyous and excited and so turned on I'm surprised I haven't slid right off the bench. "Yeah, probably."

"I like you, Scottie." Her voice is frank. Solid. Sure. "It's weird and totally unexpected, and I don't quite know what to do with it or about it, but it's the truth. I like you."

"I like you, too," I say. "And so much same on the unexpected part. Wow."

She sits back on the bench and crosses her legs. I mimic her position, and we're both quiet for a while, just people-watching and being close together. It sounds kind of silly and unexciting, but it's far from it. I'm completely aroused just sitting next to her, my body thrumming from simple proximity. So. Bizarre.

"What if…" Marisa begins, then stops as if she's rethinking her words. Finally, she turns to me, looks me in the eye. "Would you come to dinner tomorrow night? At my house?"

"I'd love to." I don't even hesitate. Not for a second. Why would I? More time with Marisa? And on her own turf? Yes, please.

"Jaden will be home."

"Even better." That makes her smile big, and then she turns back toward the water. Her hand finds mine again, our fingers lace, and she holds them on her lap.

"I could sit here with you like this for hours."

I nod because I understand the feeling. It's peaceful. It's private. It's comfortable. And we're alone. "Same."

"Also, I'm very torn right now."

"Yeah? How come?"

She doesn't look at me, and when she rolls her bottom lip in over her teeth and wets it, I realize whatever she's thinking makes her nervous. And it's kind of surprising that I can read her so well already. When she finally tells me what's on her mind, her voice is barely above a whisper, gravelly and sexy. "I'm torn because it's Saturday night, and Jaden isn't home, so my house is empty, and I am so attracted to you I can hardly think, and there's a movie playing in my head of us. At my house. In my bed—and it's way too soon, and I know that and also the baggage, and Jesus, I can't believe I just told you that." She covers her eyes with the hand not holding mine and shakes her head slowly, back and forth.

I absorb everything she's said for a couple seconds, then reach for the hand covering her eyes and gently pull it away. "Hey." I wait until she looks at me before I grin. And grin, I do. Because holy shit, did you hear what she just said? "I get it," I tell her and squeeze her hand. "I get it because I feel it, too. Trust me. I can't remember the last time I felt this attracted to somebody this fast. It's dizzying. But in a good way. You know?" She nods, her eyes still focused on mine. "Let's take our time. Yeah? I don't know about you, but I have jumped into things in the past that I maybe should've examined a bit more first." I tip my head and raise my eyebrows poignantly, and I'm pretty sure she gets what I'm talking about. *Who* I'm talking about. "Let's have dinner tomorrow night and not worry about anything beyond that yet. Okay?" Who am I? Who is this person who sounds so incredibly reasonable? And why is she turning down a night with this gorgeous woman whose tongue was in her mouth not fifteen minutes ago? Yep. It's me. Hi. I have instant panic that I just said all the wrong things, and it must show up on my face because Marisa laughs out loud right then.

"You should see your face right now. You are so cute." She squeezes my hand. "And you're right. We'll go slow." She kisses me softly, then sits back, and we stay there for a little while longer. There is something about sitting near her that tickles all my senses, puts all my nerves on red alert. I feel almost electrified.

A little while later, we're back in the parking lot of Get the Scoop, which is closed now. Even Adley's car is gone, and I'm glad to see that. My bestie works too hard. Marisa glides her SUV to a stop next to my piece-of-crap car and shifts it into park.

"So," she says as she turns to look at me.

"So," I say back, and then it's my turn to make the move, and I can't not, because my God, she's beautiful. It boggles my mind that, not only am I sitting in her car, but I'm leaning in, and then I'm kissing her, and she's letting me. And kissing me back, and holy shit, she's good at it. It's funny—once the first kiss is out of the way, and all the nerves that come with it have eased up, there's time to really notice. Really feel. And feel, I do. Marisa takes her time when she kisses. She moves slowly. I have kissed other women who literally push right in, but not Marisa. She takes her time and brushes her lips against mine. When her tongue enters the activity, it's just a little. Just a taste, a tease, and it ratchets my arousal up higher and higher with every moment, slowly, like the burner on a stove that's increasing the heat, but just a touch, and by the time she presses her tongue all the way into my mouth, I'm ready to explode. I grab her head with both hands and give as good as I've gotten. I can feel her hands on my bare stomach under my shirt, and it's like fire, that touch. Everything about us is hot. Sizzling. And oh my God, it would be so easy to keep going. To go home with her. To tell her I changed my mind, drive me to your house, I can't get enough, please don't stop.

We wrench apart as if we both had the same thought, that things were getting a little too hot and heavy. The windows are completely fogged up, and I look around the car at them and then laugh.

"Oh my God, we're like teenagers," Marisa says, joining me in laughing. "And also, you're an incredible kisser. Jesus. Sorry about that. I didn't mean to get so carried away, but God." She shakes her head, her dark eyes wide.

"Right back atcha," I say, and it occurs to me that I'm still panting, my breaths ragged. "Wow." I wait for a moment until I catch my breath and the blood rushing through me slows to a normal speed. "Okay. I'm gonna go now." I jerk a thumb over my shoulder to indicate my car. "Can you—"

"I will be right here until your car starts."

"Perfect." I open the car door, and the overhead light seems rude and super bright, and we both squint. "Text me your address for tomorrow and what I can bring."

"I will."

I sit there, my hand on the door handle, and I just take her in. Her overall beauty. Her flushed cheeks and kiss-swollen lips. Her hands. God, she's got gorgeous hands, resting on the steering wheel, her nails painted a deep purple, which looks fab against her skin tone. She's simply…breathtaking. I swallow down the resurgence of arousal that I feel and say, very softly, "Bye."

She says it back, and I drop to the ground and shut the door. Once in my own driver's seat, I wish I could take a few moments and just catch my breath, relive the evening, gather myself before I go home. But she's still there, dutifully waiting to make sure my car starts.

It does.

I wave to her and give a thumbs-up, and then I watch as she backs out of the spot and drives away. And then I say it out loud.

"Ho. Lee. Shit."

CHAPTER THIRTEEN

A re you sure you know what you're doing?"
        My head snaps around to my grandmother because to say I'm surprised by the question is a massive understatement. "Grandma! You're the one who told me to stick out the dance lessons. *The playing field is now level.* That's what you said."

Grandma stirs half-and-half into her coffee. She doesn't mess around with milk or Coffee mate fake powdery chemical crap. No way. She puts the good stuff in hers. That's where I got it from. The spoon tings the sides of the mug as she nods. "I did say that. But we were talking about dance lessons. Not *dating*."

The way she says the word *dating* makes her worry clear. And that's what it is, worry. I know my grandmother well enough, and she's fully accepting of my sexuality. In fact, she was more welcoming than both my parents at first. So I know her concern isn't about me dating a woman. It's about me dating Marisa.

And I stop with my own coffee cup near my lips and just freeze for a beat. Because is that what I'm doing? Am I dating Marisa? I mean, last night was a date, right? And then today, that's a date, too. Do two dates qualify as dating? My coffee makes it to my lips, and I take a sip before I answer. "It's just dinner, Grandma. That's all."

She turns with her cup in both hands and leans against the counter while she studies me. I hate when she does that. I feel like she sees right into my head, into my brain, into my thoughts. Like I can't hide a damn thing from her. Finally, she brings her own cup up, and just before she takes a sip, she says, "If you say so."

Yeah, if that's not code for *I don't believe you*, I don't know what is. I sigh quietly.

Grandma squeezes my shoulder as she walks by me, likely heading out onto her deck where she likes to sit most mornings in nice weather. "I just worry about your tender heart. That's all." Then she drops a kiss onto the top of my head, and I hear the sliding glass door off the dining room open. I eat my Fruity Pebbles—because I'm a six-year-old when it comes to cereal—and try to ignore the tiny prickle of worry my grandmother just created.

A little after noon, I'm pushing through the back door of Get the Scoop because I really need to talk to Adley.

"Hey, Scoot," she says, not looking up from her laptop open in front of her.

"How'd you know it was me and not some crazy burglar breaking in to steal the world's best ice cream?" I slide an iced chai latte from Starbucks in front of her, and she makes a little sound of delight because it's her favorite and I know that.

"Please," she says with a snort as she pokes the straw through the lid. "I can hear that piece-of-shit car of yours rumbling along from down the block and around the corner."

"Valid." I open the lid of my Vanilla Sweet Cream Cold Brew and take a sip. Pretty sure I can feel the extra caffeine hit my system like an injection.

"How's the fam?" she asks, and I realize that's my cue to talk to her about random stuff for a bit while she finishes up what she's doing. I'll save the Marisa stuff for when I have her full attention.

"Jordie's dance went well, from what I could squeeze out of my mother. I got two whole pictures sent to me, but then she posted, like, thirty of them on Facebook." I take a sip of my coffee. "I was kinda bummed not to hear back from Jordie herself, though. I sent a couple texts, but she didn't answer."

Adley looks up at me over the screen of her laptop. "Oh, sweetie, don't take that personally. She's thirteen. The world revolves around her right now."

"True." She's right and I know it, but it still stings. "There were a couple photos from later in the evening and her hair still looked great, so…" I lift one shoulder.

"Of course it did. You're fantastic at what you do."

Okay. That makes me feel a tiny bit better. Just a smidge.

Get the Scoop opens at two on Sundays, so I'm happy to have Adley to myself for a bit before her employees start to arrive. "I bet today will be busy. It's fucking muggy out there already." And it is. It's unusual for mid-June to get quite so uncomfortably humid, but when I left Grandma's to get in my car, I felt like I was breathing through gauze.

Adley holds up two hands with crossed fingers and grins at me. She takes a pull from her straw, then meets my eyes and asks, "So? What's up with the Dancing Queen?"

A laugh shoots out of me. "The Dancing Queen?"

"Yup. That's what I call her in my head. She's the Dancing Queen."

"Just a touch." I sip more coffee. This is why I came here. To talk about Marisa. "Well." I swallow, and Adley stops what she's doing to stare at me.

"Uh-oh. This is serious. You look serious. What's up?"

"We kinda…made out last night." Before I can say anything more, Adley jumps out of her seat, lets out a loud whoop, and does a little spin as she throws her arms up in the air, clearly joyous. "Oh, that makes you happy, does it?"

"Are you kidding me? Hell, yeah! When's the last time you were kissed? It was Pen, wasn't it?"

I nod. Of course it was Pen. That bitch.

"That bitch," Adley adds. "And now? You're sucking face with her ex. That's"—she squints at me—"not weird at all."

I sigh and drop my chin down to my chest. "I know. I know. It's not ideal."

"No. But how was it? What's she like? What led up to making out? Is she a good kisser? Are you seeing her again?"

I laugh at the barrage of questions, and I tell her the whole story, from start—sitting with Marisa after Adley left the bar on Friday night—to finish—coming here last night, then heading to the lake, the walking, the sitting, the talking, the kissing. Adley listens quietly, which is very unlike her, her chin in her hands, a sweet, dreamy smile on her face.

"I love this whole story," she says when I finish. "I take it back. It's not weird. It's perfect. She sounds awesome."

"I like her a lot."

"And? How was the kissing?"

I let my head drop back toward my shoulder blades and let out a long, low groan. "Oh my God. *So* good." I lift my head and meet Adley's gaze. "I could kiss her forever. It's just…" A shake of my head because finding the right words to describe what it felt like to kiss Marisa, to be kissed by Marisa, is nearly impossible. "Hot. Toe-curling. Limb-melting. Exciting. Tingly. Just so fucking sexy that I get all turned on just thinking about it."

"That's exactly how it should be," Adley says, still grinning like crazy. She's happy for me, and I can see it clearly. "What now?"

"She invited me to her house for dinner tonight."

Adley drops her head to the stainless-steel counter in a pretend faint. "Amazing. I expect a full report."

"Yes, ma'am."

We're quiet for a bit as Adley goes about getting things ready to open, pulling tubs of ice cream from the freezer and hauling them out into the store area. I know how this all works, so I pitch in, restocking cones and bowls and spoons, making sure the window-service counter is wiped down and not sticky. Once we have the main stuff ready to go, Adley starts mixing the batter for the house-made waffle cones that make the whole place smell warm and sweet and inviting. As she works, she looks at me and narrows her eyes as if she's studying me.

"What?" I ask.

"So…" She blinks a few times, kicks out one hip and parks her hand on it. "How do you *feel*? About all this? About things with the Dancing Queen?"

I blink back at her. "Well. I haven't really given myself a ton of space or time to get into that."

"Because the strangeness of who she is overshadows it?"

I inhale and then let it out slowly. "I guess that's probably true." And before I can say more, as if she's privy to every move I make and every word I say, my phone pings a text notification. I slide it from my back pocket, glance down, and feel a jolt zap through my body. I hold the phone up so Adley can see it. "Pen."

"Oh my God, again? She's still texting?"

I nod. "Yep. This one says, *Happy Sunday. I bet you're seeing Adley today at the shop. Eat some ice cream for me.*"

"Okay, that is fucking creepy." Adley shakes her head, her dark eyes wide.

"I mean, it is and it's not. I always come see you on Sundays, so it's likely just a lucky guess." Adley narrows her eyes at me again, but this time adds tapping her forefinger against her pursed lips. That's my bestie's thinking face. I know it well. "What?" I ask.

She seems to choose her words carefully. Slowly. "You don't think this is some weird revenge plot on Marisa's part, do you? I was thinking that before the text came, and I can't really see how Pen would be involved in that, but…" She lets the sentence trail off and lifts one shoulder.

"What, you think her plan is to seduce me and then…what? Dump me? Kill me and hide my body in the basement of the dance studio?"

She gasps. "Or *keep you prisoner* in the basement of the dance studio!"

"You watch too much Lifetime, my friend," I say with a chuckle but don't share the quick little visual of being tied up by Marisa that zips through my head. And then zips lower.

I spend the rest of the day with Adley's words about some kind of revenge scheme hanging out in the back of my head. I'm ninety-five percent sure that's not at all what's happening, but that other five percent keeps tapping at the inside of my skull. I shake it away because I honestly don't think Marisa is unhinged like that.

Of course, she was with Pen for a few years.

Of course, I was also with Pen for a few years.

A little while later, Marisa texts me her address and says I don't need to bring anything but my smiling face. Then she asks if there's anything I don't like, and I tell her I'm not a huge fan of steak, so I'm relieved when she tells me her plan is to make salmon. That also allows me to choose a proper wine, because no way am I showing up empty-handed.

Grandma is off with her friends tonight—book club, I think—so I feed Salty and Pepper their dinner, grab the bottle of Chardonnay the girl at the wine store recommended, and check myself in the mirror on the door of the coat closet. I realized as I was getting dressed that I have no idea how Marisa feels about humidity or whether her home has central air, so I had to futz around a bit with what to wear. I opted for a cute pair of tan capris with a buttoned pocket on one leg, and a deep green V-neck tank. I made sure I was shaved smooth, and now as I stand in front of the mirror and study my reflection—with far too critical an eye, Bash would say—I think I'm okay. I grab a lightweight chambray shirt, just in case Marisa does have AC and she has it set to arctic tundra, as many people tend to do in my life, and I'm on my way.

It's funny, I'm actively thinking about how not nervous I am, being all impressed with myself, until I'm about a block away from where my GPS says Marisa's house is, and it's like the robot voice telling me to take a left triggers all those butterflies that have been hanging out in my stomach and napping. They instantly pop awake and start fluttering all over the place, and suddenly, my armpits start to sweat and my legs tremble, and for a good twenty seconds, I think I might have to pull over and throw up on the side of the road. But then I follow the directions and pull into Marisa's driveway, and she's sitting in a rocking chair on a cute little front porch, and her face lights up and her smile blossoms, and just like that, everything settles.

Really, really weird, that.

"Hey you," I say as I get out of the car with my purse and my bottle of wine.

"Hey yourself," Marisa says as she stands up, and I'm taking her in—her black shorts that are letting me see way too much leg, her simple white T-shirt, her bare feet, her hair in a ponytail, revealing a very long, gorgeous neck—when I hear my name shouted loudly and then what I think must be a cannonball in the shape of a little boy comes barreling out of the house, hits me, and wraps my waist in a tight hug.

"Wow. That is quite a greeting," I say, ruffling Jaden's hair with my free hand. I glance back up at Marisa and tease, "You could take a lesson."

Her smile gets wider. "Noted."

I really want to kiss her hello, but when she makes no move

toward me, I decide she must not want Jaden to see any PDA, which I get.

Marisa's house is a cute little Cape Cod, light blue with white shutters and a small white front porch. She leads me inside, and the first thing I notice is the smell. It's soft and subtle and warm. Inviting. Vanilla? Sugar? I can't tell, but once we pass through the living room and into the kitchen, it's replaced by the glorious smell of dinner cooking.

"Oh my God, that smells delicious," I tell her.

"Thanks." She opens a drawer and takes out a corkscrew. "Want to open that?" Her eyes indicate the wine still in my hand.

"Scottie, come and see my room," Jaden says, little-boy excited.

I look to Marisa, waiting to tailor my response to whatever lead she puts forth. With a grin, she takes the wine and corkscrew from my hand. "Only for a couple minutes, J," she says. "Scottie and I are going to have dinner soon. Your chicken nuggets will be done in five, okay?"

"Okay," Jaden says extra loudly, even as he's tugging me toward the stairs.

Marisa looks at me and mouths, *Sorry*, and I shrug and grin back at her and mouth back, *Totally fine*. Then out loud, I say, "See you in five minutes."

Jaden's room has typical little-boy decor. Race cars and dinosaurs and spaceships. His bed is twin size, covered neatly with a navy blue bedspread and red pillows with steering wheels and tires printed on them. In the corner is an enormous beanbag chair with a shelf of books next to it.

"Is this your reading nook?" I ask him.

He scoffs in a way only little kids do when they think adults are being dorks. "It's not a nook," he informs me. "It's a beanbag chair."

"*Oh*," I say, rather than correct him. "What books do you have?"

Jaden begins pulling books off his shelf to tell me a little about a few of them, but then he gets bored and turns to the racetrack set up on the floor. He hands me a bright yellow car. An older model VW Bug. "Here, you can be this guy. I will be *this*."

"Wait a minute," I say and give him a look. "You get to be the coolest, purplest, biggest tires, most awesomest car there is, and I get to be"—I hold up my car—"this jalopy?"

Apparently, *jalopy* is the funniest word Jaden has ever heard because he cracks up so hard, he falls over on the floor and just lies there laughing and repeating, "Jalopy," over and over. By the time Marisa comes up to get us, we're both lost in a fit of giggles.

"Clearly, I'm missing all the fun," she says, looking from one of us to the other and back again, amusement apparent on her face.

"Scottie said *jalopy*," Jaden says, enunciating the word slowly and carefully, pointing at me as he does, and then he's lost again.

I look at Marisa and shrug. "What can I say? I'm hilarious."

"Sure seems like it." She shakes her head. "All right, you two clowns. Dinner's ready. Let's go."

Fifteen minutes later, Jaden is parked in the living room in front of the TV with his chicken nuggets and Tater Tots, watching a cartoon I don't recognize. Meanwhile, Marisa has set her small dining room table for two, complete with linen napkins and a bouquet of fresh flowers. The wine is poured, and our meals are plated, and it's all gorgeous.

"I can't remember the last time somebody besides my grandmother made me dinner," I tell her as I sit. "This looks amazing. Thank you so much."

"It's nice to cook for somebody who eats more than chicken nuggets and pizza." She pulls out her chair and sits as I lift my glass.

"To new friendships, dance competitions, and whatever life is planning for us." Is that too much? Is the word *friendship* too generic? Is the assumption of a future too, well, presumptuous?

I must look panicked or confused or both because Marisa smiles softly and says, "I'll drink to that." The relief that surges through me as she touches her glass to mine is almost embarrassing.

We dig in.

"Do you cook?" she asks me as we eat the most amazing, buttery salmon I've ever had in my life.

"I can. I mean, not like this." I point my fork at my plate. "But I won't ever starve."

"And your grandma?"

"She's an amazing cook, but I think since my grandpa passed away, she's lost a bit of passion for it. He was always the best person to cook for." I laugh as I recall his big eyes and overdone expressions. "Everything anybody made for him was the absolute best. I remember, I made cookies once when I was a kid. And we figured out later that I'd added salt instead of sugar."

"Oh no," Marisa says with a laugh.

"Yeah. Horrific cookies. Absolutely awful. But you should've seen my grandpa eat not one, but two of them, like I was Betty Crocker herself and they were the best cookies he'd ever had in his life. It's one of my happiest memories of him."

"That's really sweet."

"What about you? Is Ms. Tina's mom your grandma?"

Marisa shakes her head. "No, she's my aunt by marriage. All four of my grandparents are still around and live within about fifteen minutes of here."

"That's awesome. My grandma Templeton is my dad's mom, and she's the only grandparent I have left, believe it or not."

"Really? You're only—what?—thirty?"

"Bless you," I say and hold up my glass in salute. "Thirty-four. And you?"

"Thirty-six."

"Interesting."

And here, our eye contact holds for a beat or two longer than it would if we were just friends. And I admit to flashing back to her tongue in my mouth the night before and wonder if my face is turning as red as I feel like it might be.

"You're blushing," she whispers, answering my own unspoken question.

"Yeah, I was afraid of that."

"Don't be. It's really cute."

We get back to our plates for a moment or two, letting those last couple lines hang in the air like vapor. Sexy vapor. Erotic vapor.

"Aunt Mar?" Jaden calls from the living room.

Marisa gives me a half grin, half grimace. "Yeah, honey?"

"Can I have more nuggs?"

I mouth *nuggs*? Because how cute is that?

"You sure can. Bring your plate into the kitchen." She turns to me. "Don't go anywhere."

"No, ma'am," I say, vaguely wondering when I became a polite girl from the South. I continue to eat as I listen absently to the two of them in the kitchen, talking quietly, and it's all so wonderfully domestic that it almost brings tears to my eyes.

I swallow that down and top off our glasses and wait for Marisa to return.

❖

I don't expect to stay overnight at Marisa's, given that Jaden is there, so it's no big deal when we say our good nights. But I also don't expect her to kiss my face off on her front porch. Because holy crap, that's exactly what she does. She walks me to the door and hands me my purse, which I haul up over my shoulder, and a foil-wrapped package of leftovers. I turn to thank her for dinner, and the next thing I know, my face is in her hands and her mouth is on mine and my legs are turning to jelly because oh my God, the woman can *kiss*.

I'm surprised I'm able to actually walk to my car, given the unreliability of my own balance after that, and I can feel Marisa's eyes on me, which doesn't help me concentrate. I drop into the driver's seat with relief and blow out a huge breath. This woman is going to be the death of me. I just know it.

Marisa waves as I back out of her driveway, then goes inside, and I head home. My knees are still weak, and my lips are still buzzing, and my underwear is uncomfortably damp, and the smile on my face is so wide, I can actually feel it. I'm actually aware of the fact that I am alone in my car, smiling like some kind of weirdo.

It's awesome.

Grandma's not home yet when I arrive, so I make myself comfortable on the couch and channel surf. Salt curls up in the crook of my knees and starts purring so loudly; I can feel it vibrating through my legs. Pepper sits on the floor near the end of the couch where my head is and stares at me. For a long time. I try not to make eye contact, but it's hard, and when I do look at her, I swear to God, it's like there's a little human in there. It's freaky. I reach out to pet her, and she takes a swipe at me.

"Why are you such a bitch?" I ask her, not for the first time. "What do you have to be bitchy about?" She blinks at me once, then slowly turns and walks away just as my phone pings from its spot on the coffee table. My excitement at the possibility of it being Marisa sends a wave of arousal through me, flashes me back to being kissed senseless on her front porch not long ago.

What are you doing with your Sunday evening? Hanging with Grandma?

Not Marisa. Pen. And for the first time, I start wondering if she's spying on me. Which I guess makes me feel less pathetic than being totally predictable. That being said, there's also an element of annoyance. Of irritation. And before I realize what I'm doing, I type back to her.

What do you want? Why do you keep texting me?

My first thought after clicking Send is *Adley's gonna kill me. So is Bash. And Demi. I'm dead three times. And probably Grandma. Four. Murdered four times.*

Pen, of course, has just gotten exactly what she wanted, which I realize about a second and a half too late, and she wastes no time texting again. *Just thinking about you. Is that so wrong?*

"Oh my God," I whisper to the empty living room. "Seriously?" And then I'm torn. Torn between ripping her to fucking shreds—via text, of course—and ignoring her completely. *I doubt your fiancée would appreciate that.* I send it and then groan loudly because I clearly don't know what I'm doing. I should block her again.

Her response comes back quickly.

Probably not... As if the three dots aren't enough, she adds a laughing emoji and an emoji with a finger to its lips. So, basically, keep my secret is what she's saying.

"Jesus Christ, Penelope." Okay, enough. I silence the phone, put it facedown on the coffee table, and turn the volume up on the TV. Pen is getting no more of me tonight.

I'm annoyed with myself, but at the same time, not surprised. What I don't do is text Adley. Or Bash. Or Demi. Because I know exactly what each of them would say. They'd scold me, first of all. Bash would be gentle—Adley and Demi, not so much. They'd tell me how I have to be firmer, that Pen is no good and probably just wants something from me, and they're likely not wrong. But I don't think they understand the pull to my heart. I loved her once. With everything I had. I really thought we'd be together forever, that she was my person. And I'm still angry and hurt over the breakup, and I know we'll never get back together—I know that. But there's still a part of my heart that doesn't want her to hurt. That wants to be there if she needs a friend. That hasn't quite let go all the way.

Stupid. Yes. Whatever. I know it.

How I manage to fall asleep with the TV so loud, I have no idea, but I hear Grandma come in, and when I turn my phone over to see what time it is, over an hour has passed. I have three missed texts from Pen.

And two from Marisa.

I turn down the TV just as Grandma rounds the doorway. "How was book club?" I ask her.

She rolls her eyes. "I think two of us actually read it."

"Well, you guys are much better at drinking wine than reading books." I push myself up to sitting.

"True. You fall asleep?"

I nod and yawn like I'm proving the point.

"And how was dinner?"

"It was great." I don't go into detail with Grandma right then because I'm just not ready to. It's not her. It's anybody. I'd like to just sit with it for a while. Sit with my memories of the evening, of teasing Jaden, of how Marisa looked across the table, of how absolutely, one hundred percent comfortable it all felt. I don't know what to do with it yet, and I decide just to keep it for myself, at least for a little while longer.

Grandma gives one nod. "Well, I'm heading up."

"Right behind you," I say and follow her to the stairs. Once in my room, I take a look at my missed texts. Not the ones from Pen. Those can wait. The ones from Marisa.

Had a great time with you tonight. Hope you did, too. Let's do it again. Soon?

The question mark after *soon* kicks my heart into overdrive. She wants to see me again. Soon.

Her second text came about forty minutes after the first. *Did you go to bed already? Sorry I missed you.* Then a sad emoji. *Sleep well. Dream about us.* That's followed by an emoji blowing a kiss.

And then I'm so annoyed that Pen made me miss these wonderful sweet texts. I growl low in my throat, which makes Salt lift his head and look at me with concern. I type, *Sorry! Fell asleep in front of the TV.* Not a lie. Not a lie at all. *Tonight was awesome. And yes, let's do it again soon. Sweet dreams.* And, not to be outdone, I add three emoji blowing kisses.

I plug my phone into the charger and set it on the nightstand while I do all my nightly stuff—take off my makeup, brush my teeth, lotion up. By the time I get back to my bed, it's nearing midnight, and no return text from Marisa tells me she's probably asleep. Even though it's summer, she's got Jaden all day tomorrow. Me? It's my day off.

I slide under the covers. Normally, I'd turn my own TV on very low, turn on some mindless reruns like *The Big Bang Theory* or *Modern Family*. Since I've been alone—meaning not with Pen— I've had trouble falling asleep, and the TV helps. Maybe it's the sound, other people talking so I don't feel quite so solitary. But it helps. I drift here and there and remember seeing the clock at 2:21 before finally falling all the way to sleep.

My dreams are filled with salsa music and beanbag chairs and an old yellow VW Bug that I'm driving with Marisa in the seat next to me, her hair blowing sexily in the wind.

CHAPTER FOURTEEN

Two things surprise me at the next dance class, which is our eighth.

First, Ms. Tina is back. The wave of disappointment that flows through me is almost disturbing in its intensity. I don't want to dance with Ms. Tina, no offense. I want to dance with Marisa. I haven't seen her since dinner Sunday night. We texted a bit, but she had a crazy day with Jaden, getting him signed up for summer activities, buying him some new clothes because he is apparently "growing like a weed," she said. I spent my day off chilling, trying to read a new novel I've had for weeks now, and attempting not to spend the entire afternoon fantasizing about Marisa and what she might look like naked. I was really looking forward to tonight, and I get here, and Ms. Tina smiles at me.

Damn.

I drop my crap at the edge of the room like always as Ms. Tina chats away with Davis and Linda about how well Davis's knee has been holding up, as the rest of the class trickles in. I'm looking down at my phone, making sure it's on silent, when that voice tickles the back of my neck.

"God, you smell good."

And you know what's weird? My entire body reacts to her voice. *My entire body.* I get this, like, full-body shiver that flows through me like a wave. Every nerve is at attention. My legs are instantly weak, jellylike. The butterflies in my stomach are suddenly awake and zipping around like crazy, bouncing off my ribs. My mouth has gone dry.

"How do you do that?" I whisper to her as I turn and meet her dark eyes.

"Do what?" I can tell by the look on her face—she knows exactly what *what* is, but I answer anyway.

"Make every nerve in my body sit up and take notice."

"Is that what happens?" Her eyebrows rise in what looks like honest surprise, and I kind of like that.

I nod. "Every time."

"Huh." It's all she says, but she's smiling like a weirdo, so I know it made her happy.

"Um, what are you doing here?" I ask as the rest of the class mills about, waiting for Ms. Tina to get things started.

Marisa blinks at me. "I'm your partner. Duh."

And before I can respond, Ms. Tina starts talking about tonight's class, so I stand there and it's my turn to smile like a weirdo. Marisa came to class specifically to dance with me. Yeah. Kinda giddy, not gonna lie.

Class number eight will go down in history as something incredibly memorable. I can tell even after ten or fifteen minutes in. Dancing with Marisa when she's not teaching the class is…it's different. And dancing with her after we've made out a few times? Yeah. It's more sensual. *Way* more sensual. She is completely focused on me. Her hands are warm and sure where they touch my body. Her eye contact is steady, sometimes intense. And being so close to her like this? With our bodies touching so often? God. I don't even have words. It's almost erotic. I'm painfully aware of the other members of the class, and I have to consciously not swoon as Marisa leads me around the floor, and I follow her obediently. We move beautifully together, and I'd say that even if I didn't have a huge thing for her. We really dance well together. We're almost fluid, and it's so perfect and natural that I don't notice right away that the rest of the class has stopped to watch. I keep my eyes on Marisa's, and it's kind of incredible how easy it is to be led by her. I know instinctively where she wants me to step and which way. I'm not even sure how she's doing it, but I can feel it. That's the crazy part. I can *feel* her direction. Which, I suppose, is how dancing works, but it's incredibly sexy, something I didn't count on when I signed on for this with Bash what seems like ages ago.

When the music ends, we get an enthusiastic round of applause from the others in the class, and I can feel my cheeks heat up.

"That was amazing," Katrina says, and Pete, her partner, nods his agreement. "You guys move together like you've been dance partners for years."

A little buzz goes through the rest of the class as Ms. Tina smiles and says, "Don't they? That's why they're going to represent our studio in the local competition in September." She waves her arm at us with a flourish, like she's introducing us. Which she kind of is, I guess. My face gets hotter as the applause kicks back up. I glance at Marisa and she's smiling, a little flushed, and just fucking gorgeous.

I can't believe I get to dance with this woman.

A few minutes later, as the other students begin filtering out, Marisa turns to me.

"Do you have some time right now, or do you have to get home?"

What do I have to get home to? My grandmother and a couple cats? I don't say it out loud, but I think it. I shake my head. "No, I have time."

"I thought we could talk a bit about our dance for the competition, since Aunt Tina's here. She has ideas."

"Oh, okay. Sure. Let's do it." I was kind of hoping that she wanted to do something, just us, but this is good, too. More time with Marisa, even if Ms. Tina is around, is never a bad thing, as far as I'm concerned.

For the next hour, Ms. Tina does more talking and explaining than Marisa and I do dancing, and I suppose that was to be expected. She plays us the music, an upbeat Latin song that sounds vaguely familiar to me. The pace slows to an almost ballad and then picks back up again. It's a shortened version, and Ms. Tina informs me that it's two and a half minutes long. That's our dance time. That's everybody's dance time.

"It seems short now," she tells us, "but trust me. When you're out there dancing in front of people, it'll feel like an hour."

In front of people.

Oh my God, I haven't even thought of that aspect of a competition. Wow. I glance at Marisa, who bursts out laughing.

"Forgot about that part, did you?" she asks.

"Little bit," I reply with a shake of my head.

She squeezes my shoulder. "Don't worry. I've got you." Her hand stays there for a beat, and I notice that Ms. Tina notices. I'm not sure how to feel about that.

We set up time for the following week when Ms. Tina will start us on the actual moves, and for whatever reason, *now* I'm nervous. We pack up our stuff and walk out together while Ms. Tina hangs back to finish some paperwork, she tells us.

"You got a little deer-in-headlights back there," Marisa says, amusement in her voice. "You okay?"

I laugh quietly. "Yeah, just...I don't think I thought the whole thing through before I agreed."

Her face falls. "Do you want to back out? You can. There's plenty of time."

"No," I say, probably too loudly, and grasp her upper arm. "No, not at all. I just need to readjust my expectations. No, I'm good. I'm in. I'm all in." I realize the double entendre there and look away from her quickly.

"It'll be fun," she says, but her voice has gone soft. "I promise." Our gazes hold for a few seconds before she says, "I have to go get Jaden from my mother's."

I nod. "Okay. Can we...?" The words catch in my throat, but Marisa smiles.

"Get together soon? Definitely." And then she leans forward and bends slightly until her lips meet mine. We're the only ones in the parking lot, and it's dusk and it all feels so clandestine and exciting, and it takes everything I have not to reach up for her neck and pull her in tighter...and then I do just that. And she lets me, a soft whimper escaping her mouth. It's a sound that does things to me. Sexy things. My heart rate picks up speed. A surge of wet hits my underwear. Everything below my waist tightens deliciously.

Marisa pulls back enough to make eye contact, and she tips her head the smallest bit as if scolding me just a touch. "You're bad," she whispers, then runs her fingertips over my swollen lips. "I have to go."

"I know," I say. She looks apologetic, so I add, "I get it. I do. As long as I can see you again. Soon."

"Promise." She gives me a quick peck, then points in the direction of my car. "Go."

"Yes, ma'am." I walk backward toward my car, not taking my eyes off her, and she waits, standing there in the same spot, and lets me look. Eventually, I back right into my own car, sigh, and turn to get in. Marisa hasn't left yet, and it takes me a moment to realize that she's probably waiting to make sure mine starts. It takes four times tonight but finally turns over.

I wave one last time to her and point my car toward home.

❖

That Thursday, I get a text from my brother Kai asking if I'm coming to his soccer game. I need to learn to let go of the irritation that neither of my parents ever seems to request my presence and just be thankful that my siblings think about me. I had planned to have dinner by myself, so I figure it can't hurt to hit the soccer field and grab a hot dog or something from the concession stand.

Kai runs like the wind. I've never seen a kid that fast, and I'd say that even if he wasn't my little brother. He's a streak of lightning on the field. Nobody can touch him. I remind myself that he's only ten, so he may not always be the fastest, but it's fun to watch him now. My mom and Stephan sit next to me in folding chairs, alternating between cheering while sitting and screaming while jumping out of said chairs. Just like when I went to Noah's Little League game last week, I'm reminded of the dichotomy of their dedication to kids' sports now and their apathy when it came to mine.

I unfold my own chair and sit it next to my mom, who smiles at me and gives me a quick air kiss. "Hi, honey."

I give Stephan a wave around her. "How's he doing?"

"No goals yet, but his dribbling has way improved," my mom says, her eyes on the field.

Kai is lanky, tall for his age, and I think that's why he's so fast already. He's all legs. I wonder what will happen when the other boys start to catch up to him, but until then, I'll watch him fly up and down the field.

Unpopular opinion: soccer is dead, dull, boring. At least I think so. The goals are so few and far between, that it's generally just watching people run up and down the field for what feels like hours. But people love it, I know I'm in the minority, so I sit and watch and don't say such things out loud. Plus, he's my brother.

"Where's Jordie?" I ask my mom after a while.

"At Emmajane's today." My mom doesn't take her eyes from the game.

"Emma Jane?" Another new friend I have yet to hear of.

"No. Emmajane. One word."

"Oh. Okay." Interesting. After a few more minutes, my stomach reminds me I haven't eaten since before lunch by doing that thing where it feels like it's eating itself. "I'm gonna get something to eat. Want anything?"

My mother shakes her head, so I stand and head toward the brown building at one end of the field that houses the concession stand. Since this is a summer league and not a school league, we're not at a school. We're at a large recreational park that has five baseball fields and two soccer fields, so it's busy and it's crowded. I wait in line and people-watch, and I'm amazed by how invested some of these parents are in their children's games. They're cheering and yelling and shouting insults at officials. It's a little ridiculous.

I buy myself a hot dog with mustard and a Coke and begin making my way back to the field. Just as I get to my chair and sit, I hear my name and turn to look behind me. Regina from dance class is smiling and waving at me and heads my way.

"Hey you," she says when she gets to me. She must've come right from work because she's wearing a pale green pantsuit and looks very professional. I'm used to seeing her in leggings and tennis shoes. "What are you doing here?"

"My little brother plays," I tell her, finding Kai on the field and pointing him out to her, and my mom is actually paying attention, I notice. "Oh. Regina, this is my mother, Maggie, and my stepdad, Stephan. You guys, this is my friend Regina from dance class."

My mom's eyebrows climb up in her hairline, and it occurs to me right then that either I didn't tell her I was dancing—though I'm sure I did—or she didn't listen when I told her, which is much more likely.

Regina reaches to shake hands with both of them, saying how nice it is to meet them. "Are you going to come to the competition in a few weeks to see your daughter dance?" she asks, all smiles, and that's when it occurs to me that it won't just be strangers watching Marisa and me dance. It'll be my fellow classmates as well. Holy mother of all that is holy, what have I gotten myself into?

"Of course," my mom says, and my head whips around to meet her eyes so fast, I'm surprised it doesn't fly right off my body. "Wouldn't miss it." She smiles at me, then asks Regina, "You have a child in the game?"

"On the other field," Regina says. "My son." She shrugs. "I'm late." She says good-bye, waves to my parents, and makes her way toward the other soccer field. I finally feel like I can bite into my dog, since I didn't want to be rude and eat in front of her, and as I'm chewing, I realize my mother is staring at me.

"What? Do I have mustard on my face?" I use my napkin to dab at invisible stuff on my lips.

"Dance competition?" my mother asks. "Were you going to tell us? When is it? Why is it? When did you start dancing?"

Yeah, okay, so maybe I didn't say anything to her after all. I make a mental note to analyze that later, the fact that it ticks me off that my mother never tells me anything, and am I purposely not telling her things so we're on a level playing field? God, the human psyche is a giant bowl of spaghetti, all tangled and entwined, isn't it?

"Sit." My mother points to my chair, and I dutifully plop down like the obedient good girl I am. "Explain this dance competition. Details. Now." She's not mean about it, but there's something that flashes behind her eyes, and it takes me a moment to realize what it is: hurt.

I chew my bite of hot dog, which feels like a lump in my stomach when I swallow it. Then I clear my throat and launch in.

"Well, Bash wants to surprise Lydia at their wedding by knowing how to salsa dance, so he asked me to go to lessons with him."

Mom makes an impressed face and nods, and I'm kind of shocked she's actually listening to me. Like, paying attention. Eye contact and everything.

"So, we went to two lessons, but then he broke his foot."

"Is that why he was in a boot when we came by?"

Seriously, does she see more than I think she does but just doesn't say anything? It's kind of freaking me out. I nod. "Yes, and he couldn't dance. But since the lessons were paid for, he told me to go ahead and keep going if I wanted to. And honestly, it gave me something to do, to get out of the house, and"—I half shrug—"I kinda liked it."

"You always did have rhythm," she says, completely contradicting what I thought I knew about myself. "So, what's this competition?" Her eyes have been on me for this entire conversation, and my level of freakedness has inched a little higher.

"Well, since I didn't have a partner to dance with, I ended up dancing with the instructor. Who was Ms. Tina, the owner of the dance studio, to begin with. But she had a family emergency and had to go out of town for a bit, so then it was her niece, Marisa." I take a moment and weigh the pros and cons and necessity or not of explaining to my mother exactly who Marisa is. I decide on not. I can tell her later. Or never. "Turns out Marisa and I dance really well together, and when Ms. Tina came back, Marisa stayed on as my dance partner. Then Ms. Tina came to me last week and told me that every year, the dance studios in and around the area have a friendly little competition to show off some of their students, and she asked if I'd be interested in representing her studio and dancing with Marisa in the competition." There. Done. Told. Mostly.

"Honey, that's fantastic. Wow." She elbows Stephan next to her. "Did you hear that?"

He nods. Unlike my mom, his eyes never left the game, but it turns out he was listening. "Dance competition. When is it? Can we come watch?"

I blink at them. Am I in some parallel universe? Am I in the Upside Down? Who are these people, and when did they start giving a crap about my life? I know I should be grateful, and I will be. Later. After I'm done being stunned into silence.

"It's in September. We started rehearsing this week, but just a sort of overview. I don't know the dance yet."

"And you're dancing with a girl?" Mom asks. "That's progressive." She's not being sarcastic at all. I have lots of issues with my mom, but acceptance of my sexuality isn't one of them. It took her some adjusting, but once she did that, she's always been super supportive.

"Right? I'm excited. And nervous. Like, really nervous."

"Why? You're gonna be great."

I don't tell her that I'm more nervous about dancing with Marisa than dancing in general, but to be honest, having this kind of support from my mom has come as such a surprise that I'm feeling a tiny bit, well, fucking blindsided. Like, what is happening?

"You let us know when and where, and we'll be there," she says and gives my knee a squeeze. "Oh, go, Kai!" she shouts and jumps to her feet, and I shift my attention to the field just in time to see my little brother score a goal. The crowd goes wild.

I jump up with them and clap and scream, and for the first time in longer than I can remember, I actually feel like I'm part of this family.

It's been a long time.

CHAPTER FIFTEEN

I think Marisa has taken a step back from me.

We've texted some the past few days and over the weekend, but I haven't seen her. I know she has Jaden, and I'm sure that keeps her busy, but there's been something about the tone of her texts. A bit…cooler. Not as flirty. Makes me sad.

Dance class doesn't necessarily confirm my suspicions but doesn't rule them out either. Marisa dances with me and smiles at me and even makes a joke or two, but it feels like there's a space between us that wasn't there before. I do my best to ignore it. Or at least tuck it away until I'm home alone when I'm sure I'll take it back out and analyze it to freaking death.

The rest of the class has left, and now it's just me, Marisa, and Ms. Tina, and it's the first true rehearsal for our competition dance. Ms. Tina turns on the music, that same Latin song that I like now but suspect I will want to never hear again by the time we reach our last rehearsal. She directs us through a fairly easy move, my hand in Marisa's, my hand on her shoulder. I can feel her fingers at the small of my back. I can also feel the heat coming off her body. Her eyes are dark, but they seem a little shadowed. At one point, Ms. Tina walks away from us to start the song over again and I catch Marisa's gaze.

"Hey, are you okay?" I whisper.

There's a split second of surprise, as if she didn't think I'd notice. Then she smiles and nods. "Yeah. Fine." And then Ms. Tina is facing us again, and I return my focus to the moves.

Speaking of moves, even when she's clearly preoccupied with

something—whether it's Jaden or her job or me or some other thing I don't know about—Marisa is fluid. Her moves are smooth and graceful, and just like before, she leads me easily, her very subtle tugs or pulls or shifts telling me exactly where she wants me to go. It still shocks me how easy it is to follow.

"These are just the basic moves," Ms. Tina says as our time draws to a close. "We're going to add some more complex things as you two become familiar with the dance. Another week or two, yeah?"

I nod, near the wall where my stuff is. "Sounds great."

Marisa nods, too. "Okay." She picks up her water bottle and sips.

"Sweetheart, I have to scoot," Ms. Tina says to her. "Can you turn off the lights and lock up?"

"Of course."

"You're the best. Thank you, darling. Scottie? See you next week."

"You will. Bye." And like she's being swept out on a slow, graceful wave, Ms. Tina floats out the door of our studio. I wait until I hear the main front door click closed before I turn to Marisa, who doesn't look at me, just gathers up her stuff and heads toward the door. I follow her, and as she clicks the lights off, I ask, "Are you sure you're okay? Because something is clearly bother—" I don't get any farther before Marisa grabs my face in the dark with both hands and backs me into the wall, and I let out a small *oof* as I make contact. I absently notice the sound as all the things we were carrying drop to the floor with a clatter, and then she's kissing me.

Except, no.

She's *kissing* me.

Like, full-on making out with me. No buildup. No preamble. Her tongue pushes into my mouth, and her entire body presses mine into the wall, and a small whimper comes from one of us. I'm not sure which. And do I fight her? Please. What am I, a fool? No, I don't fight her. I grab at her—at her hips, her shirt, her hair—and I give as good as I get, even as I feel her hands wandering and one slides up under my T-shirt. When I feel it close over my breast, I wrench my mouth away and gasp. Loudly.

I think it startles her because she pulls back just enough to see my face.

"I…" She blinks several times. It's dark, but the lights from the parking lot out front send shafts of blue slashing across her face.

"What?" I whisper, and I stroke her cheek softly. "What's going on?" And then I notice her eyes are wet with unshed tears, so I pull her closer, the idea that she might cry making me want to cradle her. Protect her. "Baby. What is it? Talk to me."

She spends another moment with her gaze toward the front windows, still holding me, still close enough for me to smell her, feel her heartbeat. Finally, she says, so quietly I almost don't hear her, "You terrify me."

Well.

That is unexpected.

I suck in my bottom lip because, the reality is, I'm trying not to smile like a dork. Marisa looks panicked, even in the dim lighting, but her admission makes me ridiculously happy, despite the expression on her face. I shoot for understanding instead of giddiness.

"I get it," I tell her, keeping my voice as quiet as hers was. It somehow feels…reverent in the studio for some reason. Like if I speak too loudly, some spell will be broken. But standing this close to Marisa is intoxicating. Literally. I feel a little drunk with arousal, a bit unsteady on my feet, and I lift my hand to touch her lips. "You scare me, too," I tell her, and it's not until that exact moment that I realize those words are the absolute truth.

And then we stand there quietly, simply absorbing the words we've each just spoken. They're big. They're admissions. We've basically just told each other that this is something. That this could go somewhere.

"Wow," I say after a moment.

Marisa nods. "Right?"

We're still standing in each other's arms. Well, it's more like I'm leaning back against the wall and she's leaning in to me. Her hips are pressed against mine, and it suddenly occurs to me just how sexy that is. I shift mine the tiniest bit, and she makes a very small sound that lets me know she feels it, too.

"What do we do now?" I ask, toying with a curl of her hair, winding it around my finger. It's silky soft, and I want to bury my face in it but manage to keep some control.

"I think…" She looks up at the ceiling, which gives me a lovely shot of her long neck, and then my control decides to take a coffee break, so I lean forward enough to run my tongue along her throat. The sound of her breath catching is a total turn-on, and then she groans, so I keep going. Kissing her neck. Tasting her skin. I can't help myself. "I think we kiss a little more," she whispers, and our mouths find each other again, slower this time, more sensually. This kiss isn't so much a make-out session as it is a melding of our lips, our mouths, our tongues. We take our time, tasting, exploring.

"And then?" I ask between kisses.

She pulls back enough to pout a little. "And then I'm afraid I have to go get my kid."

I love that she calls him that even though he's her nephew. I give one nod. "Then I guess I'd better get what I can now." I recapture her mouth with mine and then kick up the intensity. Gotta do what I need to tide me over until the next time I see her. Then I realize I don't know when that'll be.

"Are you free on Friday?" she asks me as if reading my mind.

"Who wants to know?" Yes, that's my attempt to be funny and a smart-ass, and why now, brain? Why now? I groan internally at myself.

"Me. I do. I want to know."

"Oh. Well, in that case, yes. I'm free on Friday."

"Come to my house? Jaden has a sleepover with his cousins." She makes eye contact, holds my gaze, and I understand exactly what she's saying. Exactly.

I nod. A lot. Like a bobblehead doll. Because all words have left my brain and apparently fallen out my ears to the ground.

"I'll cook," she says.

I nod some more. Finally, I manage to clear my throat and say something along the lines of, "I'll bring wine." I think. I think I say it out loud, but I'm not sure because my mind is filled with images of possibility. The possibility of staying overnight. The possibility of being naked with Marisa Reyes. The possibility of *her* being naked.

And then she's laughing quietly.

"What?" I ask.

"You should see your face."

"What's it doing?"

She takes a beat and just looks at me and I feel it. *I feel it* right down to my center, which throbs just to let me know it got the message. "It's telegraphing exactly what you're thinking. Which is exactly what I'm thinking." And with that, she kisses me and says, "I have to go get Jaden."

I nod. "Okay." And I kiss her once more for good measure. We walk out the door together, stopping so Marisa can set the alarm. Our cars are the only two left in the lot, and they're side by side, the symbolism of it touching me somehow.

"I'll see you on Friday," Marisa whispers and kisses me once more, softly, then jerks her chin toward my tin can on wheels. "Start your car up. I'll wait."

I have never wished harder for my car not to start, but of course, it fires right up on the first try. Marisa gives me a thumbs-up and a wave and she's off. I, however, sit there for a few minutes, reliving all the kissing, anticipating Friday, and generally just trying to get my body to cool down—which the reliving of the kissing is not helping with.

Finally, I point my car toward home.

❖

I wake up nervous on Friday.

It's like my body knows and wants to make it all just a little bit harder for me to get through my day. Which is supremely annoying.

How does this nervousness manifest, you might ask? Well, I can tell you that it's generally in clumsiness. I drop things. I trip over things. I spill things. I bump into things. Luckily, my friends know this about me, and they're prepared, quickly catching dropped items and ready with paper towels to clean up messes I create.

"Everything's shaved, right?" Demi asks on Friday afternoon as the three of us stand in a row at our chairs, working on clients. She just blurts it right out. Bash chokes on the Red Bull he's sipping. My head whips around to her so fast, I think I dislocate a couple of vertebrae.

"Geez, Demi," I stage-whisper. "The entire salon doesn't need to know."

She shrugs. "Nobody's listening," she tells me, though judging by the three sets of wide eyes in our three chairs, I beg to differ with her. The client in my chair rarely chats when I do her hair. She's generally on her phone the whole time. But now? Yeah, her phone is in her lap, its screen black, her attention clearly on our conversation.

I sigh. "Yes. Affirmative to that."

"Good. What are you gonna wear? You have to pull out your best underwear. And by best, I mean sexiest and tiniest, not most comfortable, yeah?"

"Oh my God," I mutter. A glance at myself in the mirror reveals exactly what I can feel happening. My face is *very* red, as are my ears. "I cannot believe we're having this conversation right now."

"Listen," Demi says, pointing her scissors at me. "This is important. You like this girl."

At those words, Bash looks at me kind of sideways and his agreement with her is clear. "Truth."

What I don't say is that I've been thinking of nothing else since I opened my eyes this morning.

No. Lies.

I've been thinking about nothing else since I left Marisa in the parking lot of the dance studio on Tuesday. We've texted and it's been a little flirty, but not a ton, and it wasn't until Thursday that it occurred to me that maybe she doesn't get terribly graphic in texts because she lives with a nearly five-year-old who might play on her phone and might also be able to read a bit. I also imagine that by the time she goes through Jaden's whole nighttime routine and gets him to bed, she's likely exhausted herself. Thus, not a ton of time or energy to be flirty.

Of course, this is all just theory, but I might ask her about it tonight.

"Hello? Earth to Scottie." Demi is waiting for me to come out of my daydream, and I give myself a shake.

"Sorry. What?"

"I asked about your clothes for tonight. You need light—'cause it's hot today—cute, sexy, and easy access." She ticks these requirements off on her fingers like she's reading me ingredients for a recipe.

"Oh my God," I mutter and cover my eyes with a hand.

"I'm thinking those cute denim cutoffs she's got." Demi says this to Bash, and he nods enthusiastically.

"Yes! She's got great legs. Those'll show 'em off. And then… I'm definitely partial to the layered look like last time." He tips his head to the side.

"Oh, the tank and then button-down over it?" Demi asks, and I'm not actually even part of the conversation any longer. I meet my client's eyes in the mirror and shrug, and she grins at me. I shake my head and continue trimming her hair.

"You got all this, Scottie?" Demi asks.

"Most of it, yeah," I say, still somewhere between mortified and amused.

"Cutoffs, white tank, that purple and white striped short sleeve shirt you bought last month, those cute sandals with the silver tie. Keep your hair casual, but your makeup a little more pronounced. Got it?"

And now they're both standing there looking at me, as are their clients in their chairs, as is my client in the mirror. Five sets of eyes staring at me with expectation. Waiting.

I clear my throat. "Got it."

"And we will be expecting a full report tomorrow." Bash says it firmly.

"Oh, you will, will you?" I ask with a chuckle. "How about a PowerPoint presentation?"

"Listen, if you have enough time to create one of those, we'll automatically know the night was a bust," Demi says, and Bash's client snorts a laugh.

Later, in the break room, my intention is to eat my lunch, but my salad sits untouched in front of me. When Bash comes in, he points at it.

"That's how we know you're nervous," he says. "You haven't eaten a thing all morning."

He's right. I'm a breakfast girl. If I don't eat something by ten, I became a cranky, hangry bitch on wheels, and all my friends know it. Today? I've eaten nothing. "My stomach is too full of butterflies for there to be room for food."

He takes the seat across the table from me and looks me dead in the eye. Bash is good at that. He's an eye contact kind of guy, which I love about him, and it also weirds me out. "You okay?"

I nod. "I am. Just, you know, like you said. Really nervous."

"And that's how we know you like this girl." He unwraps a sandwich from some foil and takes a bite, still watching me. I can smell the peanut butter.

"I do. I really, really do." And that's the first time I have admitted it to anybody. Including myself. I catch my bottom lip between my teeth and grimace at him.

Bash smiles big. "I'm really glad, Scottie. Really glad. I like seeing you like this, and I hope it works out for you. Just relax and breathe and try to enjoy yourself tonight. Whatever happens, happens. Right?"

"Right." It's good advice, and I carry it with me for the rest of the day. Whatever happens, happens. I get dressed in the exact outfit Demi and Bash chose for me, trying not to let myself be unsettled that they know my wardrobe so well. As I stand in front of the full-length mirror in my room, I shift positions, angles, scrutinizing my legs, which—Bash wasn't wrong—might be my best feature, if I do say so myself. I leave my hair down but use my curling iron to give it some texture and curl. I add silver earrings, a leather bracelet, and a spritz of my favorite perfume. Then I study myself.

"Not bad, Templeton," I whisper. "Not bad at all."

I'm slipping a tube of my favorite lip gloss into my purse when my phone pings, and I pull it out, thinking maybe Marisa has changed her mind and is telling me not to come after all. Because, yeah, that's the level of confidence I have right now. But it's not Marisa. It's Penelope.

Friday night. Going out tonight? Followed by a martini glass emoji.

I growl. Like, legit growl. No. Not tonight. I am not going to let her ruin my night. *Stop texting me. I mean it.* I grab the bottle of wine I bought earlier, lock up behind me because Grandma is out again, social butterfly that she is, and head to my car.

Do you tho? comes the next text. And a wink.

"Oh, you bitch," I mutter in the driver's seat. Let me be clear: I know I'm giving Pen exactly what she wants by engaging. At all. Any kind of contact is still contact, even if I'm telling her to fuck off. Which is exactly what I should be telling her. Well, no, not really, because that's still engagement. I need to ignore her.

God, Adley will kill me when I tell her I responded. More than once. This time, I don't. I just put my phone into my purse where I can't see it, then turn on the radio too loud and let Lizzo serenade me all the way to Marisa's.

I love her house. I didn't really give it a good look last time, but this time, I do. It's really so cute. Small, but not tiny. Neat, which doesn't surprise me. Marisa seems like somebody who's pretty put together, so I sort of expect her home to be tidy. Pretty red flowers in pots on the front steps give a nice pop of summer color, and the lawn has been freshly mowed—I can smell it.

I run a hand through my hair, fluff it up a bit, check my breath, and then stroke on more lip gloss before gathering my things and exiting my car. I'm still nervous, but there's also an unexpected element of calm that I feel settle over me as I climb the three front steps to the door. That surprises me. I feel like I'm almost used to the nerves, but I'm not sure what to do with the feeling of calm belonging. Because that's what it is. I feel like I'm supposed to be right here, in this very spot, about to spend the evening—and maybe the night—with this incredible woman. Like it's preordained. Which is corny and ridiculous, I know, but I can't shake the feeling.

The door opens before I can knock or ring the doorbell or announce my presence in any way, and Marisa's smile tells me she was watching and waiting for me. She's wearing a black tank that clings to every curve of her torso and gives me full view of her shoulders. Her shorts are khaki colored and she's barefoot, which is suddenly almost unbearably sexy. Her hair is down, and she's tucked it behind her ears. She is a *vision*. I don't know how else to say it. God.

"Hi," I manage to say.

"Hey you," she says back and kisses me right on the lips. Slowly. Softly. She lingers a bit, and I follow her mouth, not realizing I'm leaning toward her until she pulls back and I almost tip forward. "Come in." She turns and walks into the house, and my eyes are glued to her ass. Yeah, it's kinda lewd. I don't care because she has the best ass I've ever seen. In my entire life.

Oh Lord, help me get through this meal.

I send the silent little prayer up as I shut the door behind me and hang my purse on the mounted hooks on the wall because it will be a miracle if I don't rip all Marisa's clothes off with my teeth before dinner even starts.

I follow her into the kitchen with the wine. "Oh my God, it smells *amazing* in here," I say.

"Yeah? I was going to grill the chicken but decided to roast it in the oven instead." She opens the oven door and pulls out the baking sheet where four chicken breasts sit, gorgeously golden brown and seasoned with what I can't make out by sight but smells like pepper and parsley and maybe oregano? Doesn't matter. My mouth waters.

"So, I'm beginning to understand that you're a hell of a cook," I say, taking the corkscrew she hands me and going to work on the wine bottle.

She lifts one bare shoulder, and I suddenly want so badly to suck on that olive skin that I have to clench my teeth in order to keep myself from crossing to her and doing just that. "I do okay. My mom's a great cook. I learned everything I know from her. And once Jaden moved in, I realized I needed to learn how to make actual meals." She laughs softly and points to the four pieces of chicken. "He loves chicken, so I'll wrap it up for him to eat tomorrow."

I pour wine into the glasses she hands me, then she dishes up dinner. Two plates with chicken, rice and beans, and salad.

"I've got some strawberry shortcake for dessert, too," she tells me as she finishes plating. "How do you feel about eating on the deck out back?"

"It's gorgeous out. Let's do it."

We carry our dishes and wine through her dining room and out the sliding glass door to a deck I haven't seen yet. It's small, but also not, if that makes sense. She's got a nice outdoor table for four in a corner and a small grill in the opposite corner. The backyard is narrow, but long, with a swing set all the way in the back. A privacy fence that looks fairly new encloses the whole yard, and it feels like we're the only people in the world right now.

We sit, and I pick up my wineglass. "To a new adventure, a beautiful woman, and an amazing meal."

She touches her glass to mine with a soft tink. "I'm an adventure, am I?"

"The very best kind."

She nods as she cuts her chicken. "I like that." She looks up at me, and those dark eyes of hers are sparkling somehow. She pops a bite into her mouth and chews, her gaze holding mine, and I feel it. All the way down.

"You are very possibly the sexiest woman I've ever met, do you know that?" I'm surprised when the words pop out of my mouth, but it's also the truth, so I'm kind of proud of myself for voicing it.

"Even sexier than Penelope?"

And I'm more surprised by *that*, but I don't miss a beat. "Absolutely. Way sexier."

"'Cause she was pretty sexy. I can admit that, and I imagine you can, too."

I'm not sure how or why we ended up taking this route of conversation, but I also understand that it's a subject we'll need to address eventually. No time like the present, right? "She was, definitely. But in a different way."

"Different how?" Marisa sets down her fork, props her elbows on the table, and folds her hands. Her chin on them, she watches me, and I think I see a slight upturn of one corner of her mouth. This is either a test or she's playing with me. Or both.

I set down my fork, too. Okay. I can play this role with her. I look in her eyes and everything below my waist tightens pleasantly. "Pen was…loudly sexy. I almost said *confidently*, and there is an element of that, but it's more brash. Like she wants the world to see her and be collectively enamored. And they are. Everybody sees her when she walks into a room." Marisa is watching me intently, so I go on. "It's magnetic at first. She pulls people in easily. Quickly. But it becomes a lot. Too much. Being enamored goes away quickly for many if they look too closely." I pick up my glass and take a sip.

Marisa doesn't move. She continues to study me, which I admit is both incredibly erotic and also a little nerve-racking as I wonder if I'm measuring up. "And me?" she asks.

"You?" And now is when I don't need to tiptoe. I make a *pfft* sound like this is the easiest question in the world. Because it is. "You're classically sexy. You're quietly sexy, like you don't know it. And because of the quiet part, *everybody* sees it. You walk into a room, and you own it without trying. That's the best part. You don't announce your beauty or your appeal or your sexiness. You don't need to. It just…is. Everybody sees it. It's instant. You walk in and you command attention. Without commanding it at all." Her smile grows as I speak, and two little circles of pink tint her cheeks, and that's how I know my words came out as I intended. "I've never known anybody as devastatingly attractive as you."

"Devastating, huh?"

"You have no idea."

And something has shifted. I can feel it. The very air in the room feels slightly different. I smile at her for another beat or two, then go back to my dinner, and we eat in comfortable silence.

"Just so you know," she says after a few minutes, "you're incredibly attractive yourself."

"You think so?" And I immediately hate how uncertain my voice sounds. Pen did that to me, I know it.

Marisa tips her head slightly and narrows her eyes at me. "Um, hello? Are there not mirrors in your house? You work in a hair salon. I *know* there are mirrors there."

She's teasing me, but her eye contact is direct, and it makes me squirm a bit in my chair. "A couple, yeah."

Her fork goes down and her wine is picked up, and a moment or two of her studying me go by before she takes a sip, lets the wine roll around in her mouth, and swallows. "Lemme guess. Penelope sucked at saying nice things about you. It was rare for her to tell you that you looked nice or hot or sexy or whatever."

"Sucked so bad," I say with a soft laugh. "Legit terrible."

"And any time you hinted that maybe a compliment or two from her would help, she saw it as fishing and, therefore, withheld even more."

"Oh my God, yes. The *fishing* comment. And then *that* made me feel so pathetic. I mean, you shouldn't have to hint to your partner that you need occasional reassurance, should you?"

She nods. "Totally get it."

And then we're quiet because I think we both realize, yet again, how weirdly unique this situation is. We're literally comparing notes on our ex, who happens to be the same person. Also, how could anybody—not just Pen, but anybody—be partnered with Marisa and not tell her every single day that she's beautiful? That makes no sense to me, and I desperately want to change the subject.

"How long has the J man lived here with you now?"

Marisa smiles at me, and I could be wrong, but I think there's an element of relief in her expression to be talking about something else. "It's been about eight months now."

"That had to be quite a change. For both of you." I remember that first ride home she gave me from the studio when my car wouldn't start, how I mentioned that her life must've changed drastically.

She nods and chews a bite of food as she seems to collect her thoughts. "It was. We had to sell my brother's house, which meant cleaning it out. It was hard to decide what things to keep for Jaden, stuff he might want when he's older or at least want the option of deciding. Furniture. Clothes of his dad's. His mom's jewelry. Stuff like that. There's a stack of boxes in my basement, and my parents have several pieces of furniture in their attic."

"Were you already here? In this house?"

She nods. "I was, but just. I bought it and moved in last summer. The accident was in late September. Jaden moved in with me right after Halloween. He'd been staying with my parents, but we all knew that couldn't be permanent. I mean, they'd absolutely have taken him if there were no alternatives, but like I told you before, my parents aren't getting any younger, and running after a three-year-old would've been hard on them."

I nod in understanding. "Your parents are older than mine, so I'm trying to picture my grandmother, who's in her seventies, chasing after my little brothers, who are five and eight. She'd do it, make no mistake, but she'd be exhausted. They'd run her ragged."

Marisa points her fork at me in agreement. "Right? I had to convince them that Jaden living with me was the better solution. I have another older brother, but he's single and lives in Denver. I'm here. I work with kids when I teach dance. I have the room. I'm a financial planner, for God's sake, I know how to budget, and I'm secure. Etcetera." She grimaces. "I think they felt like they'd be failing my brother."

"That's so sad," I say with a frown.

"Plus, they needed to be able to mourn." Her voice has gone

very soft. "They lost their son. They deserve to grieve, but I know they wouldn't want to do that in front of Jaden."

"And what about you?" I ask, my voice equally soft. "Do you allow yourself a chance to mourn your brother?"

Her face flushes prettily. "I do. It helps that my parents take him often. Gives me a break, gives them time with him, and I get to have some alone time. To reminisce." She scoffs and picks up her wine. "Or cry or get drunk or scream in a pillow or whatever."

"I'd think you have to do all those things for a while, yeah?"

"True." She sips her wine, then takes a breath as if bolstering herself, pulling herself back from the seriousness. "But it's been great. I always wanted kids. I still hope to have another one or two. And he's my brother's kid. My nephew, my blood. I love him more than life."

I suddenly want to know so much more about her. Everything. I want to know everything. "Tell me about your brother. What was his name?" I reach for the wine bottle and top off our glasses.

"Matt. Matthew. He was forty when he died. His wife, Sheri, was thirty-five." Marisa takes a deep breath, and I can tell this isn't a subject she broaches a lot. That being said, it also feels like one she wants to. She doesn't look sad. In fact, she looks kind of radiant. Bright eyes, a soft smile. "He was my protector. He looked out for me. He was a senior when I was a freshman, and he never let any guy even close to me." Direct eye contact then as she says, "Which was fine by me, since I liked girls." We both chuckle at that. "He was funny and kind and helpful and smart and just a really, really good man, you know?"

"Sometimes seems hard to find those."

"It really does, but he was one of the good ones. I want to make sure to raise Jaden to be like that."

"Well, from what I've seen, you don't have anything to worry about." True, I don't really know. I've been around Jaden exactly three times. But he's a good kid. I feel like you can tell when a kid is a good kid, and I definitely get that vibe from him. And it feels important to tell Marisa that.

"I hope you're right."

"Does he ask about his parents?"

"Not a lot. But he'll randomly say something about them, like he did when we drove you home. He'll tell a stranger his parents are in heaven or that they're watching over him. My mom tells him that all the time, and I'm not sure he gets it, but it seems to comfort him." She sips her wine, swallows. "He has nightmares, though."

I clench my teeth and make a face because the thought of a tiny human as adorable as Jaden screaming out in terror in the dark is almost too much. "Oh no."

"Yeah. He'll wake up screaming for his mom and"—she waves a hand in front of her body—"he gets me instead." A deep breath in and a loud exhale follow, and I can see her uncertainty all over her face.

"I still say he's lucky to have you. And time will help, don't you think?"

"They have gotten less frequent. And he has a great therapist, which is probably at least part of why."

And then I'm just looking at her, at this big-hearted, warmly caring woman, and I feel my own heart swell up with whatever it is I'm starting to feel for her. She glances up at me, smiles, and gives herself a full-body shake, like she's trying to escape the heaviness of the topic.

"Anyway," she says. "Are you ready for dessert?"

I hold her gaze and let the double entendre hang in the air between us before I nod.

I see exactly when she catches it because her cheeks get pink again, and I decide in that exact moment that making this put together, supremely confident woman blush is one of my favorite things in life.

"Come with me," she says, her voice suddenly very low and husky. I follow her into the kitchen because I am a smart girl.

She pulls a bowl of strawberries from the fridge, then slices two biscuits that look homemade in half and sets the bottoms in small bowls. As she spoons strawberries over them, she asks me to get the whipped cream from the fridge, and I'm delighted to see it's one of those spray cans that I loved so much as a kid. "Oh my God, I love this stuff." And before she can comment, I spray a little on my finger and eat it.

Marisa's eyes have gone slightly hooded, but she blinks rapidly and clears her throat and sets the tops of the biscuits on the strawberries. I hand her the whipped cream, and she sprays a generous amount on each dessert in a cute little swirling shape. And then, without missing a beat, she sprays a little more on her fingertips, turns quickly, and smears it on my lips. I don't even have time to be happily surprised before she's chasing it with her mouth. With her tongue.

I hear my own breath catch in my throat before I feel it, and Marisa makes a sexy humming sound before deepening the kiss. It feels like this is what the entire evening has been leading up to. Like all the conversation was just stalling. The combination of the sweet whipped cream and the heady taste that I've grown to understand is just Marisa is almost too much for my body to handle standing up. Thankfully, she seems to read my mind and pulls away just far enough to look in my eyes.

"I can't wait anymore." I feel her hand slide down my arm and grasp my hand. "Follow me."

"Anywhere," I say.

She turns back and over her shoulder, mischievous glint in her eye, and orders, "And bring the whipped cream."

CHAPTER SIXTEEN

Sex with Marisa is going to be intense, in the best of ways. I can tell that immediately. Her bedroom is fairly large, her bed neatly made and color coordinated in greens and yellows and so many pillows and everything looks soft and inviting, and that's all I get to take in because my face is in Marisa's hands and her mouth is on mine, and dear sweet Lord in heaven, how can anybody completely undo me with just a kiss?

I've never thought of myself as somebody who's particularly easy, but right now? I would do anything she asked of me if it meant she'd keep kissing me. Anything. Crawl across the floor naked? No problem. Cluck like a chicken? You got it. Howl at the moon? How loudly?

Her tongue is in my mouth, and her hands are pulling at my shirt. I blindly find her waist with both hands and pull her in to me more tightly, so our hips collide. She lets go of a quiet gasp, and it thrills me that I'm having an effect. In the next moment, my tank is pulled up over my head, and I'm standing there in front of her in my white bra and denim shorts and nothing else. My heart is pounding, and my blood is rushing through my veins, and my center is throbbing so intensely, I wonder if she can sense it. If she can feel it under her hands.

She looks at me. Just looks at me. It's nearing dark, but the curtains are open, and the ambient light from outside is enough for me to see her clearly. Her rich brown eyes follow the lines of my body, and I swear to God, I can feel them, feel them roam over me, over my shoulders, my chest, my nipples, my bare stomach.

"God," Marisa whispers. "You're so beautiful." And then she reaches behind me and in an impressively swift flick, unclasps my bra and pulls it off. "So beautiful."

I let myself bask in the glow of somebody being clearly attracted to me for one more moment before I say to her quietly, "You're overdressed," and I reach for her.

Underneath the black tank is a black bra, and underneath the khaki shorts are black panties, and when I've left Marisa standing before me in just those two things, I can hardly breathe. I've read a hundred times about a person taking somebody's breath away, but this is the very first time I have honest-to-God felt it. Like she reached right into my lungs and simply stole all the air. She is, quite literally, the most breathtaking sight I've ever had the privilege of laying eyes on.

"My God," I say, barely audible. "Marisa…"

She steps closer so she's in my space. "I love the way you say my name."

I lift a hand and slowly let my fingertips touch the skin on her chest, run them along her collarbones. She's soft and smooth, and I can't wait any longer to kiss her again. I slide my hand up and around the back of her neck, pull her head down to me, and kiss her. Hard. Push my tongue into her mouth. One of us whimpers slightly, and her hands slide down my stomach to my shorts, where she unbuttons them and lets them slide to the floor at my feet. We make short work of what's left of undergarments, and then we're both naked.

My mind sends me a flash of the little fantasy I had the other day about the possibility of standing naked with Marisa, and I must grin without realizing it because she tips her head and asks, "What?"

I wet my lips, my focus glued to her gorgeous bare breasts, full and round, her nipples brown and hard and begging for my mouth. "I'm just remembering how I fantasized about this. About seeing you naked."

"Yeah?" She's clearly amused. "And…?"

I force myself to meet her gaze, and I hold it for a moment before I whisper, "My imagination didn't even come close."

I hear the breath leave her lungs, and then she's on me. Literally.

In a flash, I'm on my back on her bed and she's above me, her knee between my legs, her tongue pushing into my mouth, and I can't get enough of her. I wonder if I'll *ever* get enough of her.

We're kissing so deeply, I'm so focused on her mouth, that I'm almost startled to feel her hand close over my breast. Knead it firmly. Zero in on my nipple and tug. A sound comes from my throat, and Marisa switches to the other breast, the other nipple, back and forth until they're so hard they're almost painful. In the best way. I decide to return the favor and find one of her breasts. They're larger than mine, and they fill my hands perfectly. Her nipples are already at attention, and I slide myself under her a bit so I can take one into my mouth and suck. Hard.

She moans and it's so damn sexy, so I do it again to the other one. Back and forth. Back and forth. When I stop to glance up at her, she's watching me, watching my face, and we lock eyes. It's deep and intimate and speaks of things I'm not sure I'm ready to handle yet, let alone even think about.

She pushes herself up, so her knees are on either side of my hips, and she looks down at me with a smile and a glint in her eyes.

"What?" I ask. "What's that look?"

And she stretches to her right, and when she straightens up, she's got the can of whipped cream in her hand.

"We have props. Did you forget?"

I totally did, and sweet baby Jesus on a skateboard, if there has ever in my thirty-four years of life been a sexier sight than naked Marisa Reyes straddling my nude body with a can of whipped cream in her hand, I have no idea what it could possibly be.

The hiss. The cold hits my nipples. I gasp.

Marisa lowers herself slowly, her eyes locked on mine. Her tongue comes out and takes a swipe at the whipped cream, and my nipple gets impossibly harder. I watch as her mouth closes over nearly my entire breast and it's like there's an electrical wire that runs from my nipple down to my throbbing center. Every pull from Marisa's mouth, I can feel between my legs, and soon I'm squirming beneath her. I've lost control of my own hips, and they push up toward her, straining for some kind of release.

I slide my hand down her stomach, my fingers itching to touch her, and oh my God, she's soaked. But the second I touch her, her body freezes. I glance at her, and there's something in her eyes I can't identify.

"What?" I ask softly. "Did I hurt you?"

"No," she says, and the only way I can describe her expression is sheepish.

"Tell me."

"I haven't…" She clears her throat and her eyes dart away from mine. "I haven't been with anyone in a very long time."

I smile, doing my best to make it reassuring. "Me, neither." It's true. I haven't been with anyone since—

"Not since…" She catches her bottom lip with her teeth and grimaces a bit, like she's waiting for me to call a halt to everything we're doing.

I wait until she meets my gaze before I say, very softly, "Me, neither."

Seems that was the right thing to say because her mouth crashes down on mine, and she kisses me. Hard and rough and dominantly and a rush of wetness floods my center. She pulls back and slides her fingers through my wetness, and my entire body arches, I can't help it. I hear her gasp as her fingers touch me, slide around between my legs, and then they're gone. Suddenly. My hips drop, and I'm about to cry out at the loss when I hear the hiss again. And then shocking cold against the most heated part of me makes me catch my breath.

Marisa's hands are on my legs, and she lifts them both, drops them over her shoulders, and her mouth is on me before I have time to brace myself, and the sounds I make…I've never made them before.

Her tongue is everywhere. It glides around in the wetness and the whipped cream, slides through the folds, and pushes into me. Deeply. There go my hips again. Up, up, looking for anything to relieve the pressure building in my body. Marisa closes a hand over one of my breasts and pumps the nipple in rhythm to the movements of her tongue. I'm so close, but just when I'm ready to drop over the edge, she eases up, and my hips start to relax. This happens three times before it occurs to me that Marisa is doing it on purpose.

"You're teasing me," I manage to grind out between clenched

teeth. I have fistfuls of bedding in my hands, and when I speak, Marisa glances up at me with that mischievous glint and pushes her shoulders so that my legs are higher, spread wide for her. Our gazes hold, lock, and she's looking right at me as she pushes her fingers into me. "Oh my God," I grind out and slam my head back against the pillows.

She knows she has me now. I can feel it in her movements. In the rhythm of her stroking tongue, in the speed of her pumping in and out of me, and it's only another moment or two before she releases me to fly. Colors explode behind my eyelids as a cry rips from my throat, and my hips once again push up off the bed, taking Marisa with them. She grabs my hips with one hand, and she does a fabulous job staying with me as I come, a chunk of her hair clenched in my fist, my other hand flat against the headboard above me, pushing me into her as firmly as I can.

I am boneless.

I am soaring.

I don't know how long it lasts, to be honest. Time becomes meaningless. All I'm aware of are the contractions and spasms in my body, and every single place Marisa is touching me. I come down slowly, my breathing ragged and my limbs like jelly, and without looking, I know that Marisa's fingers are still deep inside me, her tongue is still pressing against my wet flesh but no longer moving, no longer exploring. I let out one more moan and open my eyes, and she's looking at me. Watching me. Gently, she removes her tongue but leaves her fingers where they are.

Her smile is radiant as she says, "Wow." One simple word, but it goes right through me, straight to my heart, and I don't want to think about that, but also can't help it. "That was something to see, can I just say?"

"You should've been in my seat," I say, my voice hoarse. "That...I just..." I shake my head, at a complete loss for words.

"The whipped cream was a good call, if I say so myself."

"Holy shit, yes," I say with a laugh and cover my eyes with one hand.

"I've never done that before," she says.

I pull my hand away and meet her gaze again. "Me, neither," I whisper, and what the hell? What is happening here? Marisa and I are saying things and doing things, and this is the second first that we've admitted to. I shake my head a little, and her smile grows.

"It is a little sticky, though," she says as she rolls her lips in and licks them, scrunches up her face as if trying to feel her skin without using her hands.

I keep my eyes on hers for a beat before saying, "Maybe we need to shower together, then."

Her eyebrows climb up slightly. "Maybe we do. Of course, then I'd have to move." And with that, she gives her fingers a wiggle, sending an electric charge through my body and making me gasp.

"Only long enough for us to get to the bathroom."

She seems to debate this for a moment, then finally nods once. "Acceptable." But she takes her sweet time slipping her fingers out of me, and she watches me the whole time.

This woman is going to be the death of me. I just know it.

I grab her hand and lead her to the bathroom.

❖

Why I thought I could sneak into Grandma's house early Saturday morning to shower and dress for work without her knowing, I have no idea. My grandmother doesn't miss a trick. She's also up before the birds. So it shouldn't surprise me when I walk in the side door into the kitchen, and there she is, sipping her coffee with a look on her face that's a combination of amused and knowing, barely containing a grin. But it does, and I let out a little squeak when I see her.

"Nice night?" she asks.

"It was fine," I say, but I can actually feel the blush crawling up my neck to cover my whole face. My ears are so hot, it wouldn't make me blink an eye if they burst into flames right now.

"I bet." She gives one nod as she lifts her cup to her lips. "You're blushing and your shirt's inside out."

"Gah." I turn and run quickly up the stairs, pretending I don't hear my grandma's satisfied laughter coming from the kitchen. Listen, Grandma and me? We're tight. We talk about a lot of stuff.

Love? Sure. Fine. Fire away. Sex? Are you fucking kidding me? No. Hard no. Absolutely not.

I'm running late because leaving Marisa was hard. Like, not just kind of difficult, but really, really super hard. If I had a different job that wouldn't have involved calling ten separate people and telling them I have to reschedule their appointments—and then manage to take the time to actually do that—I might've called in sick. But Marisa gets it, seems to be a person with a strong work ethic, and tempting as it was to stay, she sent me on my way this morning complete with a travel mug of coffee and a make-out session in her front doorway that really, really had me rethinking my own work ethic. People can find a new hairstylist, right? How hard can it be?

I'm taking a quick shower when I start having flashbacks of the one I took last night with her, and yeah. That sends my body along for the ride, making my stomach tighten, my fingertips tingle, and my center wet for reasons that have nothing to do with the shower water.

Penelope never wanted to have shower sex. I suggested it many times, but she would wave me off, saying showers were for alone time, for washing and shaving and thinking about the day ahead.

Sex.

One of the many differences between Pen and me. I've learned a lot about myself since our breakup. She wasn't my first girlfriend by any stretch, but she was the one I was most in love with. The only one I ever saw a forever with. When I look back now, I roll my eyes and can't figure out how I would've thought those things, but while I was in the midst, Pen was all I could see. Being away from her has been healthy. I know that. I'd become a shell of myself, some watered-down version that Pen transformed me into so she'd be sure to always be the standout in the relationship. One of those methods was by controlling our sex life. We did it when and where Pen wanted, and I rarely got a say.

Marisa is completely different, and oh my God, I can't begin to explain how lucky I feel in finding her. One of the things I learned about myself in the time I've been away from Pen is that I'm sexually adventurous. Not that I've been with anybody since her, but I had a lot of time on my hands after we ended. I did a lot of reading and a lot of watching TV and movies and, yes, a little porn here and there, and the realization just came to me one day—the realization that I'll try just about anything once. I *want* to try just about anything once. And though it wasn't a discussion, yet, I get the feeling Marisa is the same way. Now, as I sit in my car in the parking lot of the salon, I flash back to that shower last night. The sight of Marisa's water-slicked olive skin bared before me, her dark hair wet and brushed back off her face and beyond sexy. Her back against the cold tile of the shower wall, her hips rocking toward me as I held the showerhead between her legs, set to pulse. Kissing her deeply and thoroughly as the warm water slowly brought her to orgasm. The way she wrenched her mouth from mine to arch her neck, her head back, a low, husky groan coming from deep in her throat.

Jesus, I'm gonna need to change my pants if I keep reliving last night. I'm already on my second pair of panties since I got dressed. Officially pathetic, yup, that's me.

"Morning," I say to Bash as I put my purse in my little cubby near my supplies. He's still in his boot while he's working on a guy named Jeff who comes in regularly and—I think—has a crush on him. I mean, who doesn't?

Bash narrows his eyes at me and follows me around my chair with his gaze as I prepare for my first client, who's sitting in the waiting area. I pretend not to notice his stare, but I can feel it, like he's poking me, and I finally meet his eyes.

"What?"

He waves his comb at me, up and down in front of me. "Something's different." A glance over his shoulder and Demi is also looking at me, her chair empty for the moment. She looks at me for no more than three seconds.

"She got laid," she says matter-of-factly with a half shrug to punctuate it.

Bash ignores my soft gasp. "You think?"

"Totally. She's all glowy."

"Oh my God, you're right!"

"You stop that," I say with great vehemence, casting a glance toward the waiting area, which is only steps from my station. "Both of you."

"Hey, I am simply reporting the weather, ma'am," Demi says, but she's smothering a smile.

"And?" Bash asks in an exaggerated whisper. "How was it?"

I want to hold on to my anger, I do. But the smile comes all on its own, and I can't even begin to help it. I feel my cheeks flush—I guess I'm a regular blusher now—and I glance down at my feet as I say softly, "It was incredible." No lie. "I think my legs are still rubbery, and I got about three hours of sleep."

"That good, huh?" he asks, pulling out his electric razor to shave the back of Jeff's neck.

"So good I don't even have words." And I don't. I've been thinking about that since I left Marisa standing in her doorway in her red silk robe, completely naked underneath—another thing I've been thinking about since I left.

"When do you see her again?"

"We're going out tonight. Jaden is at her parents' for the weekend." I give him a look that tells him we're tabling the conversation for now because my first client is Mrs. Haversham, who is in her eighties and does not need to hear all about my dating life.

Aside from a couple of whispered, teasing comments as the day goes on, Bash and Demi obey my wishes. Marisa, however, does not. Texts come from her sporadically all day long, starting off innocuous enough—*I miss you* or *I'm thinking about you* or *Last night was incredible*—to things like *My inner thighs are sore* and *I can't wait to touch you again* and *I just took care of myself while thinking about your naked body.*

Seriously, how is a girl supposed to get any work done when those messages are coming at regular intervals? I'm lucky I don't chop somebody's hair completely off, I'm so distracted. I need yet another pair of panties because I've soaked through these. When I finish with my last client at about five, I just grab my crap, hop in my jalopy that takes four tries to start, and head to Marisa's house, doing my best not to speed, but my foot on the gas pedal seems to be doing its own thing, and I'm apparently just along for the ride.

Marisa opens the front door before I even have a chance to slow my pace up her front steps, and in the next three seconds, she grabs me by my shirt, kicks her door closed, and slams me against it before her mouth crashes into mine and we're full-on making out in her foyer.

"God, I've missed you," she whispers between delicious kisses. "What took you so long?"

"I had to work," I tell her. "But I'm quitting tomorrow."

She laughs, takes my hand, and drags me upstairs to her bedroom, and forty-five minutes later, we are both naked and breathless and spent.

"Holy shit," I say, on my back, my arms still over my head where Marisa had pinned them before she finished me and rolled off. There's a fine sheen of sweat covering my torso, and my center is still throbbing. Marisa's head is pillowed on my stomach, and I can feel her ragged breathing.

"Right?" she says, then lifts her head to meet my eyes. "Have you…" She seems to take a moment to find the right way to phrase her question. She clears her throat, and I think she's hesitant to say what's on her mind, so I reach down and play with her hair. Which, by the way, is the softest hair I've ever felt in my life. I wind my finger in it.

"Have I what?" I ask, gently prodding.

"Has it ever been this good for you?"

I snort-laugh. No, it's not pretty, but it shoots out because is she serious? "God, no. I don't think I even knew it *could* be this good."

"Oh, thank Christ," she says with a laugh and lays her head back down. "I was really hoping it wasn't just me."

"Hey." I say it softly and give her hair a little tug. When she looks at me again, I tell her to come up, and then I watch as she uses one fingertip to wipe the corner of her mouth. Which sends everything below my waist into pleasant tightening. Soon we're snuggling, her head on my shoulder even though she's taller. I squeeze her to me and press a kiss to her forehead. "I promise, it's not just you."

That seems to make her happy because she snuggles in closer and we're quiet for several moments, just *being* with each other.

"Scottie?" she asks after a while.

"Hmm?"

"Do you struggle at all? With this? With, like, who we were to each other versus who we are now?"

I bark a laugh. I can't help it. It just shoots out of me. "Oh my God, yes. Yes. A lot. It's so weird." And now is probably a good time to tell her about the texts that have been coming pretty regularly now from Penelope, but I just don't want to spoil the mood, so I decide I'll tell her later.

"*So* weird." We laugh together over it, and then she asks what I want to do tonight.

"I'm torn," I say honestly. A glance at the clock tells me it's just past six. "It's Saturday night and I want to go out with you, but I also want to be in with you."

"Same."

"Also, I've just worked up one hell of an appetite."

That makes her laugh, that beautiful, musical sound. Almost lilting. She lifts her head, props it in her hand, and runs soft fingertips along my stomach, up and around each breast, and back down. She's driving me a little crazy, to be honest. In the best of ways. "What if we go out and grab some dinner, then come back here and watch a movie?"

"Can we watch it all wrapped up on your couch?"

"Oh, I think that's a requirement."

"I'm in."

It's another hour before we manage to get dressed again.

CHAPTER SEVENTEEN

Whatever weekend is closest to the Fourth of July, that's when Northwood has its street festival. They shut down all the roads in and around Jefferson Square, so people can set up vendor booths of art and crafts and food and music, and it's just one of my favorite things in the world about summer in my small city.

But walking through it with Marisa? *That* has become my favorite thing in the world about summer. At least this summer. We stroll slowly, stopping at different booths—Marisa likes the jewelry vendors and seems partial to silver, which looks incredible against her olive skin, I have to say. I make a note. We hang out at each musician's location, listen for a few minutes, drop a couple dollars in their guitar cases, then move on. We've had kettle corn and warm cinnamon almonds, and I'm sure that's not the last of the food. Not by a long shot, because festival food? The. Best. I still plan on getting an Italian sausage with peppers and onions, and maybe a hot dog and also maybe ice cream. And a funnel cake. I think Adley has a booth here. And if there's anything deep fried, I'm there. Thank goodness Marisa doesn't seem turned off by the fact that I become a bottomless pit at festivals and carnivals. It's a thing.

Last night was amazing. We went out to dinner, just simple burgers and fries. Then we came home, cuddled up on the couch, and attempted to watch an action flick together. All I can tell you is that I don't remember one damn thing about the movie, but I have marks on my body to remind me of every single part of me that Marisa touched, stroked, licked, or nibbled on. Couch sex? Check! I'm sore today. I want to be sore every day, just like this.

As we get beers and a funnel cake to share—and I mentally check that off my festival food list—it occurs to me that I'm feeling a bit more secure in this thing with her. Not totally secure—let's not go overboard—because it still feels a little bit like she's way, way the hell out of my league. But a little more secure, and that means I can look around at other people now instead of being totally focused on how I might mess things up. What do I notice? I notice that Marisa turns freaking heads. Holy moly. It's not a surprise. Of course not. She turned mine. But wow, just about everybody checks her out—men, women, kids—and the fact that my hand is in hers makes me stand up a little taller. *Yup, that's right. She's with me. Suck it, losers.*

Listen, I never claimed to be mature. Or cool.

"Scottie!" I hear my name called out in a little kid voice, and when I locate its source, I'm shocked to see my little brother Drake running his five-year-old legs toward me as fast as he can until he throws his arms around my waist.

"Hey, buddy," I say, hugging him back. I run my hand over his soft, little boy hair as my dad and my stepmother, Connie, come toward us. "Hi, Dad. I didn't know you were coming to this." I spoke to him on the phone only a couple days ago and he said nothing.

"Oh, yeah, last-minute decision," he says, but his eyes dart away from mine and land on Marisa.

"Marisa, this is my dad and stepmom. Dad, Connie, this is Marisa." I purposely don't qualify who she is because…I'm not sure how to do that. Friend? Girlfriend? Hot chick I'm sleeping with? While they're all shaking hands and saying how nice it is to meet each other, I look down at my little brother, who's still got his arms around me. "What have you eaten so far, little man?"

He counts things off on his fingers. "Cotton candy. Funnel cake. Candy apple. Fried Oreos."

"Ooh, where are those?"

He points vaguely behind him and waves his arm around. His eyes are wide.

"So, no sugar high for him, huh?" I joke to Connie.

She grits her teeth and makes a face. "Getting him to bed tonight will be interesting."

I laugh. "Where's Noah?"

"Sleepover," my dad says. "We're headed to get him soon."

We talk a little more about mundane, surface-y things, then say our good-byes and head in opposite directions. A few minutes go by, and before either of us can say anything, I hear my name again, this time from a teenage girl. Jordie is with a couple friends, and she waves at me from the hot dog stand.

"You're here, too?" I ask as she high-fives me, too cool for hugs in front of her friends.

"Too? Who else is here? Did you see Mom?" She sips from her soda and doesn't bother to introduce me to her friends. 'Cause, you know, thirteen.

"Mom's here?" I ask and look around.

Jordana nods. "With Dad and Kai." She turns in a circle. "Somewhere." I'm sure she'd rather avoid them, and I don't even bother to introduce Marisa because the gang of girls is on their way, and I don't want to cramp Jordie's style.

"Both your parents are here," Marisa observes.

I nod. "And neither of them told me they'd be here." I say it quietly, and Marisa must sense my hurt, which I've been trying to tamp down, but I don't think it's working.

"And didn't invite you."

"No."

"Does that happen a lot?" The question is soft and gentle.

"All the time," I tell her. "They have new lives and families. I'm the old one. There's not a lot of time for me. There hasn't been in quite a while." I swallow down the hurt that I inevitably feel when this kind of thing happens. "You'd think as time goes by, it would get easier, but…" I shrug.

"It still stings."

I nod, surprised she gets it. Happy that she gets it. *Relieved* that she gets it. She takes my hand in hers again, and we continue walking down the fairway. We play a couple games, and Marisa wins me a stuffed penguin that I immediately name Peter and decide will live on my bed forever. Marisa shakes her head at me, but her smile tells me she likes that. We run into a couple of her friends, and she introduces me as her friend Scottie, and I think I'm relieved at that. It's too soon to think of each other as girlfriends, even if I want to. Patience, I tell myself. I rushed into things with Pen. I don't want to do that with Marisa.

Speaking of Pen, I have three separate moments of thinking I see her. The third time, Marisa asks me what the matter is, and somehow, for whatever reason, it feels weird to tell her the truth. So I shrug and shake my head and tell her I thought I saw somebody I knew—which isn't a lie, by the way—but I must've been wrong.

"I need to grab some cotton candy to take home to Jaden," she says when we've decided we've eaten so much we might explode.

"When's he come home?" I ask as she pays and takes the bag of blue sugary goodness.

"Tonight. My mom will drop him off after dinner." She doesn't say so, but I feel the cue that our time is over, and she needs to focus on Jaden now.

"Well," I say as we get into her SUV, "I've had an amazing time with you this weekend."

She stops with her hand on the ignition button, turns to gaze at me, and smiles so tenderly, it almost brings tears to my eyes. "Me, too," she says in barely a whisper. "I wish we could see the fireworks together tonight and tomorrow, but I promised Jaden we'd spend some time just the two of us and…" She trails off, clearly not wanting to voice what she's thinking, but I get it.

"And you're not ready to let him in on us yet."

A nod. "Exactly." She makes a face, like she's worried I won't understand.

"It's okay. I get that." And I do. Doesn't mean it doesn't sting, and I'm smart enough to know that it only stings because my heart is already raw from the wounds my own parents served up to me today. I completely understand not telling Jaden anything yet. Yes, he knows me. Yes, I've been to his house for dinner. But that's it. As far as he's concerned, I'm his aunt's friend, and I've cut his hair. Telling him anything more would be premature. We have no idea where this is going, and it's irresponsible to bring a child in on things when they might not work out. Right? I think about how my parents never really introduced me to their now-spouses. They were both just…suddenly around. And it was a bit weird for young me. Makes me even happier that Marisa is so careful with Jaden. At the risk of sounding like a petty teenager, Marisa is already better at parenting than either of my parents was with me.

Not long after that, she drops me at home with a sweet kiss good-bye and tells me she'll text me later. I go inside to see a note from Grandma that she's watching the small fireworks display a few towns over with her friends and will be back late. I take Peter the Penguin inside, pour myself a glass of rosé from the open bottle in the fridge, and head out to the backyard. I still have another two and a half hours or so before it goes fully dark, so I stretch out on a lounge chair and simply sit. Sip my wine. Try to work out when I'll ever be chosen first. By anybody. My mother? My father? Even Marisa.

Unfair. Or is it? She has a child, and I can't be expected to be chosen over her child. That's immature and selfish of me. And again, I know I'm only feeling this vulnerable because both my families were at the street festival today, and neither thought it would be nice to include me.

Not for the first time, I vow that when I have a child of my own, I will never, ever let them feel as insignificant as my parents make me feel sometimes. I will never, ever let them feel unchosen.

My eyes well up and I hate that. I *hate* it. I'm thirty-four fucking years old. Far too old to be crying over my parents' divorce two decades ago and their lack of attention now. Far too old to think that children don't deserve attention over me, a grown-ass woman.

A grown-ass woman with a stuffed penguin in her lap, but a grown-ass woman just the same.

❖

"Kinda weird that we're both home today," I say Monday morning as I pour myself a cup of coffee. It's July Fourth. Grandma is sitting at her kitchen table with her iPad, scrolling through the news. "Why don't you have plans with some of your seventy billion friends?"

She lets go of a quiet sigh that I'm not sure I'm supposed to hear. "I kept the day open because I thought your father was coming over with the boys. I was pretty sure we'd talked about it. But yesterday when I texted him to remind him, he told me they're going to Connie's parents' instead." I know Connie's parents live about a two-hour drive from here, so catching both sides of the family in one day would be nearly impossible.

I scoff. "Glad to see I'm not the only one." I say it softly, but Grandma hears.

"What do you mean?"

"I mean I ran into him yesterday at the street festival. I also ran into my mom. Apparently, it didn't occur to either of them that I might have fun there with my siblings."

"Oh, honey, I'm sorry." And the pity in her voice is almost too much.

"No," I say with an edge of firmness to it. "Ignore me. I'm being a baby."

"You're not being a baby. Being an adult doesn't mean your parents can't still hurt you."

"Truth."

"I say we spend the day together, you and me. We'll play games and cook on the grill, and then if you feel like it, maybe we'll drive into town and watch the fireworks. What do you say?"

And suddenly, pretty much everything feels better again. "I say that sounds like the perfect Fourth of July."

And it is. We spend some time reading. Then we play a game of gin on the deck, and Grandma kicks my ever-loving ass, as she does every single time we play. She grills us up some delicious cheeseburgers while I make a potato salad that comes out rather wonderful, if I do say so myself. There's a little wine—beer for me—but we keep it to a minimum because we've decided we want to see the fireworks. We have time to kill, so we go back to playing gin. I get an occasional text from Marisa, but they're fairly generic, and I remind myself that she's spending the day with Jaden.

"Texting the dancer?" Grandma asks as I slip the phone into the back pocket of my jeans.

"Yeah, little bit."

"Why aren't you with her today?"

"She's spending time with her nephew." There must be something in the tone of my voice because Grandma turns her focus from her hand of cards to my face. I'm not looking at her, but I can feel her looking at me.

"Things okay?"

I nod as I try to figure out what has me so edgy today. It can't really be my parents excluding me yesterday—and today, really. I mean, yeah, it sucks, but it's also a regular occurrence. So I don't think it's that.

"You seem pretty taken with her."

Taken with her. Am I taken with Marisa? Oh yes. I am so much more than that, and I realize, right then in that very second, *that* is what has me so edgy today. I inhale slowly and blow it out. "I am. I'm very taken with her. More than I care to admit." To my horror, I feel my eyes well up, so I bow my head a bit and pretend to concentrate on the cards in my hand. I think my sniffle gives me away, though, 'cause Grandma reaches across the table to squeeze my hand.

"Does she feel the same way?" Grandma asks softly.

I shrug. "I have no idea. And it's so early in this relationship. God, I don't even know if I can call it that yet, *that's* how early it is. But…"

"You've got big feelings." Grandma says it with love and a delicate smile, and I can see the worry behind it. "Just be careful, honey, okay? I don't want to see you hurt."

"I don't want to see me hurt either," I say with a chuckle.

"Patience. Just have patience."

"I'm not good with patience."

"Oh, I know. You've been impatient since you were little. You want what you want, and you want it now. You're like the girl who wanted the golden goose in *Willy Wonka and the Chocolate Factory*." She lays down her cards. "Gin."

"You call me Veruca Salt *and* beat me at cards? Wow. You are hard, Grandma. Hard, I tell you."

"And don't you forget it."

It's still slightly before dusk when we head to Jefferson Square. Since the street festival continues, the Square is still blocked off. You have to park elsewhere and wander into it carrying your chair and whatever else you need. Adley gave me a cute little cooler bag for my birthday last year. It holds a bottle of wine and two glasses and slings over my shoulder, so I carry that and two folding chairs.

"Give me one of those chairs," Grandma says, reaching for one as I turn my body so she can't grab it. "I'm not an invalid, you know."

I stop and hand her the cooler instead. "Here, take this. I've got the chairs."

She sighs like she is *very* put-upon, but I grin at her, and she playfully swats me.

Here's another thing about my grandmother: she knows everybody. She. Knows. *Everybody.* It doesn't matter where we go. Park. Grocery store. Ball game. Fancy restaurant. She will inevitably find somebody she knows, and we'll have to stop and chat. This happens four times before we even find a place to set up our chairs, and space is filling up fast.

"Grandma, I'm going over that way to set up our chairs." I jerk my chin in a direction of vaguely over there, and she nods and promises to catch up. I also take the wine from her because she could be chatting with random friends for the next hour, and I'm not waiting that long to have a glass.

I find an open square of space and set up our chairs, relieved to be settled. There are tons of people here, likely because the weather is beautiful. Not swelteringly hot and humid like last year's celebration. Not pouring down rain like the year before. No, it's lovely and warm, and there's a gentle breeze that just ruffles the leaves in the trees around us.

I wave to a couple of people here and there, some that I don't quite recognize, and that's a funny tidbit about my job. My clients will come up to me in stores, at parties, at the theater, and say hi, shoot the shit, ask questions. And there have been times when I have very little recollection of the person. Nine times out of ten, they turn out to be a client whose hair I've done once or twice. But it makes sense if you think about it. I have well over a hundred clients, but those hundred clients only have one hair stylist. I have learned to nod and smile and ask general questions like, "How's life treating you?" Usually, in answering that, I can glean enough info to jolt my memory.

I flop down into my folding chair and unzip the wine cooler bag. The bottle Grandma chose is a very buttery Chardonnay—the only kind of Chardonnay I'll drink—and it has a screw top, so I open it, pour two glasses, and set one in the cup holder of Grandma's chair.

"Well, that's a nice set-up you've got there."

Ugh. That voice.

Pen.

I don't look at first, just close my eyes for a second to let myself acclimate to the sound of the voice I used to love and now kind of despise. I actually take a sip of my wine before I acknowledge her, which makes me kind of proud of myself. "Thanks." One word. That's what I offer.

"I noticed you at the festival yesterday with Marisa. That was interesting." I stiffen. I *knew* I'd seen her.

"And not even a little bit your business." It's Grandma. She's clearly finished chatting and comes around her chair to sit, her eyes focused on Pen and shooting daggers. I'm actually kind of surprised Pen isn't clutching her heart—or the place where her heart is supposed to be—and dropping to her knees.

"Mrs. Templeton," Pen says with a nod. "Nice to see you."

"Wish I could say the same," Grandma tells her, and I have to roll my lips in and bite down to keep from laughing.

"No fiancée tonight?" I ask, something I never would've done, but Grandma's emboldening me.

"She's got a prior commitment."

She's lying. It wasn't something I could ever see when we were together, but now? It's plain as day. Her left eye twitches the tiniest bit, and she glances off to the left. Lying. Something about that gives me a tiny surge of satisfaction. Trouble in paradise, looks like, and I'm not an asshole. I don't wish ill on Pen…anymore. I don't want to see her in pain. But I can't help feeling that there's a little karma at work here.

She stands there and looks at me for a moment, and I can tell there's a ton she wants to say. But Grandma's making her squirm a little, so she says simply, "Well. I'm over there with some friends." She makes a gesture and points vaguely in a direction. "Enjoy the fireworks."

"You, too," I say, and I don't watch her go. When I'm sure she's out of earshot, I turn to Grandma. "You are a beast."

She shakes her head. "That woman is trouble. I knew it from the first time I met her."

I gape at her in surprise. "You did?"

"Sweetie, you don't live as long as I have without developing a very accurate bullshit detector. And that girl?" She points in the direction Pen walked. "Set it off immediately."

"And you didn't think to tell me?" My voice is a little high. Possibly a bit shrill.

Grandma tips her head. "Scottie. Would you have wanted to hear that while you were in love with her?" Her eyes are soft, and I swallow. "You'd have hated me and stayed with her. I had to let you see her for yourself, and I had to be ready when either you decided you'd had enough or she moved on to the next. You were going to need me."

The words are tender and gentle and bring wetness to my eyes. She's not wrong. I needed her badly. "I'm glad you were there."

"Me, too." She holds her glass toward me. "Now fill me up, barkeep."

CHAPTER EIGHTEEN

I'm one of those people who jumps. Leaps. Dives right in before taking all elements of a thing into consideration. Relationships, for example.

So, it's now July fifth and I've had sex with Marisa more than once and all I want now is to be with her. To spend time with her. To talk about the future. Our future. But I also don't want to scare her away by being clingy or needy or pushing too hard, too fast. I did that with Pen, and look where it got me. No, I'm going to slow down. Relax. Just breathe. Chill. I'm breezy. Easy breezy.

"How are things with the hot dance instructor?" Bash asks as we sit in the break room having our lunches. I have a peanut butter and jelly sandwich. Bash has a bento box filled with sushi, and it looks freaking delicious, and I'm extremely jealous. I want sushi.

"They're good. Rehearsal tonight."

"*They're good. Rehearsal tonight*? That's all you have for your best friend? They're good. Rehearsal tonight? I'm insulted." And he is, I can tell. He's playing it off as a joke, but his feelings are hurt. "I feel like ever since you started seeing this girl, I have to pry any and all info out of you. What's that about?"

"I'm sorry, Bash. You're right. I've been kind of a closed book, haven't I?" I take a bite of my sandwich, happy I used crunchy peanut butter instead of the smooth Grandma prefers, and chew thoughtfully. Because Bash is right, and I hadn't really considered it before.

"To put it mildly, yes. What's going on with you?" He's gone from hurt to worried, and that makes me love him even more. "Can I help?"

I reach across the small table and squeeze his arm. "No, but I love you for asking. I'm okay. Just…" I hold up both my arms and try to make some kind of gesture that encompasses everything over the past two months. "Lotta feels going on, you know?"

He smiles, and I'm reminded for the millionth time just how handsome he is. He recently trimmed up his beard, so he looks neat and put-together. "I've met you, yes." Then he grows serious. "You like this one. A lot. I can tell."

"I do," I say, and I'm kind of surprised I admitted it so easily. But talking to Bash has always been a salve for my aching heart. "Too much, I'm afraid."

"Why do you say that?"

"Because"—and it's definitely a whine—"it's too soon."

"You just said it's been two months. I don't think that's too soon."

I blink at him. "You don't?"

He makes a face and then scoffs. "No. In this technology laden, everything moves at six hundred miles an hour world? Two months is a lifetime."

I can't tell if he's kidding, but it does actually make me feel a little better. "Huh. I never thought of it like that."

"Well, you should listen to me. I'm kind of a genius. Even Lydia says so."

"I mean, if Lydia says so…"

He stands up and clears his lunch stuff. "Stop worrying, Scottie. You're fine. If you like this girl, then instead of freaking out about it, try just liking her." He grins at me and heads back out into the salon, leaving me alone with my sandwich and my thoughts. And none of his sushi, damn it.

But it's dance lesson day, so that keeps a smile on my face and my steps light all afternoon, and when I get to the studio and see Marisa's SUV in the lot, that tightening in my belly happens. It's a feeling I'm beginning to expect, but hope I never get used to. And I hope it never stops.

I'm the last one to arrive. Regina and Dale are practicing their moves. There's no music yet, but they've become so good. They flow. They glide. They're so smooth—it's fun to watch. Unlike Davis and Linda, who don't exactly flow so much as...clomp. But they're having fun. I can tell by Linda's laugh and the way Davis's eyes have started to sparkle a bit. Plus, he's moving much better on his new knee than he did the first couple of classes. The other three couples are chatting in a group, and I join them—something I don't usually do.

"Where's your partner?" Katrina asks just as Marisa breezes through the door in leggings and a teal racer-back tank top. Her hair is pulled back, the rubber band doing a commendable job holding it all, and then I chew on the inside of my cheek as I let myself dwell on the fact that I know exactly how thick and lush that hair is because I've had both hands in it. It's like my own little secret. "Never mind. She's here." Katrina lowers her voice. "It should be illegal to be that good-looking. Seriously."

Nods and murmurs of agreement rumble through the seven of us as Marisa's gaze meets mine, and she smiles. Ms. Tina gets her attention, so I stretch a bit along with the others, and soon we're in the midst of lesson number ten. There are only two more left, and I can't believe it's been ten weeks already.

Ms. Tina gives us some new steps, and I notice we all pick them up pretty quickly, which says a lot about how far we've come. Even Davis gets it down fast, surprising even himself if his wide eyes are any indication. We clap for him, and his round face turns very red, which is adorable.

When class ends, I'm a little sweaty, but looking forward to it being just me and Marisa. These rehearsals alone with her? Yeah, they're such a turn-on. Being close to her. Looking in her eyes—an important part of dancing, it turns out—holding on to her hand, her shoulder, her body. I already have that tightening below my waist, and it only gets more insistent as our rehearsal looms.

Along the wall where my stuff is sitting on a bench, I grab a sip of water and glance down at my phone. A text notification from Pen appears.

You home tonight?

Ugh. What the hell does she want now? I pick the phone up as another comes through.

Was nice to see you last night. And then a heart-eyes emoji. I sigh. God, I wish she'd just go away. I don't answer, just set the phone down on top of the sweatshirt I took off and trot back out to the center of the room where my gorgeous dance partner holds out her hand to me. I put mine in hers, and she pulls me in close.

"Hi sexy," she whispers in my ear because I'm pretty sure she hasn't told Ms. Tina about us yet.

"Hi beautiful," I whisper back, and then we're off, Ms. Tina starting our music.

For the next forty-five minutes, we step and spin and I falter and Marisa catches me and we laugh and we focus and we dance. When the song ends for what feels like the millionth time, I'm breathless, and I bend over with my hands on my knees.

"You have water in your bottle?" Marisa asks. "Mine's empty."

I nod and gesture toward my stuff with my chin.

Ms. Tina pats me on the back while I'm still bent over, catching my breath. "You are doing great, you know that, yeah?" I stand up and meet her gaze, and the pride on her face is so clear, it almost brings tears to my eyes. "I hope you know how proud I am to have you representing my students at the competition."

"Well, I'm honored." And then she surprises me by pulling me into her birdlike arms and wrapping me up with surprising strength.

"Let's call it a night," she says, a little louder so Marisa, who's still at the bench by my things, can hear.

She nods. "Okay. I need to pick up Jaden from my mom's anyway."

"Good work tonight, girls." Ms. Tina closes the laptop and rolls the cart out of the studio.

"I'll catch you later, okay?" Marisa says and heads for the door. Wait, what?

"Hey, wait," I say to her back.

She raises a hand but doesn't look at me. "I really have to run." And just like that, she's through the door, leaving me completely confused. And a little ticked off, if I'm being honest.

My crap is scattered along the bench, so I scoop everything up and into my bag as fast as I can and head out after her, but she must have literally run because she's pulling out of the parking lot when I reach the front door of the building.

"What the actual fuck?" I whisper into the night, watching her taillights disappear. What just happened? I stand there for a second or two, all my stuff gathered in my arms, hurt, surprised, confused. I push through the door and walk to my car, uncertain what to think. Once inside, I dig out my phone so I can text her and make sure she's okay. When my screen comes to life, I gasp. There's a text notification on the screen from Pen.

So, you and Marisa…it's revenge, isn't it? Creative…

I can't see the rest of the text unless I unlock the phone. Which means Marisa couldn't see the rest of the text, but that was more than enough, I'm sure. Especially since I haven't told her Pen's been texting me.

"Oh fuck," I say to the empty car.

I should chase her down, right? Follow her to her house? But then I remember she has to pick up Jaden from her mom's, and I have no idea where that is.

I feel heavy as I drive home. That's the only way to describe it. I feel like all the weight of life has come to settle on my chest, constricting my lungs, making it hard to breathe. My heart hurts.

Adley's car, I notice, is still parked at Get the Scoop, which is closed. I do a quick turn and park next to it, then push through the back door, not happy that it's unlocked.

"Hey," I say, and Adley literally jumps in her seat.

"Jesus Christ," she says, hand pressed to her chest. "You trying to give me a heart attack?"

"Maybe lock that door when you're here alone, huh? That'd be a good idea, don't you think?"

"Okay, Mom," she says, but her grin takes away any sting. "What are you doing here?" A glance at her watch. "Don't you have dancing tonight?"

"Did. Regular lesson and rehearsal."

Adley pulls her glasses off and closes the laptop in front of her. "What's up?" she asks, her voice soft. "You look stressed."

"This might be a job for ice cream." I pull up a chair and sit next to her at the stainless steel countertop.

"Every job is a job for ice cream." She doesn't ask me what kind I want or how much. She simply scoops us some ice cream into a couple of cardboard bowls, adds chocolate sprinkles to mine because she knows me well, and slides it in front of me. Then she sits close and says, "Talk to me."

I sigh, and it feels like my whole body deflates. My shoulders drop, my legs relax, and my lungs empty. I take a spoon of what turns out to be chocolate almond coconut and let it sit on my tongue for a moment. Then I spill it all out to Adley, who has worries of her own, I can tell by the tension in her eyes, but I need somebody who knows me to listen and guide me because I don't know what to do. So I tell her everything, right down to Marisa running away like the building was on fire tonight.

"Fuckin' Pen," Adley mutters once I finish. "She just can't help herself, can she? Bitch is a walking wrecking ball."

"I think she's struggling," I say, and as soon as the words are spoken, I know it's true. I'm also surprised by the note of sympathy in my voice. "She doesn't want to get married. She never has. She said yes to the woman she's with now and can't figure out how to get out of it."

"So she's gravitating back to the girl who told her she didn't need marriage to be happy." Adley gives me a look. Yeah, I said that toward the end. I would've said anything to keep my relationship from ending, but it was a lie. I do want marriage. I want a wedding and kids and a family life. But when I knew I was losing Pen, I became desperate. Said things I didn't mean. "Well, we've solved Pen's motives. What do we do about Marisa?"

I sigh again. I'm doing a lot of that tonight. I add a head shake just to round out the picture of pathetic and sad. "I really, really like her. Like, *really*. I might be falling in love with her."

At that, Adley's eyes go wide for just a second. "Yeah? Wow."

"I know. It's so soon. But, Ad, we click on so many levels. We talk and we like the same movies and have the same values, and we're fucking volcanic in bed. But we have this thing hanging over us."

"The thing that's tall and blond and can't commit?"

"That *is* the thing. And we've talked about her a bit, but we probably need to do that more."

"You should've told her Pen was texting." Adley keeps the accusation out of her tone, which I appreciate, because I already know this.

"I know. You're right. But I wasn't answering much, it wasn't like we were having in-depth conversations, so I didn't think it mattered." I eat some of my ice cream. "But it matters now."

"It does, clearly. You need to talk to her."

Not shocking advice, but solid. "Yeah." We eat the rest of our ice cream in silence. "That was excellent," I say when I've scraped the last of it out of the bowl and into my mouth. "Thank you."

"You like the coconut?"

"I do. Nice addition. Gives it a subtle flavor and some extra texture." We're quiet, and I decide to steer the focus away from me for a moment. "You okay, Ad? You seem kind of tense lately." Here I've been burying my best friend with all my problems, but I'm starting to think she's dealing with some of her own.

Her cheeks puff as she blows out a breath. "Business isn't great," she says, a variation of the same thing she's been telling me, but doesn't offer more.

"I'm sorry. Anything I can do to help? Want me to stand on the corner with a sandwich board? Dress up as an ice cream cone?"

"Would you? That'd be great." She grins at me, and just the sight of her smile makes me feel better. "It's fine. I'm figuring some things out. No worries."

"I don't believe you."

Adley shrugs but doesn't look me in the eye, so I wait her out until she does.

"I've been dumping my entire life's worth of problems into your lap. The least I can do is listen." I tip my head. "Talk to me."

She's quiet for a moment, and just when I think she's going to stay silent, she speaks. Softly. And her voice carries an edge of emotion. "Business could be better. That's all." I squint at her because she's told me this several times, but never elaborates. That's Adley for you. She glances up at me from her bowl and gives me what I suspect she thinks is a grin, but looks more like a grimace. "I'm working on it. Figuring it out."

"Can I help? Tell me what you need. Anything." I don't like seeing her so uncertain. Adley's a rock. Seeing her wavering is unsettling.

"When I figure it out, I'll let you know."

"Promise?" She nods. "No. Say it." She releases a big, clearly annoyed sigh. "Don't you sigh at me, young lady."

That makes her laugh. "Fine. I promise."

"Thank you." I watch her for a few more seconds, but I know Adley, and I also know this is all I'm going to get from her today. I push to my feet and take both our bowls to the garbage. "Thanks for letting me spew," I say and kiss the top of her head. "Don't stay here too late."

"I won't. Tell your grandma I said hi."

I get in my car, and now I'm worried about Adley as well as Marisa and myself. I sit there for a few moments. It's getting late. I'd love to drive over to Marisa's and hash this out, talk it through, tell her everything I should've already told her. But I know she's got Jaden and there's a routine, I'm sure, and me busting in on them likely wouldn't go over so well. And would probably put me farther into the doghouse, if I'm being honest.

I turn the key in the ignition. Then I do that five more times until it finally turns over, breathing a sigh of relief because I don't want to have to go back in and ask Adley for a ride home. I shift into drive and the car sputters a couple times before catching and moving forward.

A couple hours later, and I can't sleep. Not surprising, given the whirlwind of thoughts that is my brain tonight. I sent Marisa a couple of texts earlier. One saying I'm sorry and another saying it again.

She didn't respond to either.

It's now after midnight, and I am wide awake. I have tossed and turned, much to the irritation of Pepper, who finally huffed at me and left my room completely, me hissing, "Sorry!" after her. I pick up my phone, open my texts to Marisa, and start typing. I don't even care how I sound at this point. I'm going a little mad and it's making me delirious.

I'm so sorry I didn't tell you Pen texted me. I've only responded a couple times and it wasn't even a conversation. I'll show them to you. Please, Marisa. Just talk to me. At least give me that. A chance to look in your eyes and talk.

It's pathetic and I know it, but I send it anyway because I don't know what else to do. I set the phone down and turn on my side away from it, not expecting the ping that sounds after only a minute or two. I whip back over and grab it. Open the notification from

Marisa: *I think maybe we were right when we said this was too weird.*

That's it. Nothing more. And you know what? It makes me angry. I want to text back, to beg her not to step back because it's pretty clear that's what she's doing. But I'm not going to beg. No. I promise myself right then that I won't beg. I'm tired of having to ask to be chosen, and that makes me mad, and it's the anger simmering in my gut that keeps me from texting back. Instead, I turn the phone off completely, then toss it across the room with a clatter to remove the temptation. I stare at the ceiling, blink a few times, angry at Pen and at Marisa and at myself.

And then the tears start.

"Goddamn it," I whisper, but I let them flow because what else can I do? I'm sad and confused and mad and my heart hurts. I lie in bed and cry silently.

CHAPTER NINETEEN

I can be stubborn. Just ask my grandma.

But here's the thing—I'm not stubborn just to be stubborn. No, I'm usually the most stubborn when I'm hurt. For example, if I've hurt you and you refuse to give me a chance to explain myself, I can be just as stubborn as you. Meaning—and I'm sure you can see where this is going—that Marisa hasn't answered any of my texts at all since Tuesday night. I tried all day on Wednesday and heard only crickets. So I stopped trying. Because I'm stubborn. And all of Thursday went by with nothing from either of us. And now it's Friday and I'm incredibly hurt—now as much my fault as it is hers…well, almost as much. Which, in my case, manifests as cranky.

When Demi arrives, she says, "Triple Threat," tossing out a name for our salon.

"Seriously? No. That sucks," I snap unnecessarily because I'm *cranky*.

That's not something Demi takes well, so she mutters, "I liked you better when you were getting laid," and even though I deserve it, it clobbers me. I excuse myself to the bathroom, thankful I'm between clients, and do some more silent crying. Apparently, it's my thing now, sitting on the lid of a toilet while tears roll quietly down my face. I've done it at home several times, and this is the third time here. I'm a mess, and I don't know what to do about it.

When I come out of the bathroom and am headed to my chair, I swipe my hand across Demi's shoulder. "Sorry," I say quietly, and she nods and gives me a half smile, and I know we'll be okay. If anybody gets the ups and downs of dating, it's Demi, she of the three guys at one time. "Hey," I say as I return to my station to wait for my next client, "how are things going with Guy Number Three?" And then I can't believe what I'm seeing. Demi's cheeks blossom pink, and I look at Bash, whose eyes are as wide as mine must be. "Is she blushing?" I ask him.

"Why, yes," he says, "I do believe she is."

Demi's blush deepens as she half-heartedly tells us to shut up. Demi is so not a blusher, so it's clear things with Guy Number Three are going *very* well. "He's good for me," is all she says.

"That's great, Dem," I tell her. "I'm happy for you." And I am. Envious, yes. But happy for my friend.

Clients arrive, and the three of us get back to work, the hum of business filling the air around us. Conversation, running water, electric razors, scissors clipping. It's the soundtrack to my job, and I normally love it, but today it feels super loud. Extra annoying. And I can't get away. But I have to because, by three in the afternoon, I feel like I'm going mad. I'm open right now, but I have clients at four thirty, five, and six, and I make the decision in that moment to do something I rarely—if ever—do. I call them all and reschedule them for next week. Because I have to get the hell out of here. I feel like ants are crawling under my skin, and I don't want to lose my shit in front of my coworkers and clients alike. I make the shift in my schedule, then sidle up to Bash.

"I have to get out of here or my head's gonna explode," I say quietly as he paints color on the hair of a woman in her fifties.

He stops all motion, and his eyes snag mine. "Sweetie, are you sure you're okay? I'm worried about you. What can I do?"

I lean in to him, against his strong shoulder, and for a moment, just absorb his warmth, his love. Then I press a kiss to that same shoulder. "I'll be okay. I just need some time." And that line calms me, because I think that is what I need. I mean, aside from talking to Marisa, which is really what I need. I don't deal with rejection well. I deal with heartache even worse. So I think I just need to go home, order a pizza, watch some mindless horror film. Maybe I can convince Grandma to watch with me, if she's around. After all, it is Friday and she's probably got plans. That doesn't mean I can't order pizza and watch horror by myself. Salt and Pepper will keep me company.

It takes me fifteen minutes to get my car started, and honestly, I'm expecting it not to start at all because that would be the icing on the shit cake of my day. I pull out into traffic and my phone pings a text notification. As always, my heart surges in the hopes that maybe it's Marisa. But no. It's Pen. Fucking Pen. Still texting me.

You're on my mind today…

Goddamn it. I feel like, somehow, this is the last straw. I'm on her mind today? Seriously? What the hell am I supposed to do with that? She left me. She's engaged, for Christ's sake. I hit the microphone icon on my phone and scream, *"Stop fucking texting me!"* at the top of my lungs. I should have blocked her long ago because blocking her now is a stupid thing to do.

I glance up just in time to see the taillights of the very large truck that's stopped dead in front of me before I plow right into it.

❖

Have I ever had a headache this bad?

I don't think so.

My skull feels like it's about to split open and spill my brains out all over the floor. The word *pounding* doesn't begin to describe it. My head is in a vise, and somebody is slowly squeezing it. I would open my eyes, but I'm afraid the light will pierce them like lasers and melt them in my head, so I keep them closed and try to figure out where I am and why.

I take stock of my body first. I can feel all my limbs, so that's a good sign. Between the antiseptic smell of my surroundings and the soft electronic beeping, not to mention the murmur of muffled conversation, it's not hard to ascertain that I'm in the hospital. I search my memory but can't figure out why I'm here. Something must've happened.

I think my door is open because I can hear activity out in the hall, clear, but removed. People walking by. A rolling cart. Medical folks chatting.

But just as quickly as I woke up, I start to feel drowsy again.

Which is funny since I have yet to open my eyes. At the same time, I sense somebody has walked into the room, and now that I want to open my eyes, I can't. I'm too sleepy. They want to stay closed. But who's here? A nurse? Doctor? Grandma?

"Hey," comes a soft voice. "You okay?"

Pen? What? Why? Why is she here? I feel her hand on my arm.

"You scared me, Scottie. Jesus." I hear the scraping of what sounds like a chair being pulled close. "Listen, I've been doing a lot of thinking. A lot of thinking. And"—I hear her swallow—"I don't have much time 'cause your grandma just went to grab coffee, and well, I'm pretty sure she hates me." A bitter chuckle.

You're goddamn right she does, I want to say. But it's only in my head. My voice stays quiet.

"I think…I'd like to give us another shot. I was messed up when I left you. I didn't know what I was doing. And maybe it took this car accident to wake me up…" Her words trail off and I hear footsteps coming into the room. "Oh," Pen says, her tone surprised. "Hey there."

A loud sigh from the newcomer. Then she speaks. "Really? You're here? I guess I should've seen that coming." Marisa! It's Marisa! God, why won't my eyes open? I feel like it's been forever since I've seen her.

"Seen what coming?" Pen asks.

"This little revenge plot of yours? I saw your text the other day." Marisa's voice is low, steely.

A beat goes by, then two, then three before Pen speaks again. "I don't know what plot you're talking about. I'm just here to tell Scottie that I think we should give it another shot."

A snort from Marisa. "Of course you do. Because it's all about you. It's always all about you." Pen says nothing and I wish I could see her face, but any connection my brain has to my eyelids seems to be malfunctioning because they stay closed. A moment of silence goes by before Marisa says one more thing. "As for Scottie? She deserves better than you."

I hear her footsteps retreat, and inside my head, I'm screaming, *No!* But nobody hears me. I feel Pen take my hand in hers, but I can't stay awake any longer, even just in my head, and everything fades into silent darkness.

❖

I feel awful.

Sore and tired and embarrassed and so damn lonely. Maybe it's the medications I'm on. Maybe something inside me got cracked. I don't know. I feel sad and broken and confused, and I am on the edge of tears all day on Saturday.

They brought me in yesterday, after I rear-ended a stopped truck, then was rear-ended myself by the guy behind me. My car is totaled—I guess that's one way for the Universe to force me to get a new one, huh? The airbag went off, thank God, but my face is a mess. Those things are brutal. Nobody tells you that. I have a broken nose and two black eyes. I sprained my wrist and have a pretty good concussion, but other than that, I'm okay. They kept me here overnight for observation, but I get to go home sometime today. Once all the paperwork is done. Which means maybe by midnight.

At least I'm sitting up in bed. The room is filled with flowers, even though I'm only here for one day. Bash and Demi. The dance students. Adley. They all sent bouquets. Adley is sitting next to me right now, and I'm telling her about Pen and Marisa both visiting yesterday.

"Are you sure you didn't just dream that up?" she asks, keeping her tone gentle, I assume so I don't think she's mocking me. "Your grandma was here all day, and she didn't see either of them."

I mean, I *was* positive they were both here, but now Adley has me wondering. And the idea that maybe Marisa wasn't actually here sends me plummeting farther into depression so fast, I don't even realize it's happening until my eyes are already wet. That's when my mom walks in. Or rather, scurries in, like she's late.

I don't know what happens to me then, but there's something about seeing my mom, seeing the worry on her face, the dark circles under her eyes, that sends the wetness in my eyes spilling over and I'm crying. She comes right up to me and wraps me in her arms, and I smell her perfume—Obsession by Calvin Klein, the same scent she's worn for years—and her shampoo and her hairspray, and all of a sudden, I'm just sobbing in her arms. My face hurts, but I don't care.

"Oh, my baby," she murmurs as she sits on the side of the bed, not letting me go, and then she does that gentle rocking thing that moms are so good at. She holds me and rocks me and strokes my head, and suddenly, words are spilling out of me, muffled against her chest, but still clear.

"I know you're busy and I know you have Jordie and Kai and Stephan, and I know Dad has the boys and Connie, but please don't forget about me. Please? I miss you both so much and I feel so lost and alone without you." And then I'm sobbing some more, and where the hell is all this emotion coming from? The other side of the bed sinks with weight, and then hands are on my back, and when I peek out from my mom's embrace, my dad is sitting there looking at me with soft, wet eyes and a sad smile.

They hold me for a long time.

❖

I don't get discharged until dinnertime, but that's fine. I just want out. I miss my own bed. I will not miss people poking and prodding me every two hours. My head is killing me, but I'm told that's normal for an airbag concussion. Adley tells me I probably shouldn't look in the mirror, but I do and then wish I'd listened to her. The entire top half of my face is black-and-blue and my nose is swollen and all taped up. I look like a prizefighter. Who just got her ass whooped. And is lying facedown in the ring while her opponent jumps around her celebrating.

My parents are still here, which is weird, to say the least. But I'm grateful. Strangely, both of them were out of town with their other families, which is why they didn't come to the hospital last night. Grandma called them and they each sped home as fast as possible to be here with me. Surprising. At least something good has come out of this disaster.

I have no car now, so my dad drives me home to Grandma's, and my mom and Adley follow. Grandma has the couch all set up with blankets and pillows. On the coffee table are the remotes for the TV and cable box, a box of tissues, a huge glass of water, a cup of tea, and a package of Oreos, my favorite. I mean, I'm not an invalid, but Grandma seems to think I should be downstairs rather than up in my bedroom, and she clearly went to such trouble to make me a nice spot that I don't have the heart to argue. I take my place on the couch, and it's in that moment that I realize just how tired I really am. Between the medication, the pain, and somebody coming into my room every two hours last night, I got very little sleep. As if they know it's safe to do so, my eyelids suddenly get really heavy, and it feels like it takes every ounce of strength I have just to keep them open. I had hoped to take a shower when I got home, but there's no way I could stand up long enough. It'll have to wait. My mom helps me get settled on the couch, takes off my shoes, covers me with a blanket, and that's the last thing I remember.

The next time I open my eyes, it's fully dark outside. It's dark in the living room, too, except for the light from the TV. Adley is sitting in the chair by my feet watching it, but when she glances over at me and sees that I'm awake, she sits up and says hi.

"How do you feel?"

"Like I got run over by a train." My mouth tastes like ass, my back is sore because the couch is too soft, and my stomach rumbles to remind me I've had very little to eat in the past twenty-four hours. Also, I don't smell great.

"I mean, you're not far off." Adley grabs my toe and gently wiggles my foot under the blanket. "What can I help you with?"

I'm sure the shame is clear on my face, but I don't have a choice. "Can you help me shower?"

"Absolutely." She doesn't even hesitate, and for that, I'm so grateful.

"I think I can wash myself, but if you can stay in the bathroom in case I fall on my ass?"

My wrist isn't in a cast, so I'm able to unwrap it and wash myself pretty well. It takes much longer than normal, and that's mostly because washing my hair hurts. Like, my hair literally hurts. Adley sits on the toilet lid and talks to me, peppering her stories with quick *How's it going?*s and *Doing okay?*s. At one point, I hear a muffled conversation and realize that Grandma has brought some supplies up to my room. I can't hear the actual words, but the tone of her voice is dialed to concerned, so I call out to her.

"I'm okay, Grandma. Don't worry."

Adley helps me into bed, and I'm all tucked in, have taken my medication, and have both Pepper and Salty curled up with me by eleven. My hair is wet, but I don't have the energy or the desire to dry it. I'll deal with it in the morning.

"Are you sure you don't want me to stay the night?" Adley asks. "I'm happy to."

I squeeze her hand. "Thank you. I so appreciate that offer. But I'm good. I think I'm past the point of *might pass out* and more into *has a splitting headache*. I'll be fine. Go home."

She does. I listen until I hear her car start up and pull away. Grandma checks on me once more before she goes to bed and gives me a kiss on my forehead, very softly, which makes me feel like a small child. In the best of ways.

I'm very tired, but I lie there in the dark for what feels like a long time. I replay what I remember about hearing Pen and Marisa in my hospital room. Could I have imagined it? Grandma didn't see them, but I know she left a few times. To use the restroom. To get coffee. I sigh. I don't know.

Both cats are purring, their soft, furry bodies up against me on either side. I reach for my phone on the nightstand. When it lights up, it's like an ice pick stabbing through my eyes and into my brain. I blocked Pen, so there's nothing from her. I pull up Marisa's name in my texts, and before I can second-guess myself or talk myself out of it, I send one short sentence.

I miss you.

Then I turn the phone completely off, snuggle into my bed—as much as I can, given I can't lie down fully or my nose will swell up—and close my eyes. Thanks to the wonders of drugs, I fall asleep in minutes.

CHAPTER TWENTY

It's been a week and a day since my accident. I really want to get back to work, but the doctor ordered me to take at least a full week. And to be honest, even though my face is healing up nicely, it's still kind of that purplish-yellow color of bruises after a while. Makeup covers quite a bit, but not enough. The splint thing is off my nose, but I have to be really careful. It needs another two or three weeks before it's healed completely, and if I brush it accidentally or bump it at all, my entire head feels like it's going to explode. But I can get around, and I can breathe, and those are two very good things.

It's a beautiful warm afternoon in July and I'm sitting in Grandma's backyard, on the deck where there's shade. It's already quite hot today, and I could really use some color. Let me clarify— some suntan color, not the various shades of black, blue, purple, and yellow I've been sporting for the past week. But the last thing in the world I need right now is a sunburn on my face. So I dutifully sit in the shade, sipping a beer and chatting with Grandma.

My mother has called me every day for a week, and my dad has stopped in three times so far. Every time I hang up from Mom or say good-bye to Dad as he drives away, I then look at Grandma with shock, shake my head in wonder, and tell her I don't understand. She has laughed every time, shrugged, and told me wonders never cease. I guess she's right. I can't explain it, but I'll take it. Maybe my tearful pleas to them in the hospital finally got through. I have no idea. But I like that they're around more all of a sudden. It's good.

The phone rings from inside, and Grandma and I look at each other. We both have cell phones. Nobody uses the landline. It's basically for emergencies.

"Probably a telemarketer," she says, but pushes to her feet and goes in to get it. When she comes out, she looks puzzled, but shakes it off. "Wrong number, I guess."

For the next half hour or so, we sit quietly and read. Well, Grandma reads. I read for a bit but start to get a headache, so I put my book down and just watch the yard. Grandma has three bird feeders out, and they're always overpopulated with sparrows. But occasionally, something colorful will show up. A deep red cardinal or a bright yellow goldfinch. A squirrel here, a chipmunk there. I love to watch them, and they sort of lull me into a light doze in my chair. In my brain, I start salsa dancing with a partner with no face—because that's not creepy and weird, but I am startled awake by a knock on the fence and then Grandma's back gate opening to reveal Penelope. She looks sheepish, but not sheepish enough to keep her from coming into the yard uninvited.

"Hi," she says, looking from me to Grandma and back. "I was wondering if we could talk for a bit."

What the actual fuck?

I'm at a loss for a few seconds. Grandma doesn't say anything, but when she looks to me, I can tell it's a struggle. She literally has her lips pressed together like she's working hard to keep them closed and keep the words she wants to say from shooting out. I sigh and nod at her. "It's okay, Grandma. This'll only take a few minutes."

Grandma picks up her phone as she stands, gives Pen a look that would slice through her skin if it was tangible, and begins typing on her phone as she heads into the house. I wait for the door to slide closed before I turn to Pen and sigh like I am very put-upon. Because that's how I feel.

"You blocked me again. I had to call your grandma's landline to see if anybody was home."

"What do you want, Pen?"

She takes the wooden ottoman that goes with the Adirondack chair across the deck from me and drags it so it's in front of me. She sits down with her forearms on her knees and studies me for a moment. I don't like it, and I do a kind of shifty squirm to tell her so.

"I'm sorry, Scottie." That's how she starts, and I already hate it. "I'm so sorry for how I treated you. For breaking up with you."

"You are?"

"Yes. Very sorry."

"What else are you sorry for?"

She squints a bit and seems to try very hard not to look puzzled. "For breaking up with you…"

"Yeah, you said that. How about for kicking me out of my own home?"

"That, too."

I sit up a little straighter. "And how about for telling me for over a year you didn't want to get married and then getting engaged to the first person you date after me"—I tip my head and make a show of looking up at the sky—"or that you dated while you were with me." She looks surprised for a split second, and I laugh bitterly. "Yeah, that one wasn't hard to figure out."

We hold one another's gaze for several moments. The birds are in the bird feeder still. I hear a car door slam somewhere out front. A dog barks.

"Give me another chance," Pen says suddenly, and I'm shocked. Seriously shocked. I did not expect this.

"What?" Are my eyes bugging out of my head? I feel like they are.

She hangs her head, and I can't help but think it's a practiced move, one she rehearsed. I know her that well.

"I screwed up, Scottie. I did. I know it, and I'm so sorry. Give me another chance. We can start slow, and you can see how it feels. What you think. And then, maybe you can move back in…" She's looking me in the eye right now, and I see the sincerity on her face, and for one split second, I almost take her hands in mine, but three things occur to me all at once, like they're crashing into each other in my mind.

One, Pen's fiancée has left her. I don't know how I know that, but I do. It's almost something palpable in the air. Maybe Pen cheated on her. Maybe she found Pen's texts to me. Maybe she saw Pen for what she really is. Maybe she's just had enough. But I suddenly know beyond a shadow of a doubt that she's gone.

Two, Pen can't be alone. She never has in her entire adult life.

She goes from woman to woman, house to house, but she's never been on her own. Not once. That's why she's here. Not because she wants me back. Because she wants *someone* back.

And three, I want Marisa. More than I can put into words. I miss her so much that my body literally aches with the pain of missing her. With longing for her presence, her touch. Hell, I just want to lay eyes on her. That would be enough right now.

I look at Pen. I smile. I place my palm against her cheek, and she leans in to it, closes her eyes, and moves her face into my hand. "You need to go," I say. My voice is steady. My tone is calm.

Her eyes fly open. "What?"

I stay cool and calm and resolute. Steady. Factual, not mean. Clear. "You heard me." Strangely, I don't want to hurt her. I'm past that, and I realize it in this very second.

"But…" Pen sits back on the stool, eyes wide, and blinks at me. Clearly, this isn't how she saw the conversation going, and part of me is thrilled to have been unpredictable. "But why?"

"Because I'm over you. And I deserve better." Again, not mean. Not hurtful. Factual.

She stares for a beat, and I watch, fascinated, as the surprise leaves her face, and she rearranges her features into bored-slash-knowing-slash-accusatory. Anything to not let on that I have the upper hand now. Which I do. "You think you deserve Marisa?" she asks, and she doesn't spit the name, but she's not happy about saying it either.

I laugh softly, bitterly, and shake my head. "No. I don't. I don't think I deserve her at all." I inhale slowly and let it out. "But I'd like to deserve her. I'd like to spend the rest of my days being the kind of person who deserves her. I would work on that forever if it meant getting to spend just a little bit of time with her."

Pen looks at me blankly. Because of course she does.

"You know, for the past week, since my accident, I've sat here wondering how you could have possibly left her. And for me? Seriously? What is wrong with you?" I give a soft laugh again. "But then, I could ask the same about you leaving me, couldn't I? And I realized that your leaving wasn't about either of us. Not about Marisa and not about me. It was about you. Because it's always about you."

Pen's expression changes then, and it's a weird combination of being insulted by what I said and of the shame of knowing I'm exactly right.

"I can't really blame you for messing up things with Marisa because it's what you do. It's totally to be expected. But I can blame *me* for messing up what *I* had with her. One simple lie of omission. Just one. I never told her you were texting me. It didn't matter that I'd barely answered you." Pen gives a little snort at that. "All that mattered was that I kept it from her. One lie of omission and that's on me." The truth of the words makes me sad. "And I miss her more than I can put into words. I wish I could fix it." The words hang between us in the silence that follows.

"Well," Pen finally says and pushes herself to her feet. She brushes herself off like she just got a little dirty but is recovering. Or maybe she's wiping her hands of me. Could go either way at this point, but the beautiful part about it is: I don't care. She stands there for a moment, and I almost feel bad because I think she's feeling a little bit humiliated, which wasn't my intention. But I also feel something else. Closure. Finally. It's something I've needed from this situation since moving out.

"You take care of yourself, Penelope."

She looks the slightest bit flustered but gives me a nod, then heads out of the yard the way she came. Through the gate. I sit there, shaking my head slowly and trying to reconcile all that just happened, but I hear muffled voices coming from the other side of the gate where Pen just went. It's to my right and at an angle that I can't see, but I figure she must've run into a neighbor or something and is being polite. I lean my head back against my chair and close my eyes, hoping to fend off the headache that's been pounding softly and threatening to blossom into something bigger since Pen's arrival. I'm trying to decide whether to call out to Grandma and ask her to bring me some Motrin.

"Hi." A quiet voice intrudes upon my impending headache.

I open my eyes with a start. The sun is behind her, so she's backlit, and I swear to everything holy, she looks like an angel. To my own horror, my eyes well up. "Marisa. Hi. What are you doing here?" I give myself a shake. "No. I mean, I'm so happy to see you, I'm just…confused."

She smiles that gorgeous smile of hers, accentuating her cheekbones. Her hair is hanging loosely, swooping near one eye, and I have never seen a more beautiful sight in my entire life.

Marisa grabs a chair and slides it so it's close to mine, then takes a seat. "Seems your grandmother and my aunt know each other?"

I blink at her in surprise, then vaguely remember Grandma possibly saying something about that when I first started taking dance lessons. I'd totally spaced on it, though. "Okay…" I draw the word out, still confused.

Marisa looks down at her hands. "Your grandma texted my aunt, who, as luck would have it, I was with at the time. My aunt then told me to, and I quote, get my sorry ass over to your place, along with the address, in case I couldn't remember."

The pieces click into place. Grandma on her phone the second Pen arrived. She set Marisa up to hear me talking to Pen. She knew I'd send her packing. She had that faith in me. I crane my neck around to see Grandma standing at the sliding glass door. She smiles and waves at me, then turns and walks away into the kitchen.

My eyes are still wet. Maybe wetter now.

"So," Marisa says. "Here's me and my sorry ass."

I sniffle and lift one shoulder in a half shrug. "I mean, your ass isn't sorry. At all. It's actually a really, really excellent ass."

She returns the grin. "Yeah?"

"Absolutely."

"Good to know."

We sit there quietly, but it's not uncomfortable. I don't think I've ever been uncomfortable in Marisa's presence. She reaches out and gently touches her fingers to my cheek, featherlight.

"Your poor face," she says, and her fingers linger. "I heard what you said to Pen." She nibbles on her bottom lip and meets my eyes. "Is it true? Do you miss me?"

I swallow hard. "More than I can say. Yeah."

"Oh, I miss you, too." And now her eyes are wet.

"You do?" My shock must register on my face because she laughs.

"Of course I do, you weirdo. Do you think this means nothing to me?" She moves a finger between the two of us.

And right then, in that exact second, I understand that nothing but full and total honesty is acceptable here—nothing but full and total honesty is acceptable if we want *anything* moving forward. "You left pretty fast," I say softly, doing my best not to sound accusatory.

"I know. I know, you're right. And I'm sorry about that. I have no excuse other than I freaked the hell out." She looks off into the distance and blows out a breath. "There's so much, Scottie. Not even counting Pen. I'm dealing with so much. Jaden and grieving my brother and my parents aren't getting any younger and I have two jobs...and then you come along. Like this ray of sunshine. But we're going so fast. My God. It's all so fast, but there's a part of me that doesn't care because I think..." She swallows and glances away for a moment, as if she needs to take a break for couple seconds. When she looks back at me, the wetness in her eyes has spilled over, tears tracking down her cheeks, and something inside me cries out at the sight. "I think we could really have something. I think we could be good. Great. Excellent." She chuckles. "So, yeah, it all has me freaking a bit. Well, a lot. It all has me freaking a lot. But then you got in an accident, and I freaked out even more because..." She stops, closes her mouth, and I hear her swallow again. And then I remember that her brother died in a car crash, and I reach for her hand.

"I'm okay. Marisa." I wait until she returns her gaze to mine. "I'm okay. I mean, my nose may never be the same, but..." I shrug and she laughs.

"Does it hurt?"

"Not as much as it did."

"Airbag?"

"Yes. Brutal, those things. Nobody tells you."

"They don't." She pauses. "As soon as I found out, I ran to the hospital, but when I got there, fucking Pen had beat me and I freaked some more. I kept thinking you took Pen from me, and now Pen's going to take you from me. And I couldn't get away from that. So I left."

"You *were* at the hospital! I knew it!" I'm so relieved to have that cleared up that I want to laugh.

She looks at me, puzzled. "You were unconscious."

"I heard you. I was sure of it, but nobody believed me."

A small chuckle bubbles up from her throat. "Yeah, nobody saw me. I was in and out pretty quick."

We're quiet for a moment before I say, "I'm really sorry I didn't tell you Pen was texting me."

"But you hardly responded to her." Marisa gives me a sly grin and nods toward the gate. "Eavesdropping, remember?"

"I hardly responded, it's true!" I laugh because I suddenly know that we're going to be okay. Just like that, and the relief that floods through me is like a drug. "But I promise you, if we can try this again, I will never, ever lie to you again. Ever."

"Those are pretty big words."

"I've got pretty big feelings for you." I freeze, realizing what I've just said, but Marisa squeezes my hand and holds my gaze.

"I've got pretty big feelings for you, too," she says very softly.

It's way too soon for the L-word, and I think we both know it, but it's there. Not far off in the distance, and we're well on our way to it. I know it. I can feel it, just as sure as I can feel my own heart beating in my chest. It's both scary and reassuring, and I have a hard time figuring out how that's possible.

"Where's Jaden?" I ask.

"Playdate."

"So you have some time?"

"I do."

"Wanna hang out with me?"

Again she reaches out and touches my face. I feel her touch radiate through me, filled with warmth and love. "I would love nothing more." She slides her chair around so that we're side by side, then takes my hand and entwines her fingers with mine. We sit there quietly, holding hands and watching the birds.

I turn to her. "I'm keeping you. I just want you to know that."

Her dark, sparkling eyes meet mine. "Yeah? Well, that's a relief, because I'm staying right here next to you."

I squeeze her hand as the birds flit and chirp, and I can't remember a more perfect moment in my entire life.

EPILOGUE

Two months later

I'm so fucking nervous. God, I don't think I've ever been this nervous in my entire life. Ever. Not when I graduated from high school and had to walk across the stage in front of people. Not when I took my final test for my hairdressing license. No, this tops both of those by a lot. My heart is pounding in my chest as I stand off to the side in the dark. I adjust my neckline, wiggle my toes in my shoes with the slight heel. I swallow the ball of nerves that's lodged itself in my throat. Swallow again because it didn't go all the way down. And then the spotlight comes up on the stage, and before the announcer begins to speak, I look across to the other side of the stage. I make eye contact with Marisa, and she smiles at me, makes a gesture with her hands, palms down like she's pressing them toward the floor. It's her sign language for *relax*, and suddenly, everything is right. Everything calms. I take a deep breath in, hold it for a count of seven, then let it out slowly.

"And now, representing Ms. Tina's School of Dance, please welcome Marisa Reyes and Scottie Templeton!"

That's our cue, and just like that, I have confidence. But it's not coming from me. It's coming from Marisa's dark eyes, and she walks across the stage, and we meet in the middle as the applause and whistles fill the small theater where the dance competition is being held. She holds out her hand, and I put mine into it. She looks…incredible doesn't even begin to scratch the surface. Her dress is black and red and sequined, and every time she moves, she sparkles. The bottom is soft and flowy, and the top? The top is a jacket and bow tie, very tuxedo-ish. She wanted it to be clear to the audience that she's leading, in the traditional male role, and she looks so incredibly hot, I'm already entertaining fantasies of undressing her later.

Reel it in, Scottie, my brain tells me.

Marisa's hand is warm and strong, as always, and she gives mine a gentle squeeze as I smile back at her. We set up, my back against her, her arm around my waist to our linked hands.

"Ready?" she whispers in my ear.

I give a tiny nod. Because I *am* ready, and it's crazy to me how everything in my world calms right down when I have her arms around me. I don't worry about how many of my friends and family are in the audience right now. All our fellow students came to watch, plus my grandma, Adley, Bash and Lydia, Demi and Ben, and—shock of all shocks—both of my parents and their families. I'm not sure how everybody found out—I'll be having a chat with my grandmother about that later—but for now, I feel incredibly loved. I don't worry about the steps because I know this dance backward and forward. I could do it with my eyes closed. We've been practicing nonstop for weeks now. My accident sidelined me for a bit while I healed, but once I could stand up and move around without my head swimming, we were right back at rehearsal, and it was different. There was a new level of comfort between Marisa and me, and it's stuck. We see each other at least a couple times a week. I only stay over when Jaden isn't home. We haven't told him yet. But we will. Soon.

Because this is it for me. Marisa is it. I don't know how I know that, but I do. There's no longer a doubt in my mind. And the weird, wonderful thing about it? I feel chosen. It doesn't matter that she has Jaden, that his needs come first. She still chooses me. For the first time in my adult life, I feel chosen. This woman, standing behind me with her arms around me and holding my hand? She's my destiny.

Corny? Maybe. True? Absolutely.

The Latin beat starts up to the song I've heard a million times now. Maybe more. And we start to move.

We don't dance so much as glide. Ms. Tina told me that once, and I didn't quite understand what she meant until after my accident.

Until Marisa and I had talked about our feelings and rose to a new level of trust with each other. Because that's what dancing with a partner is about: trust. When you trust your partner, that's when you make the move from dancing across the floor to gliding.

We move like we've been dancing together for years. I feel it, which means I know the audience can see it. Marisa spins me, sends me out away from her, but never drops my hand, and then she pulls me back in. I've never felt so safe with somebody and also so free to be myself. I never had that with Pen. She never made me feel protected, but Marisa does.

I spin back into her arms, and her smile is radiant. I don't know how else to describe it. Her eyes are always on me. Always. And every time I meet her gaze, there's a little twinkle that I know is there just for me. We've danced around the bigger words for a few weeks now, but it's just silly because I know how I feel. I have fallen fast and hard for Marisa Reyes. And I'm never letting her go.

The music builds to a crescendo. Our big finish. Marisa spins me out, tugs me back in, and then she dips me over her knee, and we both stretch out one arm in our finishing pose. The music stops, and there's barely a split second before the place erupts in applause. I'm breathing hard, still bent over her thigh, looking in her eyes. She smiles down at me, her face just beautiful, her happiness clear, and I can't help myself.

"I love you," I whisper to her. I doubt she heard me over the applause, but she saw me say it. Her eyes go soft. As I watch, they well up with tears.

"I love you back," she says, and I don't hear her, but I see the words. I feel them as they flow right into me, right into my heart.

She pulls me up to standing, and we take a bow together. Then another. The audience is giving us a standing ovation. Ms. Tina is in the front row looking ridiculously proud of us. We take another bow and then Marisa leads me off, stage left.

I want to say wow, to exclaim how great that felt, to apologize for the one misstep I took and thank her for covering it for me. But I'm unable to do any of those things because the second we're off the stage, Marisa grabs my face in both hands and kisses me. Not hard, but not softly. Firmly. Like she's telling me something.

And she is.

"That dance was amazing," she says, her nose almost touching mine. "You are amazing. I love you so much, Scottie. Let's tell Jaden this weekend. About us. Okay? I don't ever want to be apart from you. I want us to be together, to be a family, to raise our kids and grow old in the same place. I don't ever want to be apart from you. It's you and me, from here on out." She says it all in one breath, and when she stops talking, she inhales, then lets it out slowly. She's still holding my face and still looking in my eyes. "Say yes."

I don't realize I'm crying until her thumb brushes across my cheek to wipe a tear. I'm honestly worried my heart is going to burst because I've never been this happy. "Yes," I say softly. "Yes, yes, yes." And I throw my arms around her neck and feel hers go around my waist, and we stand there like that, wrapped up in each other. It's a moment I know I'll never forget.

"I have one question for you," she says, her lips close to my ear.

"What?"

"Where should we put our first-place trophy?"

And I laugh. Loudly. It bursts out of me. "A little overconfident are we, Ms. Reyes?"

"Nope. Just incredibly, appropriately confident in the gorgeous moves of my girlfriend. Trust me." She kisses me again.

And you know what? She's right. Not twenty minutes later, they announce the winner of the competition, and Marisa and I place first. Ms. Tina is ecstatic. Our friends and family scream their heads off for us as we link hands and hurry onstage to take a bow. The emcee hands us a trophy, and we bow again. As we're standing there in the spotlight among the thunderous applause, I tug her to me and say, "How about in our bedroom?"

Her entire face goes radiant, as if she's glowing from the inside. She nods.

"I think that's perfect. I love you, Scottie."

And now I know why I had to go through all the pain, confusion, and uncertainty in my life. To get me here. Now. Standing next to Marisa, the love of my life, with my hand in hers. "I love you, too."

And then the music starts up again so that all the contestants can come out onstage, dance some more, take bows, wave to friends in the audience. Ms. Tina runs up onstage to greet us. She gives us hugs, thanks us for the great representation of her school. Marisa hands her the trophy.

"Can you hold this for a minute?" she asks her aunt.

"Absolutely." Ms. Tina grabs it from her and runs off to show the others, I assume. I watch her go, laughing, and when I turn back to Marisa, she's holding out her hand.

"Dance with me?" she asks.

"For the rest of my life," I say and put my hand in hers.

And we dance.

About the Author

Georgia Beers lives in Upstate New York and has written more than thirty novels of sapphic romance. In her off-hours, she can usually be found searching for a scary movie, sipping a good Pinot, or trying to keep up with little big man Archie, her mix of many little dogs. Find out more at georgiabeers.com.

Books Available From Bold Strokes Books

Curse of the Gorgon by Tanai Walker. Cass will do anything to ensure Elle's safety, but is she willing to embrace the curse of the Gorgon? (978-1-63679-395-5)

Dance with Me by Georgia Beers. Scottie Templeton mixes it up on and off the dance floor with sexy salsa instructor Marisa Reyes. But can Scottie get past Marisa's connection to her ex? (978-1-63679-359-7)

Gin and Bear It by Joy Argento. Opposites really can attract, and as Kelly and Logan work together to create a loving home for rescue cat Bear, they just might find one for themselves as well. (978-1-63679-351-1)

Harvest Dreams by Jacqueline Fein-Zachary. Planting the vineyard of their dreams, Kate Bauer and Sydney Barrett must resist their attraction while battling nature and their families, who oppose both the venture and their relationship. (978-1-63679-380-1)

The No Kiss Contract by Nan Campbell. Workaholic Davy believes she can get the top spot at her firm if the senior partners think she's settling down and about to start a family, but she needs the delightful yet dubious Anna to help by pretending to be her fiancée. (978-1-63679-372-6)

Outside the Lines by Melissa Sky. If you had the chance to live forever, would you take it? Amara Rodriguez did, and it sets her on a journey to find her missing mother and unravel the mystery of her own heart. (978-1-63679-403-7)

The Value of Sylver and Gold by Michelle Larkin. When word gets out that former Boston homicide detective Reid Sylver can talk to the dead, the FBI solicits her help on a serial murder case, prompting Reid to assemble forces once again with Detective London Gold. (978-1-63679-093-0)

When It Feels Right by Tagan Shepard. Freshly out of the closet Marlene hasn't been lucky in love, but when it comes to her quirky new roommate Abby, everything just feels right. (978-1-63679-367-2)

Lucky in Lace by Melissa Brayden. Straitlaced stationery store owner Juliette Jennings's predictable life unravels when a sexy lingerie shop and its alluring owner move in next door. (978-1-63679-434-1)

Made for Her by Carsen Taite. Neal Walsh is a newly made member of the Mancuso crime family, but will her undeniable attraction to Anastasia Petrov, the wife of her boss's sworn enemy, be the ultimate test of her loyalty? (978-1-63679-265-1)

Off the Menu by Alaina Erdell. Reality TV sensation Restaurant Redo and its gorgeous host Erin Rasmussen will arrive to film in chef Taylor Mobley's kitchen. As the cameras roll, will they make the jump from enemies to lovers? (978-1-63679-295-8)

Pack of Her Own by Elena Abbott. When things heat up in a small town, steamy secrets are revealed between Alpha werewolf Wren Carne and her human mate, Natalie Donovan. (978-1-63679-370-2)

Return to McCall by Patricia Evans. Lily isn't looking for romance—not until she meets Alex, the gorgeous Cuban dance instructor at La Haven, a newly opened lesbian retreat. (978-1-63679-386-3)

So It Went Like This by C. Spencer. A candid and deeply personal exploration of fate, chosen family, and the vulnerability intrinsic in life's uncertainties. (978-1-63555-971-2)

Stolen Kiss by Spencer Greene. Anna and Louise share a stolen kiss, only to discover that Louise is dating Anna's brother. Surely, one kiss can't change everything…Can it? (978-1-63679-364-1)

The Fall Line by Kelly Wacker. When Jordan Burroughs arrives in the Deep South to paint a local endangered aquatic flower, she doesn't expect to become friends with a mischievous gin-drinking ghost who complicates her budding romance and leads her to an awful discovery and danger. (978-1-63679-205-7)

To Meet Again by Kadyan. When the stark reality of WW II separates cabaret singer Evelyn and Australian doctor Joan in Singapore, they must overcome all odds to find one another again. (978-1-63679-398-6)